I0633137

COLORADO MYSTERY MERGE

CRIME FICTION COLLECTION 1

SISTERS IN CRIME COLORADO CHAPTER AUTHORS

CONTENTS

NOTE TO READER

This short story anthology will probably be unlike anything you've read before. We're starting out with an overarching mystery ("Murder at the Twelve Mooses Ballroom" by Becky Clark) involving a fictional Colorado icon who gets murdered at a fundraiser where he was to be honored.

We're calling this the "mystery merge" because the subsequent short stories—completely unrelated to the overarching mystery—will each merge for a moment, dropping a pertinent clue for you to use in solving Doctor Dictionary's murder. Well, the stories are not *completely* unrelated. They all take place in Colorado during the same week as Doctor Dictionary's murder. The characters from the other stories will hear some tidbit about the investigation from a news source of some kind—newspaper, radio, online, whatever—because you know how it is when there's a high-profile murder … you can't get away from the news no matter what else is going on in your life. The same is true for the characters in all these short stories.

Use the following character sheet for "Murder at the Twelve Mooses Ballroom" and take notes as you read the anthology. By the time you finish all the stories, you should have enough information to take a stab at solving Doctor Dictionary's murder.

After you make your prediction, check your work by reading the denouement at the end. No peeking, Sherlock!

We had a ton of fun creating this book and we hope you enjoy this selection of stories from some of the members of the Colorado Chapter of Sisters in Crime. Rest assured you won't be confronted by any overt gore, violence, sex, or language in these pages. All the mysteries stand alone and cover many genres under the crime fiction umbrella.

If you solved the murder of Doctor Dictionary, let us know by visiting the anthology page at SistersInCrimeColorado. org/anthology. (There might even be a surprise for you there!)

If you enjoyed this anthology, please drop a review—no spoilers, though—and tell your friends!

"MURDER AT THE TWELVE MOOSES BALLROOM" CHARACTERS, IN ORDER OF APPEARANCE

WENDALYN "WENDY" BILBERSTEEN — worked with Doctor Dictionary at the local news TV station back when he was just Leo Linder. She got stuck as "Wendy the Weathergirl," but worked her way up to News Director. She tried to get out of being the emcee for the event due to the scars she still carried over Doctor Dictionary's treatment of her, but couldn't. Was vengeance in the forecast?

CHARLOTTE WEBB — CEO of KIDDO (Kindhearted Individuals Dedicated to Dreams and Opportunities) honoring Doctor Dictionary at their annual gala fundraiser. She fought hard for a different honoree due to her deep and abiding hatred of him after their romance soured. Was her purse Glock locked and loaded? Would this event get on her last nerve?

UNKNOWN MAN — skulking about the ballroom wearing an ugly, ill-fitting tuxedo during the fundraiser. How much did it cost to rent an ugly tuxedo? What was he hauling around in that big trash bag? Why all the skulking?

. . .

OLIVIA TWIST — believes Doctor Dictionary is her father, something her mother denies, because Olivia knows he shares an unusual allergy to marijuana which causes symptoms exactly like Olivia's. Was she planning to expose him? Indulge in a bit of blackmail? Or was she simply looking for answers?

RYAN RIZZUTO — known online as The RizzBizz for his viral pranks. He crashed the fundraiser. Was he planning a dangerous new prank?

SENATOR MANFRED "FREDDIE" PASCO — using this fundraiser to try to control damage he caused himself by saying something vile during an unfortunate hot mic moment. His "Pasco Fiasco" went viral and he became the butt of many jokes, several made by Doctor Dictionary himself. Would the large donation he'd be making to KIDDO appease his critics? Would this be his opportunity to show a new side of himself?

LOIS LALANNE — reporter for the local newspaper covering the event. Turned up at the gala with her notebook and some marijuana-laced brownies. Would the right person eat them?

DOCTOR DICTIONARY — Leo Linder left the news business to become Doctor Dictionary, beloved local celebrity, hosting Knowledge Bowls, spelling bees, geography bees, mathletic contests, and trivia pub nights, much to the delight of everyone. Everyone except the person who murdered him at the fundraising gala.

READER NOTES

MURDER AT THE TWELVE MOOSES BALLROOM

BECKY CLARK

"For the ten-thousandth time, I don't want to!" Wendalyn Bilbersteen spoke emphatically to Charlotte Webb, the CEO of KIDDO (Kindhearted Individuals Dedicated to Dreams and Opportunities).

Charlotte sighed. "I understand completely, Wendy. But you're the obvious choice to emcee this gala honoring him and his work on behalf of kids. You both started out in the news business at the same time and came up through the ranks together. I know there's some animosity between you, but I was overruled."

If faces could talk, Wendy's would shout, "*Liar!*" Luckily faces couldn't talk, only mouths. And Wendy's was full of the gummy worms she kept shoving in there from the sandwich baggie she clutched.

Wendy tried to speak around her wad of half-chewed gummies, but Charlotte raised one hand. "It's too late for you to back out now." She checked her watch. "Two hours until he gets his award and I still have eight million things to do." She leveled her gaze at Wendy and spoke quietly. "After tonight, you'll never be bothered by Doctor Dictionary again."

Charlotte took a couple of steps before turning back and handing off one of the two plastic shopping bags she held.

Wendy took it from her. "I almost forgot. I picked these up from the printer today. It's those brochures I told you about."

Wendy watched Charlotte hurry away to deal with her eight million things, her lone plastic bag swinging wildly at her side. Charlotte had no idea the can of worms she'd opened when she asked Wendy to emcee this event. Wendy had drafted a polite statement wherein she'd declined Charlotte's kind offer while acknowledging how flattered she was, but before she could send it, Charlotte had published a press release listing her as the emcee. If Charlotte only knew, she'd never have asked.

But nobody really knew. Back in the 1980s Wendy got her first real job at Channel 8. She had planned to begin using her grown-up name professionally and was hired as Wendalyn Bilbersteen. She started at the station on the same day as Doctor Dictionary, who had yet to begin using his professional name. He was known then as boring old Leo Linder. She was hired as an on-air reporter, with the promise of moving up to the news desk. But when Leo Linder showed up, she was relegated to weather, even though she found out later she had better credentials than he did, since she had spent three years in college anchoring a local access daily news round-up.

When she complained to the news director, he'd shrugged and said, "Complain to Barbara Walters. Besides, if you're behind a desk, nobody'll see those gams of yours. Weather is where you belong, toots."

"I don't know anything about forecasting weather."

"No worries. Nobody does. Besides, nobody'll be listening to you anyway, just checking out those fabulous gams."

To make matters worse, the first time Leo Linder introduced her to do the weather, he called her Wendy instead of Wendalyn and it stuck. Every time after that, no matter how often or how loudly she complained, she was always introduced as Wendy the Weather Girl. Gross.

Leo Linder became locally famous for anchoring the news

but went off to become Doctor Dictionary, hosting the Knowledge Bowl for many years. Almost every kid in town was on that show at some point, whether for spelling or geography bees, mathletic competitions, debates, or any number of brainy kid-centric contests.

Wendy expected that with her seniority she'd be promoted to the anchor desk when he left, but she was told that someone named Wendy the Weather Girl had no gravitas. She was so furious, she'd had to leave the station before she did something she'd regret. All her rage narrowed to a knifepoint that pointed directly at Doctor Dictionary. Not only had he taken *Wendalyn* away from her, but he also didn't even appreciate the honor of the anchor desk job, leaving it to run some stupid kiddie program.

Of course, that stupid kiddie program was why he was being honored tonight, but still. Wendy had eventually clawed herself all the way up to the News Director position, but she never forgot how Doctor Dictionary made her feel.

But instead of telling Charlotte all of this, she'd simply said, "Fine," and shoved three gummy worms in her mouth.

Rounding a corner, her mind still in the past, she collided with a man wearing an ill-fitting tuxedo and swinging a large plastic garbage bag. Their respective bags crinkled and squeaked as they bounced off each other. "Goodness! Excuse me," Wendy said. The man's eyes were so wide, Wendy wondered if he'd lost the ability to blink. He rushed away from her without a word.

"It's going to be one of those nights." Wendy sighed and dug for more gummies.

THE SICKLY SMELL of Wendy's gummies followed Charlotte across the Twelve Mooses Ballroom being set for tonight's event. She felt sympathy for Wendy. It was clear she had some baggage with Doctor Dictionary too. Whatever it was, though, couldn't be worse than her own baggage with him. Charlotte fought valiantly for their honoree at this annual fundraiser to be world-renowned children's musical performer Big Red Doofus, but the board overruled her and chose Doctor Dictionary instead. She had a long list of reasons why they should honor Big Red Doofus, which she shared passionately and eloquently. She only had one reason against Doctor Dictionary—because she hated him like a cat hated baths—which she did not share passionately and eloquently.

Her love affair with Doctor Dictionary was something she had worked hard to forget. She truly thought they were in love. Soulmates. Kindred spirits. Her Board of Directors didn't need to know she had already asked her husband for a divorce before Doctor Dictionary broke it off out of the blue one day. Charlotte lost everything—her husband, her home, her pride, her stellar credit score.

Charlotte thought that was all behind her until the board meeting where Doctor Dictionary's name came up. After the vote, she wondered if the board members would have considered her position with more deference had she brandished her dainty purse Glock.

A clattering noise across the ballroom made Charlotte snap her head then pivot at a run toward three hotel employees staring down at flowers strewn on the floor. When she reached them, she said, "I will shoot you *dead* if that vase broke!" A puddle of water made a dark stain bloom across the carpet.

One young man dropped to his knee and triumphantly hoisted the unbroken vase in the air.

"Lucky you. You can live another day. Now get that cleaned up." Charlotte had more to say but was interrupted by a twenty-something woman wearing a fashionable pant suit. The employees took the opportunity to scatter.

"Excuse me? I'm looking for Doctor Dictionary?"

"Who are you?" Charlotte asked.

"His assistant for the event? I'm Olivia Twist."

Charlotte huffed. "They gave him an assistant? I'm the one with eight million things to do. Who hired you? I'm the CEO of this organization and I don't remember discussing anything about an assistant."

Olivia had the grace to blush. "Um … I think I have an email or something …"

"Never mind." There were so many details for this event, Charlotte had probably forgotten more than she'd remembered. And she didn't have time. Charlotte pointed Olivia to a door across the ballroom. "Might be over there."

Olivia waited until Charlotte had disappeared from the ballroom. Before she could put the plan in action, her phone rang with her mother's ringtone. She debated about answering, but knew the calls would just keep coming. "Hi, Mom."

"Hi yourself. You left before we finished our conversation. Doctor Dictionary isn't your dad. Your dad is a deadbeat biker I spent a glorious weekend with and never saw again. I told you I don't know his last name, but I'm pretty sure his first name began with an S. Steve? Sam? Snake? Can't remember. But it's definitely not Doctor Dictionary. That I'd remember. Okay?"

"Sure." Olivia laughed. "It was a pretty far-fetched theory."

"I'm glad we got that all cleared up. Where are you anyway?"

"Bowling alley near the mall. When we're done, we're going to a movie. Don't wait up, I'll probably be late. Hang on a sec." Olivia covered the phone with her hand and counted to twenty. "Abby wants me to spend the night. Is that okay?"

"Sure. See you tomorrow."

"Bye, Mom." Olivia disconnected and felt guilty for lying

for the exact amount of time it took to slide the phone back into her pocket.

She looked toward the door where Charlotte had pointed and took a deep breath. "Here goes nothing," she muttered. She'd only taken three steps when a long-legged man walked toward her. She stared at him as he passed, eyes wide, turning to continue gaping at him. "You're Ryan Rizzuto! The Rizz-Bizz! What are you doing here?"

The man turned and winked, but continued walking backwards. "I think you have me confused with someone else."

"No, I've seen your videos. They're so funny. Your pranks are so outrageous!"

"Thanks for watching." He shot her with two finger guns. "But it's not me." He winked again.

This time Olivia understood. "Gotcha. You aren't here." She used finger guns back at him.

Olivia watched as a middle-aged man spoke to him. Ryan Rizzuto didn't slow down. Olivia heard him say, "I don't know, man. Ask her," as he hooked a thumb in Olivia's direction.

A minute later the middle-aged man was in front of her. "Manfred Pasco."

"Excuse me?"

The man looked confused. "Manfred Pasco? State senator?"

"I'm sorry, I don't know him."

"Him is me. I'm Senator Pasco."

Olivia was young, but she knew his type and groaned inwardly. Full of himself. Thinks he's a party bag of flamin' hot BBQ in a world of fat-free unsalted. "Can I help you?"

"What should I do with this?" Senator Pasco thrust a large trophy in a plastic bag at her.

Olivia took it from him without thinking. "I don't know."

"Why not? You're wearing a suit. Don't you work here?" He dug a gummy bear from a small bag he pulled from his pocket. He counted the remaining ones, and with a sigh, popped it in his mouth.

"*You're* wearing a suit. Do *you* work here?" Olivia thrust the trophy back at him, wondering if he was already high on edibles. Pretty nervy, dosing in public like this. But then she remembered he was a politician. They get away with everything.

"You could have just said no," he mumbled, hurrying away, clutching the plastic-encased trophy to his chest.

Olivia continued to the door Charlotte had indicated earlier. As she grabbed the knob to pull it open, someone had pushed it from the other side. She came nose-to-ruffled shirt with a man gripping a large trash bag by its neck. "Oh, excuse me!"

The man didn't respond, and simply scurried away without entering the ballroom.

"Excuse *you*," Olivia said under her breath. Rude *and* overdressed.

Olivia saw activity across the hallway. Several people milled about, all looking like they had some important business to attend to. Doctor Dictionary wasn't one of them, however, which was perfectly fine with her. Olivia hadn't quite decided how she was going to handle him.

She felt foolish in her pantsuit. She'd wanted to look mature and responsible, neither trait she possessed, but now second-guessed her choice. Everyone else really did look mature and responsible. Especially a woman not much older than herself. It was obvious to Olivia that she was a journalist because she was speaking to Senator Pasco and taking notes in a small notebook.

He brushed off the reporter's question, looking a bit angry. The woman shrugged, watching him stride away. She wrote a bit more in her notebook, then dropped it into a messenger bag at her feet. She pulled out a large zip-top baggie that looked to Olivia as if it contained brownies. The journalist glanced around the area before placing it on the table. She patted the brownies gently before walking away.

Olivia continued to stand out of the way, trying to decide on a course of action that wouldn't draw too much attention to herself when she saw Ryan Rizzuto spy the brownies on the table. After glancing around to see if anyone was watching him, he grinned broadly and pulled a brownie from the bag. He walked away eating it.

A brownie would be a welcome treat, but Olivia glanced down at her pale blue suit, knowing the tiniest crumb would stain it. Not today, missy.

She sighed as she watched Ryan Rizzuto take a massive bite of his brownie.

WITH EACH CHEW of the brownie, Ryan Rizzuto's eyes widened. He couldn't remember the last time he'd had a pot brownie. Who made these? And did they mean to leave them out for anyone to take? And were they strong or was he simply out of practice?

He stopped walking and turned back. Nobody was pointing and laughing so it didn't seem to be a prank. Nobody was paying any attention at all. People bustled around, not seeming to care who was in the vicinity.

The brownies weren't quite in a public area of the hotel, but it certainly wasn't any kind of restricted area. But even if it was, Ryan knew all you had to do to get past any closed door was to walk confidently with purpose and look people in the eye when you greeted them. For whatever reason, that rendered you invisible.

And it was precisely what Ryan Rizzuto counted on tonight. At least up to a point.

He broke off another bite of the magic brownie and dropped the remainder in a trash can.

SENATOR MANFRED PASCO watched Ryan Rizzuto drop half a brownie in the trash. Kids these days. So wasteful.

Almost as wasteful as my donation to this organization, he thought. It would be worth it, he supposed, if it washed away the sin of his very public hot mic moment. He only said out loud what other people said to their friends. Only a joke, but these days nobody could take a joke. Plus, people held him to a higher standard just because he was a state senator. Hypocrites. The only thing worse than a hypocrite was a hypocrite with a cellphone. That eight-second video ricocheted around the entire world almost before he finished saying it. He wondered how long the *Pasco Fiasco* would be the first thing that popped up when people searched his name on the internet.

Tonight should change all that.

"Who ate one of those brownies?"

Senator Pasco turned toward Lois LaLanne's voice, a bit more shrill than when she'd interviewed him earlier. Nobody paid her the least bit of attention. Print media really might be dead.

LOIS LALANNE STARED down at the brownies. She poked at the gallon ziptop bag, to make sure one hadn't simply maneuvered around so she couldn't see it. She bent down until her nose was an inch away. Nope. One was definitely missing. She cut her eyes left and right a couple of times, but it didn't seem like anyone was skulking around, eating it, or worse, calling the cops. Senator Pasco and that girl wearing the pantsuit were staring at her so she tried to act cool.

Last night she couldn't decide if slipping someone a pot brownie was a good idea or not. On her way to the venue this morning she was certain it was. At this moment, she was equally certain it was not.

Suddenly a man in an ugly tux, complete with ruffled shirt, veered toward the table, acting like he wanted a brownie.

Lois stepped between him and the table, jostling the over-stuffed bag he carried. "You don't want one of those. I heard they're gross. Probably have nuts in them. Maybe even sugar-free." The man didn't respond so she threw in another "Gross," for emphasis.

She thought about snatching the brownies from the table but tux guy, the girl in the suit, and Senator Pasco would think she had something to do with them. She had, of course, but she preferred to keep that to herself.

The man clomped away, trash bag bumping against his leg with every step. Lois hurried the opposite direction, crossing her fingers for luck that the right person would find the brownies before they were all gone.

DOCTOR DICTIONARY CHECKED HIS WATCH. While he appreciated the honor soon to be bestowed upon him, he'd rather be at the pub. Tonight was Golden Girls Trivia and he had to miss it, replaced as emcee by a millennial who probably had never even seen an episode. Couldn't tell their Rose from their Blanche if their life depended on it.

Everyone else was scurrying around getting ready for the event. He was told the public—well, the donors—were beginning to arrive, but not by anyone official. He'd been looking forward to catching up with Wendy Bilbersteen. She'd sure done impressive things with her career, moving from weather to news director at the station.

He'd been surprised when he got the email from Charlotte Webb advising him that he'd be the recipient of this years' service award for KIDDO. After their break-up, he knew she wanted to kill him, and in hindsight, maybe he could have handled the situation better. But as the kids say, he just wasn't into her.

He had run into Freddie Pasco, who again reminded him to show a little respect and call him Senator Manfred Pasco. It tickled Doctor Dictionary to needle Freddie, so he did it at every opportunity. This latest fiasco of his was a humdinger. He teased him relentlessly about his hot mic moment for about fifteen minutes before Freddie stormed off. Doctor Dictionary felt a little bit guilty for needling him, but if a politician had such a thin skin, they should get out of that line of work.

There'd be time after the gala to apologize to him and chitchat with Wendy and Charlotte. But for now, he'd been asked to stay out of view until someone came to get him at award time, which was fine with him. A bunch of brownies had appeared, and he'd helped himself. They were delicious with a flavor he couldn't quite identify. He ate three, but never figured it out.

Suddenly his ears felt hot and he knew they were fire engine red. He took some deep breaths so he wouldn't be on stage with bright red ears. It wasn't working, but at least he had identified the mystery flavor. Who gave him pot brownies? And why did they make them so delicious that he kept scarfing them down? His breathing became rapid. Doctor Dictionary put a hand against the wall to steady himself. This had never happened before. His chest heaved. The heat from his ears began spreading through his body. His pulse pounded. His skin felt clammy.

What a stupid way to die, he thought.

WHEN TROUBLE CALLS

AMY RIVERS

Rachel glared at the television behind the bar. For more than an hour she'd zoned out blissfully, allowing the buzz of the restaurant behind her to lull her into a kind of alcohol-infused trance. Then she heard that voice, and like there was some kind of magnetism involved, her eyes fixed on the gorgeous green eyes, perfect skin, perfect hair, and obnoxious Southern accent of Laura Hansen, prime time anchor on Channel 27 News. The camera shifted to an on-site correspondent pointing a microphone at some tired middle-aged schlump in an ill-fitting three-piece suit reporting on a local murder.

"Charlotte Webb has a concealed carry permit. Every one of us on the board of directors at KIDDO knew it. At least twenty times a day she was telling someone 'I will shoot you dead!' Looks like she finally did it."

The momentary relief that came with the change in speaker—Rachel wasn't at all interested in the story itself—was gone as fast as it came. Her stomach clenched as Laura's face appeared again.

Reasons I hate Laura Hansen.

One. The obvious. She's too perfect. I mean, who looks like that?

Jealousy was certainly at the top of the list. Rachel and Laura had both applied for that anchor job, and of course

Laura got it. Not that she deserved it any more than Rachel. Their careers had paralleled each other since they roomed together in college, and Rachel was definitely anchor material —her tireless work ethic and level-headedness more than making up for lack of dramatic flair. Or so she'd thought.

Two. That accent! She's from Ohio, for heaven's sake. Who does she think she's kidding?

One evening after classes, Laura had joked about women with Southern accents having more success in broadcasting. While Rachel had laughed along, she'd always loved the trace of Midwest that colored Laura's speech, especially when she was feeling passionate about something. Which was always. Laura had always been the more exuberant of the two. Obviously.

Rachel's cheeks burned hot, and though she was only on her second glass of wine, she swayed on her stool, pretending to be buzzed to explain away her flaming face for anyone who might be looking at her, though nobody was. Instead, the eyes of her fellow drinkers were also fixed on Laura's visage as she continued her report, which only made Rachel more angry and uneasy.

Which brought her inevitably to reason three. Rachel was in love with Laura. Had been all through college and right up to the moment when Laura stole her job, sending her career into a free fall. The intensity of Rachel's feelings had nearly swallowed her whole all the years they were together, and acted like a machete to her heart when it all fell apart. Love turned to hate, or at least that's what Rachel told herself in her weaker moments.

Trouble. That's Laura Hansen.

"Hack," Rachel muttered. A man two spaces down the bar turned and frowned at her.

"What?" Blood was pumping fast in Rachel's veins and she suddenly felt like she couldn't catch a full breath. The other patron went back to his beer, and Rachel slapped some cash on the bar and hurried away. She burst through the door onto the sidewalk, and as the blustery spring air hit, she sucked in as much of it as she could handle.

She walked home, thankful for her tiny walk-up apartment only a few blocks away. Her phone vibrated in her pocket but she ignored it, half-jogging to her refuge, praying her heels wouldn't send her crashing down. She hated heels.

I'm throwing out every pair the minute I get home.

As she walked up to her third-floor apartment her phone continued to vibrate, pausing only briefly and then starting up again.

"What now?" Rachel grumbled. She unlocked her door, walked in, kicked off her shoes and sank to the floor, leaning against the wall. She pulled out her phone. The number was local but unfamiliar.

Scrolling through her call history, she saw fourteen calls from that number. All were made within the last ten minutes. The phone sprang to life in her hands: call number fifteen. Rachel hesitated, then answered.

"Rachel!"

Laura's shrill voice reached through the phone, grabbing Rachel's heart in a vise-like grip. They hadn't spoken in almost a year, but Laura's voice still did things to Rachel. They'd never officially dated, but Rachel knew Laura felt the same way. If they'd been more established in their careers, maybe things could have been different, but in a field where reputation was everything they'd never even tried.

"What do you want? And where are you calling from? Did you change your number?"

"Listen to me, Rachel." Laura's words were slightly muffled, as though she was holding her hand over her mouth and speaking quietly. "I need you to come and get me. Now!"

For a few seconds, Rachel wondered if she should just hang up. Refuse to be drawn into whatever drama Laura had cooked up, but the panic in her old friend's voice left her uncertain.

"Where are you?" Rachel asked.

"The Cleveland Room on 17th. I'm in the bathroom. Text me when you get here."

Rachel was about to protest, but Laura had already disconnected. Resigned, she grudgingly pulled her heels back on and left her apartment.

***

RACHEL HATED driving in Denver almost as much as she hated Laura Hansen. Her city apartment rendered her car nearly obsolete, but she liked to drive up into the mountains on her days off, so she kept the Honda Civic she'd had since college.

Of course, Laura knew that. They'd gone hiking nearly every weekend. Rachel was the more athletic of the two, despite her clumsiness. She had more endurance, more stamina—traits she was pretty proud of. As she drove across town, memories of picnics by the lake and summiting the beautiful Colorado mountains almost took the edge off her mounting anger.

Almost.

But her memories shifted to the day last year when she'd caught Laura sneaking out of the station manager's office. Rachel and Laura were both correspondents at Channel 27. Both competing for the open anchor spot. Both qualified. Driven. Ambitious. But in the days leading up to the decision, Laura grew distant.

Rachel's concern for her friend turned to suspicion as Laura's remoteness became full-fledged avoidance. She ignored Rachel's calls and emails, and always seemed to be busy when Rachel tried to approach her at work. When she saw Laura exiting the office that night, Rachel confronted her.

"What are you doing, Laura?"

Laura had jumped at the sound of Rachel's voice, a guilty look on her face. Instead of answering, Laura quickly pushed past, making her way to the station's back entrance.

Confused, Rachel pursued. But when she walked out the door, Laura was gone.

A few days later, Laura got the anchor job. She continued to avoid Rachel, whose sources and leads dried up. New assignments became scarce. Within a few months, she was sending out her resume. The day Rachel left Channel 27 for an online news outfit, Laura had been notably absent.

Rachel had tried hard to shake off her feelings of betrayal. After all, there were perks to taking the new job. A raise in pay. A whole new way of delivering news not bound by time slots or word counts. More freedom to investigate the stories that mattered to her. Still, it was a step away from her career aspirations as a broadcast journalist. And leaving the station came with reduced access to sources, forcing her to shift away from several high-profile projects she'd been pursuing.

As she approached the corner of 17th and Fairhaven, the glowing neon sign of The Cleveland Room came into view, bringing her back to the present. Rachel passed the entrance, looking for a place to park. She lucked out a block down Fairhaven, and was pulling her phone out to send a text when her back passenger door opened, causing her to jump. A dark-clad figure dove into the seat, slamming the door behind.

"Drive!" Laura's voice hissed from behind Rachel's seat.

Fighting to control her breath, Rachel said, "What the—?" But she was cut off by Laura's frantic words.

"Just go. Go!"

Rachel was pulling away from the curb, when she heard yelling behind her and saw two large men running along the sidewalk. They glanced at Rachel and then took off down the block.

As they merged into traffic, Rachel said through gritted teeth, "I'm driving to the park and then you're going to explain what's going on, or I'm leaving you there."

RACHEL PARKED on the far side of the lot, leaving the car idling. Her passenger had been eerily silent, leaving Rachel's mind plenty of room to spin out of control. Who were those men? Was Laura in danger? Was Rachel?

She took a calming breath. Without a glance backward, she demanded, "Start talking. Now."

Laura's head became visible in the rearview mirror. She was sitting, but kept her head low against the headrest. Her cheeks were sallow and Rachel could see deep purple shadows under her eyes. Rachel's breath caught, but she waited.

Finally, Laura spoke. "I don't know where to start."

"How about those guys running down the sidewalk? They were looking for you, right?"

"They followed me into the restaurant, but the ladies' has a window that goes out to the back alley. I climbed out." Laura chuckled grimly. "I caught my heel on the window and it slammed shut. Probably the only reason they knew I'd escaped."

"Who are they?" Rachel's patience was straining at the seams.

"I don't know." Silence followed, and with each passing moment Rachel's frustration grew, until finally she couldn't take it anymore.

"Get out," she said, surprising herself with the iciness of her tone.

"Rachel," Laura pleaded. "Please, you have to help me."

"Why?"

"I'm … I'm in trouble."

Rachel laughed coldly. "Yes, I'd gathered that much. Who'd you piss off? Those guys looked like hired muscle."

Laura sniffled, and when Rachel looked in the rearview mirror she saw tears streaming down Laura's face. In spite of herself, her anger cooled and her stomach twisted with concern.

"You're going to have to tell me something, Laura. How

can I help you if I don't know what's going on?" she asked quietly. "And honestly, I'm not sure why I should. Not after …" Rachel's voice trailed off.

"I'm sorry," Laura murmured. "I know I hurt you, but there was no other way to protect you."

"Protect me?"

"You and I, we worked together so much. I told them you didn't know anything, but they didn't believe me. And the only thing I could think to do was cut you off."

Rachel felt the blood rush to her face, a wave of fury coursing through her body. "What are you talking about?" she asked, her voice increasing in volume.

Laura winced. "If I tell you, you won't be safe."

"I hate to tell you this, but one of those guys looked me right in the eye. It's not going to take much for them to put two and two together." It took all of Rachel's energy just to keep from screaming.

Laura let out a big breath and wiped her eyes on her coat sleeve.

"It's about the gambling clubs."

Rachel's rage turned to fear. "Oh, crap."

"YOU KEPT INVESTIGATING?" Rachel asked, her voice shaking. "You found them?"

"No, but I must have gotten close. Last year, before the anchor job opened, I noticed one of my sources talking with the station manager behind the building. I barged into Connor's office later that night. I was angry, and when I confronted him about it, he tried to gaslight me. But when he figured out I wasn't going to let it go, he offered me a deal."

"A deal?" Rachel asked, but she knew where this was going.

Laura nodded her head. "The anchor job. If I dropped the story."

"Which source?"

"The bartender at Wilco's."

"My source." Rachel's mind raced. She and Laura had been investigating a string of illegal gambling clubs in the Denver area. The bartender had come to Rachel first, offering solid information. Proof.

Then he disappeared, and when Rachel asked around, she was met with stony silence from the whole staff at Wilco's and everyone else she'd been working with. Including Laura, who inexplicably seemed to have lost interest in the investigation. At an impasse, Rachel had no choice but to work on other things.

"So you took the anchor job and hung me out to dry." A feeling of resignation and defeat enveloped Rachel. "You let Connor kill the story. What's the point of being an investigative journalist if you're going to cave at the first sign of pressure?"

"It wasn't the first sign. He threatened me, and you, and a few nights later I started getting phone calls. And someone broke into my apartment. What choice did I have?" Laura pleaded. The desperation in her voice stirred feelings of sympathy and also betrayal, tightening the knot forming in Rachel's stomach.

"You had a choice, Laura. We were partners. That was *our* story, not just yours. You were handed your dream job—our dream job—and you didn't even …" A dark SUV crept down the winding drive toward the park, sending a chill down Rachel's spine. "Get down. We have to go."

Laura grumbled but sank down as Rachel backed out and slowly exited the parking lot. She held her breath, keeping the SUV in sight as she rolled toward the street. It didn't seem that the vehicle was following them, but it was moving so slowly she couldn't be sure. Either way, she wasn't waiting to find out if the danger she sensed was real.

Rachel took a circuitous route back to her apartment, making the trip twice as long as it should have taken.

"What are you doing?" Laura hissed, still hunched down low in the backseat. Rachel was on her third circle around the block, and was starting to feel silly. Without answering, she parked a few doors down from her entrance, grabbed her purse, and got out of the car.

She heard the car door close and the clacking of Laura's boots on the sidewalk as she ran to catch up. It wasn't until they were inside her apartment with the deadbolt locked and the alarm system armed that Rachel allowed herself to take a full breath.

Laura stood near the door, looking irritated. "What was that all about?"

"You're kidding, right?" Rachel huffed. "I'm the one who came to your rescue, remember?"

"Yes, but—"

"There was an SUV. I panicked, all right?"

"Oh." Laura fell silent. She looked small, standing awkwardly in the front hall of Rachel's apartment. Rachel's feelings were at war. Something about Laura's vulnerability tugged at her heartstrings, but she was too overwhelmed by the events of the evening to let down her guard.

Buying herself some time, Rachel went into the kitchen and put the kettle on. She heard Laura's footsteps and the scrape of the kitchen chair behind her, but she wasn't ready to talk. Instead, she stood with her hands on the counter, gathering her thoughts.

Rachel had tried to continue her investigation into the gambling clubs after leaving the station. But for all her efforts she'd never uncovered anything new, certainly not enough to print. She suspected police involvement in the operation. Maybe even the protection of higher officials, but she'd never been able to prove it.

"You didn't drop it?" she finally asked, still facing away from Laura.

"Drop what?"

Rachel swung around, her eyes bright with fury and

indignation. "You kept investigating. You took the anchor job and then carried on with the investigation anyway. Without me."

"You left," Laura said lamely.

"Was forced out, you mean." Rachel crossed her arms tight over her chest, trying to maintain her anger. Every time her eyes met Laura's, it was like a little chink in her armor.

"Are you implying that I made you leave?" Laura asked. The look of incredulity on her face made Rachel pause. As anchor, Laura had no control over the stories that were assigned to correspondents. But the station manager could make or break a person's career. Despite this realization, Rachel continued to argue.

"You didn't even say goodbye. And you never called," she said, but she felt less confident than she had before.

Laura stood and walked over to Rachel, planting her feet, leaving only a few inches between their faces. Rachel leaned back into the counter.

"I. Was. Trying. To. Protect. You," Laura snarled, punctuating each word with a ferocity that left Rachel breathless. "And I called. So many times. You never picked up the phone."

"I never—" Rachel started, but Laura held up a hand, silencing her.

"Just listen." Laura sighed, dropping her hand to her side. "There's a lot to unravel here, but we don't have time right now. I was at dinner tonight when those two thugs came looking for me. I don't think I was supposed to walk out of there."

"You think they wanted to kill you?" Rachel's heart beat furiously in her throat, giving the words a strangled sound.

"I don't know. I'm pretty sure I know who they work for, and let's just say it wouldn't surprise me." Laura took a step back, releasing Rachel from the grip their proximity had on her. "Last week, they found a body in the river."

"The Commissioner. Gunshot wound to the chest. The

police said he was robbed and then killed." Rachel had reported on the story, along with every other news outlet in the state.

"They *would* say that. Blame it on addicts and the story goes away. Commissioner Moore contacted me a few weeks ago. He had evidence linking several of his fellow commissioners to the gambling operation, and he implied that someone in the Governor's office was also involved."

Rachel gasped. "I knew someone was protecting them, but the Governor? Isn't law and order his platform?" She felt excitement grow as her mind connected the dots. It had always been like this, the thrill of the chase. Finding clues. Solving the mystery. Rachel's sense of self-preservation slipped to the back of her mind as she dove into work-mode. "Who knew you were still investigating?"

"No one," Laura said. "But I started to suspect that someone bugged my office the last few days. When I made dinner plans, I hinted out loud that it had to do with something I was investigating on the down-low. Seeing those guys walk into the restaurant confirmed my suspicions."

"You knew someone might come looking for you and you still went?"

"I thought someone might follow me, that's all." Laura grinned. "I expected to see the station manager or someone from work, but when I caught a look at those guys I panicked. Headed to the bathroom and called you."

"What if I hadn't answered?"

All Rachel's anger had shifted to a different uneasy feeling. After a year of radio silence, Laura had called her. Relied on her. Put her life in Rachel's hands. Why? What did it all mean? And now that Rachel had jumped into the fray, where did they go from here? What could Rachel offer Laura? What was she willing to give?

"The real question is, what do we do now?" Laura said, placing her hand on Rachel's arm. She leaned forward and brushed her lips gently against Rachel's. "I mean, if you're willing to do this with me."

Those dazzling green eyes.

"We go live!" Rachel replied, a jolt of electricity thrumming in her veins. "Tonight. Right now."

Laura gave her a puzzled look, and this time it was Rachel's turn to grin. "One of the advantages of online journalism is that I get a lot of latitude in the stories I cover, and I have access to our social media accounts. We're going live to report on what we've found so far. Even if it gets taken down, our live streams get thousands of views. Let's let the cat out of the bag!"

"But I don't have proof. Moore never gave me any hard evidence, and everything else is circumstantial."

"It doesn't matter. Don't you see? They want to silence you before you can say what you know. We have to strike first. Shift the target from you to them."

Rachel sprinted into the living room, pulling her laptop out of her bag. She sat down on the couch. Laura took the seat beside her, their arms touching. They talked through what Laura was going to say. As Rachel pressed record and Laura began to tell her story, one resounding thought filled Rachel's adrenaline-fueled brain.

Maybe trouble's not so bad.

CALL JULIE BEFORE YOU DIG

ANN DOMINGUEZ

"Call Julie Before You Dig," Cara said. "This is Julie."

"I have a complaint."

It wasn't the Breather. *Thank goodness.* Cara's shoulders relaxed. She picked up the empty Diet Coke and set it with the others against the padded cubicle wall. If she felt this way before every call, she was going to need a padded cell soon. "Yes?"

"I don't like the new traffic light on 26th Street."

"Sir, this is the Call Julie Before You Dig Hotline. You need the Public Works Complaint Line."

"I know, but they're not friendly."

"Have you tried calling 311?"

"That's just a recording. I want to talk to Julie."

"Or logging on to the City of Denver website? It has a built-in comp—"

"I want to talk to Julie!"

"Okay." She turned down the volume on her headset. "This is Julie."

His words tumbled out over each other like a waterfall. She scribbled them on a sticky note, *green arrow east from 26th onto Williams too short. Pedestrians still jaywalking.* The yellow warning light on her monitor blinked. "Can I help you with anything else? Do you plan to dig in your yard this summer?"

"I live in an apartment."

"Thank you for calling. Remember to Call Julie Before You Dig." She disconnected, pulled the sticky note off the pad, and walked across the room to hand it to Alina.

When she got back to her desk, Raj peered around the corner of his cubicle. "I'm going for lunch. What do you want?" The murmur of the city call center hummed around them like a hive.

"The usual."

"Do you want lettuce on it? Tomato?"

"No, thank you."

"Vegetables could save your life someday."

She handed him a twenty. "Let me know when you finish that nutrition degree."

The phone buzzed. Raj headed for the stairs, and she answered the call. "Call Julie Before—"

"Cara, it's me."

Thank goodness. "Hi, Mom. Are you planning to dig in your yard?"

"No, I'm not plan—"

"Then maybe you should call my cell phone."

"You don't answer your cell phone."

"Not when I'm at work. Do you need something?"

"I'd like you to come to dinner on Friday. I'm trying a new recipe I think you'll like."

"What is it this time? Pistachio-encrusted tempeh?"

"Tempeh is an excellent source of protein."

"So are hamburgers."

"Plus, there's someone I want you to meet."

Cara cracked open another Diet Coke.

"His name is Joel. He works at Whole Foods."

"Mom—" A hand gripped Cara's shoulder. She turned to look up at Maddox, the manager, and froze. Classic deer in headlights. She released her gritted teeth and pasted on a plastic smile.

"Didn't mean to startle you," he said, releasing her and moving along between the rows of cubicles.

She shivered off his touch. Her mother was still talking, double speed now. "And I wanted to tell you that Mrs. Silver saw your new billboard. She says you look great."

"That's not me. That's a model." The yellow light started blinking.

"But doesn't she have nice teeth?"

"All right, Mom. I love you. Call you tomorrow." Another call came in almost immediately. "Call Julie Before You Dig, this is Julie." *The breathing*. Wet and hot. Like a dog on steroids. Her voice rose as if she'd swallowed helium. "This call is being recorded."

"Good." He breathed into the phone. "Then everyone will hear how scared you are."

Cara ripped off the headset and threw it on the desk. The policy said they had to give every caller at least forty-five seconds, but that didn't mean she had to listen to him. She rolled her chair around a cubicle wall until the light started blinking and she could hang up.

When Raj came back, she had disconnected but was still shaking in her chair. He picked up the headset and hooked it over her monitor. "The Breather again?"

She nodded.

"How does he always know to wait till I'm gone?" He rattled the bag of take-out. "Let's eat outside."

The metal picnic tables were empty. A blizzard of white petals from the apple trees blew across the parking lot, but the sun was warm. Raj handed Cara her sandwich. "That's the third time this week. Why can't they block that number? You should call the police again."

"What are they going to do? It's not illegal to pant into a hotline." She unwrapped her burger. A blob of mayo fell on the table, oozed through the perforated metal, and splattered her new pants. Perfect. "He's called so many times I'm starting to think his voice sounds familiar. How was your morning?"

"Seven calls for new compost bins, three trash-wasn't-picked-up, and four my-neighbor-put-garbage-in-the-recycling."

Why couldn't *she* be the Garbage Hotline?

"What about you?"

"One complainer, the Breather, and my mother. She wants me to meet the guy who bags her groceries."

Laughing, Raj struggled to swallow his Vegetarian Delight on Rye.

She sighed. "Actually, I don't know he's the bagger. Maybe he works at the meat counter."

"Don't put yourself down. Maybe he's really cool, and he's in charge of stacking the produce."

"Very funny. Also, she told me my new billboard looks great."

Raj spit sprouts all over the table. They stuck to the residual mayonnaise, like grass shooting up through snow.

"I get more compliments on that billboard."

"It's terrible!" Raj wrinkled his nose. "It makes people think they're calling a phone sex hotline."

"Maddox said it would make people feel more comfortable calling in."

"No one is comfortable calling a really hot woman." Raj waved some kind of all-natural beet chip at her. "They want to talk to a real person, not an AI chatbot."

"Speaking of ... how was your date?"

"She was trying to recruit franchisees for a health food pyramid scheme. What about you, did you start your nursing school application?"

"I haven't even checked the requirements." People like her didn't get into nursing school. People like her got set up with grocery baggers. People like her had phone stalkers they couldn't get rid of.

After lunch Cara reported the Breather's call to Maddox, talked to three callers with actual plans to dig, and compiled the addresses to give to Dispatch. She wasted her break reading the news. Copper Mountain was extending its ski season till the first of May, the airport train was shutting down for repairs (again) and, in local murder news, suspect Wendy Bilbersteen hadn't even wanted to emcee Doctor Dictionary's award ceremony, telling Charlotte Webb she was sure something bad was going to happen if she had to be in the same room with him. Cara forwarded the story to her mom. If she ended up inviting the grocery bagger to dinner on Friday, at least they'd have something to talk about.

———

THAT NIGHT, she dreamt about the Breather. He was somewhere in the call center, wheezing through the air ducts, and she was trying to get away from him but couldn't. At three-fifteen, she woke up with her heart racing. She spent the rest of the night looking at nursing school requirements. She was four credits short.

"You're late," Raj told her as she dropped into her chair. "Maddox has come by twice."

She slid on her headset. "I need a different job."

"You want to run a vitamin franchise? I could connect you with—"

"Very funny."

"Maybe you should stop talking about it and actually apply for nursing school." He peered down at her over the top of the padded wall. "We'll stop eating out and put the money in a tuition fund." His phone buzzed, and he disappeared into his cubicle.

She didn't want to give up her lunches with Raj. Lunch with him was the best part of the day, but she was going to have to do something about the Breather. Her phone buzzed.

Please don't let it be him. She took a deep breath and hit record. "Call Julie Before You Dig, this is Julie."

She heard the breathing, and her skin immediately rucked into gooseflesh. She looked for Raj, but he was in the middle of a call. Panting hissed through the phone. "I love it when you're frightened, Cara. When you tremble. I'm going to make you beg."

Cara's throat closed up, but not before a little shriek brought Raj around the corner. He yanked off her headset and jammed it on his head. Cara flattened herself against the wall.

"Thank you for calling," Raj said, his voice tight. "This is Julie. Are you planning to dig in your yard?"

Cara would have laughed if she'd been able to breathe. The screen flashed *Call Disconnected.*

Raj set the headset on the desk and shrugged. "He didn't want to talk to me."

She nodded and tried to keep from trembling. That was the first time the Breather had used her name. It was like he could see her.

"I'm calling the police." Raj went back to his own cubicle.

When the officer arrived, he sat in Raj's chair and balanced a laptop on his jackknifed knees. Like a grasshopper in uniform. Just to make the whole experience more awkward, Maddox came over to listen. "How many calls have you received?" the officer asked.

Her mouth was too dry to talk.

"Maybe two a day for a month," Raj said.

"And this is the first time he used your name?"

"Y-yes," Cara managed.

"What did he say?"

Did she have to repeat it? Just thinking of it made her nauseous.

Raj nodded at her. "*Tell* him."

"He said, 'I love it when you're frightened, Cara. When you tremble. I'm going to make you beg.'" She hugged herself and tried to hide the shudder.

"He called you Cara? You're sure?"

"Yes." How had the Breather known her name? Raj passed her the trash can just before she threw up.

"You said the calls are recorded," the officer said. "Where are they stored?"

"In my office," Maddox said, pushing himself off the wall. "I'll get them for you."

Cara left early, and Raj promised to stop by after work. Only two hours to kill, she thought, not wanting to be alone in her apartment. Maybe this was a sign from the universe that it was time to leave her job. Time to do all the things she kept saying she would do "someday." Exercise. Eat vegetables. Apply for nursing school. She drove past the rec center, but the parking lot looked full. Plus, she was wearing the wrong bra. She wandered the grocery store looking for things she thought Raj would eat. Her whole nervous system was a live wire, jumping every time a grocery cart rattled around a corner. *I don't even know who to be afraid of.*

All the way home, she replayed the Breather's words. He'd known her name. What if he also knew where she lived? What if he was waiting in her apartment?

She drove back to work and played Candy Crush in the parking lot while she waited for Raj. She watched UPS go in with a dolly stacked high with boxes. She looked up how much the two classes she needed would cost at the community college and converted it into lunches brought from home. Too many.

She texted Raj. *I brought dinner. U almost done?*

Sry Maddox can't find ur calls. Still working with police.

She lost three more games before she decided to take the food up to Raj. There was a can opener in the break room. She grabbed the two plastic bags of groceries—ten cents each, because she'd forgotten to bring her own—into the lobby. The elevator opened with a ding. Maddox was about to get off but stopped when he saw her. *Of course he was still here.* Cara choked on her gum and stepped back. The plastic bags rattled against her calf.

"Are you okay?" His goatee framed a sympathetic smile. "You were pretty upset earlier."

"B-better now." The fingers of last night's dream still reached for her, but she was determined not to let him see it.

He licked his lips. "Are you going back up? I can ride with you."

"That's not—" Her brain froze, and not in the Dairy Queen way. What was she going to say, *Not a chance?* Or yet another polite evasion, like the fake smile she manufactured when he touched her shoulder or stood too close? "I just remem—the thing I—I have to get my—"

The elevator alarm cut off her babbling. He released the door, and she backpedaled with the cans banging against her leg.

"Cara, wait—"

She kept walking through the empty lobby, faster now. It was definitely his voice. The way he said her name made her skin crawl. Behind her, the elevator alarm went silent. Was he following her? She didn't turn around to find out.

She'd known Maddox for two years. He couldn't be the Breather.

Then how did he always know when she was going to be the one to answer?

She was almost to the revolving door. Where was the security guard? Raj and the cop were still on the fifth floor. If she went back to her car now, she and Maddox would be alone in the darkening parking lot. She headed for the stairs instead. She was on the fourth step when the door slammed firmly behind her.

She had just passed the second floor when she heard the door open again below her.

It was him. She could tell by the breathing. Her body responded the way he knew it would—the way he'd been training her to respond twice a day for the past month.

She kept climbing. She would get out on the third floor. Hide in a bathroom. Text Raj again. She turned the corner and saw the door, with its stupid sign that said, *NO ENTRY. EXIT AT GROUND FLOOR.*

She didn't think she was going to make it to the fifth floor. Was the fourth floor locked too? She couldn't remember.

His voice echoed in the stairwell. "Are you scared, Cara?"

No. She was done being scared. She was furious.

The fourth floor also had a *NO ENTRY* sign. What was she going to do? She had left her badge in the car. Where was Raj? Why hadn't he texted her back? What if he and the cop had finished and were on the elevator right now, headed to the lobby? She whipped up her phone, gasping as the handle of the bag, now twisted like a tourniquet, slid down toward her elbow and the cans crashed into her hip. Her phone had no signal.

She looked around for a crowbar, fire extinguisher or hose she could choke Maddox with. Nothing. Thighs burning, she kept climbing.

Who had better endurance? Maddox, who had just set a personal best in the half-marathon, or Cara, whose only personal best was in Candy Crush? She peeked over the rail and saw him halfway between three and four. He was gaining on her. She turned and sprinted up the stairs toward five. If she lived, she was going to start working out.

Another *NO ENTRY* sign, next to a red box with a lever and instructions: *PULL IN CASE OF FIRE.* Finally. She took the last four steps two at a time and wrenched down the lever.

It was so loud she had to cover her ears. So loud she couldn't tell if the screaming was her, or Maddox. She yanked on the door, hoping the alarm would somehow unlock it.

The door might as well have been a wall.

Was anyone still in the call center? If so, they'd have to come out this door. She pounded on it, but they were probably completely deafened by the alarm. Just as she was, which was why she didn't hear Maddox behind her until his hand was on her shoulder.

His breath was hot on her ear. She made out her name and wanted to rip it out of his mouth, but she was stuck in place like a fly in amber. Han Solo in carbonite.

He raised his voice. "I want to hear you beg."

Trying to move now was like thawing a glacier, but she was not going to stand here and let him destroy her. She was going to *do* something, even if it was the wrong thing. Grateful for the cover of the blaring alarm, she twisted the heavy grocery bag around her hand twice and swung the cans into his skull.

She expected him to fall like Wile E. Coyote, body stiff and head encircled by stars and tiny birds. Instead, there was a terrible moment of stillness, his eyes wide, before he crumpled on the spot. Like she'd detonated TNT at his feet. He fell in place but was so close to the ledge, he tumbled down the stairs to rest on the landing below. She was standing there, waiting for him to get up again like a zombie and come for her when the door crashed open, throwing her backwards. Raj and the police officer barreled out and barely stopped before running her over. Their lips were moving, but she couldn't hear anything but the shrieking alarm.

"It's him!" she shouted, pointing. The emergency lights flashed like a strobe, making it look like the officer jumped down to Maddox.

A minute later a fireman appeared in the stairwell. The policeman waved him up to Cara and Raj, who were now holding hands like kindergarteners on a field trip. He herded them around Maddox's body and back down the stairs. A police car and a fire truck made the parking lot a carnival of blue and red lights. An ambulance arrived, and the paramedics headed into the building with a gurney. The alarm cut out, but her ears kept ringing.

A different officer approached her. "Are you Cara Johnson?"

"Yes."

"Are you injured?"

"No." She'd have a bruise from the where the door handle hit her, but that was all. Raj let her hand go.

The cop's cell phone rang. "Don't leave the parking lot."

Cara took that as permission to walk to her car. Even if she couldn't go home, she could sit down. The plastic bag was cutting into her wrist, but the lentils in it had saved her life. Just as Raj had promised. No wonder he loved them. Cara was going to sleep with these lifesaving lentils. She was going to be buried with them, but not for a long, long time.

"Are you okay?" Raj asked.

"Yes." But Maddox wasn't, and if they couldn't find the tapes, how would she prove he was the Breather? She'd go to jail for assault with a deadly vegetable, and if—when—he recovered, he'd start breathing down the line at the next Julie.

"We pulled the tapes. You can hear the sounds of the call center."

"Of course you can. How is that going to help?"

"On *his* end. He was calling from his office."

Relief flooded through her. She felt like a piano had been lifted off her. She sank to the asphalt and leaned against her car. Maddox would be the one in jail. She would still lose her job, but even that might be for the best.

No longer was she the person cowering in front of the phone, wondering if the next caller would be the Breather. She was the person who had defended herself. Not only that, but she had climbed five flights of stairs, which was *almost* like going to the gym. Maybe she could be a nursing student. The minute she got home, she was going to sign up for the two classes she needed. She untwisted the torn bag from her wrist and stacked the cans on the pavement.

Raj sat next to her. "Can I get you anything?"

"A hamburger, extra mayo. Hold the tomato."

"You don't want to eat those lentils? I could make you—"

"Are you kidding? These lentils are evidence."

A STAGED MURDER

BROOKE CRAIG

"Brace yourself, Grace. Keep your eyes on the prize." My sassy friend and realtor partner, Anna, squared her shoulders and rang the doorbell. "This contract will help our careers take off and make us some money."

"It can't be that bad," I said, peering into the window of the massive home.

"It is … and he is."

From inside, a voice yelled out, "Janice, get the door. It's probably that sexy real estate gal and the decorator."

I looked at Anna. *Really?*

The door opened to a polished middle-aged woman. As she was about to speak, an older man sporting a diamond pinky ring, unnaturally black hair, and a bespoke suit shoved through. "No need, Janice. I'm here. Go back to cleaning." He swatted her backside as she turned around.

The paycheck, I reminded myself as I tasted the eggs I had for breakfast again.

"Hello, ladies," he crooned like some 1970s Vegas nightclub singer. "Clive Trenton. You must be the decorator."

He stuck out his hand to me, palming mine between his in a way that made me want to stab him with my keys. "Not sure why you're here to decorate. As you can see, I have impeccable taste."

Cue internal eye roll. "Hello, Clive. I'm Grace Bell, the home stager. I see you enjoy the Rococo design style. Let's walk through and see where we can move toward Colorado Modern Mountain so your property appeals to a wide local audience." I started taking some photos, coughing at some strong floral fragrance in the room. Must be some cheap air freshener.

"Like I said, honey, I have great taste. But walk around if you must. There's a great view of the valley from the master suite. Shall we start there?"

Was that a wink?

———

ANNA LEFT for another appointment and I went to my favorite Castleton Park coffee shop, the Wellsprings Cafe, to meet Madison, one of my oldest friends. We grabbed a sunny table on the patio, despite the cool April breeze.

Madison leaned in and whispered, "So he really tried to get you and Anna up to his room? What a slimebag!"

"I know. It was difficult not to smack him. But Anna's right about us needing this contract. She'll make a lot of money in commissions. And I can bill several hours of consulting time and some accessory rental fees. As sleazy as he is, Clive Trenton has a lot of connections in the real estate world, even here in Colorado, so we could get other jobs out of this."

"When I was at law school in New York, I heard a lot about his sketchy deals and disgusting behavior. It was the only time I considered working for the DA's office. I'd be wary of him, Grace."

———

EITHER ANNA'S charm or Clive's desire for more profit persuaded him to hire me for two full staging days. Anna was already at Clive's when I arrived, so I let myself in and started reviewing my consultation notes. Today was decluttering and removal. Then I'd come back with my art and accessories for styling before the photographer came.

I pulled the more ostentatious—and let's be honest, really freaking ugly—decorative pieces out of the formal living room and placed them in boxes for the packers to deal with later. As I walked past Clive's office on the way to the garage to store the items, he and Anna were having an intense conversation.

"Two percent and not a penny more. I shouldn't even be offering that since this house will sell itself."

Wow, this guy was a piece of work. How could Anna deal with him?

"Clive, our contract states a six percent commission, which I will be splitting with the buyer's agent. That's standard practice."

"You think I was born yesterday, sweetheart? I am a king negotiator, just ask anyone in New York. They're all scared of me."

I considered going in to support Anna but knew she could handle herself. I have a tendency to step in and save people who don't actually need saving.

The power saw was roaring when I got to the garage.

"Hi!" I yelled.

The guy using the saw looked up, stopped the horrendous noise, and took off his safety goggles. "Hey."

Wavy brown hair with just a hint of gray. Chocolate brown eyes. Dang, did I just step into a Hallmark movie?

"Um, hi. I'm Grace, the home stager."

"Sam."

Out of habit, I started to raise my arm to shake his hand, somehow forgetting the overly full box of ugly accessories I was holding. I tried to grab the falling box as Sam did too. We failed. It crashed to the ground, spilling the contents onto the concrete.

"Grace, huh? That's ironic," he said with a smirk.

Yeah, maybe not Hallmark worthy. Like I haven't heard the Grace-not-being-graceful joke before. I'm well aware of my klutziness, thank you very much.

"You have insurance? Trenton's going to flip out. I already got a lecture about not breaking anything while I'm here rebuilding his deck."

"Yeah, I do," I said. "Thanks for trying to help. Sort of."

I SPENT the next few hours pulling pieces out of the different rooms and taking them to the garage. I had just stopped to take a break and stretch my back when Clive walked into the living room behind me.

"Now that's a view I could get used to."

You have got to be freaking kidding me. "Mr. Trenton, it's really not okay to say that."

"What? Can't you take a compliment?"

"Mr. Trenton," Janice interrupted, a tight smile plastered on her face, "your lunch is ready in the dining room." Janice followed Clive out, but not before she pursed her lips and nodded at me in a show of solidarity.

I headed back to the garage with more decor items to stash. Sam was still in there.

"More damage to hide? Be careful not to trip over the lumber."

"Ha, ha." If he only knew tripping frequently was my signature style. I set down the box and pulled a peanut protein bar out of my pocket.

"Don't let Janice see you. Trenton has a peanut allergy. I had chocolate peanut butter cookies and offered him one. Old guy looked like he wanted it but Janice went ballistic, said she has to control everything he eats. It was just one cookie so I bet it wouldn't have hurt him."

"Some people can have a life-threatening reaction just by being in the same room."

"Well, not him."

How would he know? This guy was getting more irritating by the moment.

THE NEXT MORNING, Madison and I met at Wellsprings before she went to her law office and I went back to Clive's for the staging day. As we waited for our drinks, I started with the handsome jerk of a carpenter.

"He was so arrogant. Of course, I made a complete fool of myself dropping that box. But still."

"We'll just have to find you a nice guy somewhere else." Madison's eyes followed someone who had just walked into the coffee shop. "Hmm, there's a possibility. Wait … I think I know him."

I turned to look too. "That's Sam! You know him?"

"Yeah, but I can't place him."

Sam picked up his drink from the counter, turned and looked at me. His smirk evaporated when he saw Madison and he rushed out the back door.

"That was weird," Madison said.

"And rude!"

WITH MY MINI COOPER filled to the brim with pillows, artwork, and accessories, I drove to Clive's. As I was about to turn into the driveway, Anna's car zipped past me and out into the street. Weird. She had said she was meeting me here for the final staging day. I tried to call her, but she didn't pick up.

I didn't have time to wait since the photographer was scheduled for tomorrow. Clive wouldn't be home that morning and Janice was out of town so I could let myself in with the lockbox code Anna had already given me. Fumbling with the dreaded alphabet dial lock dredged up memories of middle school lockers and forced me to dig through my bag for my readers, but I finally got the key and went in.

I placed staging items in the living and dining rooms and then went to the kitchen. The trash hadn't been emptied and I didn't want the can showing in the listing photos, so I started to take it to the garage. I glanced in Clive's office as I walked by.

The trash can dropped as I rushed into the room. Clive was sprawled on the floor, pale with eyes wide open, not moving. "Clive, are you okay? Can you hear me?" Getting no response, I called 911. He was still warm, but I didn't feel a pulse. I started CPR.

"SO HE WAS DEAD? Was it a heart attack?" Madison asked.

"I'm not sure. The paramedics thought so."

A little kid at the next table started clapping at his tablet. "Red! Red! We love Red!" sang the tablet.

Ugh, not that annoying Big Red Doofus song.

"Sweetie, put your headphones on. Not everyone wants to hear Big Red Doofus sing," the boy's mom said sheepishly, glancing in our direction.

Madison leaned in. "That reminds me. Remember that gala I went to the other night for that Doctor Dictionary guy from the children's TV show? The one where he got murdered? Well, I was listening to the news this morning and heard that the KIDDO CEO, Charlotte Webb, really pushed to honor Big Red Doofus instead of Doctor Dictionary. At least that's what another KIDDO board member said. Can you believe that?"

"No! Doofus is so irritating. I never let my kids watch his show when they were little." I smiled at the frazzled mom near us. "You know, it's kind of creepy that we've both been in a building where a guy died this week."

"Agreed." Madison sipped her latte. "Oh, I also remembered where I knew that Sam guy from. I met his sister when I was volunteering as a victim's advocate in Denver a few years ago, before joining the firm. She had been assaulted by some powerful man when she was visiting Sam in New York but wasn't willing to testify. She never told me who the man was but I'm pretty sure Sam knew and he was super angry about it."

"Wow, small world! Did Sam move out here after that?"

"I guess."

I savored my chai latte, wheels turning. "Madison, you don't think Clive is her assaulter, do you? He's only lived here a short time, but could it fit with Sam's move out here? I mean, I know it's crazy, but maybe Sam took the job at Clive's house to get close to him."

"But Clive died of a heart attack."

"Right, but what if it was actually anaphylactic shock? He had a severe peanut allergy. And Sam knew about it. Oh my gosh! Should I go to the police? Maybe the coroner didn't do an autopsy."

"Whoa, Grace." Madison laughed, putting her hand on mine. "I think you might be jumping to conclusions. Let me see if I dig up anything on my end before you accuse someone of murder."

"You're probably right. I do tend to have an active imagination."

My cell rang as I was speeding down the curvy private lane. "Hey, Anna! What's up? I'm just driving over to Clive's to see if I can get my art and accessories back. I'm not sure if anyone will be at the house or if it's even okay to go in, but I thought I'd try."

"Can you do me a favor, please, and see if there's any paperwork in his office related to selling the house? I want to wrap this all up, but I'm in Boulder today and won't be able to get back down there."

"Sure, I can look around."

"Thanks. I also dropped off a gift and note for him at the front door the morning he died. I just couldn't bear to face him yet, so I assumed he'd see it when he returned home later that day. Did you see it?"

"That's weird. I pulled up right after you left and tried to call you. I didn't notice any note or gift sitting out."

Now I was really curious and assured Anna I would look around. When I pulled into Clive's driveway, the garage door was open and Sam was loading tools into his 4Runner. I wasn't ready to confront him about Clive's death, but it would be weird not to acknowledge him. I grabbed my stack of empty decor bins and walked to the garage.

"Hey, Sam."

"Hi." Sam didn't look up but just busied himself loading more tools. "Why are you here?"

"Same as you. Taking advantage of having access to the house to get my things before it gets closed up."

"Right. Well, see ya," he said as he walked off to the back yard.

Either he had the social skills of a toad or I was right to be suspicious.

I headed to Clive's office. I hadn't noticed anything out of the ordinary when I found his body, but it couldn't hurt to check now. The trash can I'd dropped was sitting upright in the hallway near where I'd left it. I glanced inside and noticed a card and cupcake wrappers. I didn't remember seeing those before, but maybe things shifted when I'd dropped the can. I grabbed the card and glanced inside.

Clive, I hope you enjoy your treat! I'm looking forward to discussing our contract and coming to an agreement on the terms.
Regards, Anna

So he grabbed Anna's gift and was dead a few minutes later? I put the card in my bag, not wanting to think about what it might mean and went into the office. I opened Clive's desk drawers and dug through the mess, looking for Anna's paperwork. I yanked on one of the bottom drawers but it only opened slightly, so I finagled items around. Finally the drawer pulled open and I searched through the jumble of notepads, pens, and candy wrappers. Nothing struck me as important so I started to close the drawer, except now it wasn't closing. I bent down to see the issue and found a file folder crammed against the bottom of the drawer above.

I couldn't help but open the folder, labeled "STUPID STUFF TO TAKE CARE OF" in big red Sharpie and covered with smears of food. Not to speak ill of the dead, but this guy was disgusting. Inside was a copy of a termination letter firing Anna as Clive's realtor, signed by him and dated the day before his death. Was this the paperwork she wanted me to find? *Oh shoot, Anna. Please tell me you didn't do this.*

I put Anna's letter down and frantically searched the office for evidence of Sam's connection that would give him a motive instead. I opened cabinets, quickly digging through extra office supplies. In the last cabinet, behind boxes of blank envelopes, was a portable file bin. Most of the files were labeled with New York addresses and contained real estate paperwork. The last folder was unlabeled and full of unaddressed letters.

The letters appeared to be from Clive to women he was threatening to keep quiet about something. As I flipped through the stack, my disgust growing, I heard the door from the garage open. I quickly snapped pictures of several of the letters as well as Anna's termination and put my phone in my bag.

I started coughing hard and dropped the letters. A hand covered my mouth. Everything went black.

———

I TRIED to sit up but immediately felt dizzy and nauseous. I was coughing again too. I smelled something sweet mixed with a strong floral scent.

"Just stay down, Grace. You've been attacked and I've called the police." Janice was kneeling on the floor by me, her strong perfume wafting over me.

"What happened?"

"I'm not sure. I saw Sam rushing into the garage as I walked down the hall. I had just come in the house and found you lying here. Sam's gone now but he could have killed you. You're lucky I came in when I did."

"Yeah, thanks!" Sam must have realized Madison and I knew who he was and what we suspected.

I said as much to the police after the paramedics examined me, determining I probably had been exposed to a chemical, based on how my throat was burning.

Janice and one of the officers were hovering over the letters I dropped. The officer was holding Anna's card I'd left in my bag. He dug through my bag?

———

AFTER SPENDING a few hours at the hospital and finding out it was most likely chloroform that knocked me out, I went home to rest. Could this day get any stranger? I was just drifting off for a much-needed nap when Anna called.

"They think I killed him!"

"What? Who does?" I'd never heard Anna panic before.

"The police. They just hauled me in for questioning. They knew Clive and I argued about my commission and that he was going to fire me as his realtor. He never told me I was fired! And they have a witness who said I was there the morning of the murder. I only wanted to leave the gift to encourage him to accept our contract. But I never went in the house! Like I told you, I only dropped off his bottle of whisky and the note on the doorstep. But get this … they said I gave him cupcakes with peanuts in them."

"But you don't even bake," I said.

"I know! And how was I supposed to know he was allergic to peanuts anyway?"

Why wouldn't she know? I did. Dang it, Anna. None of this made sense. I really didn't want to suspect a dear friend of murder. I also didn't want to believe she could have gassed me with chloroform.

THE NEXT MORNING, I went to the police station to give a formal statement. On the way in, I ran into my friend, the local school's resource officer, Steven, and his therapy dog partner.

"Princess Buttercup, I've missed you so much!" I got down on the floor and rubbed Buttercup behind the ears. "Do you know who poisoned me yesterday, sweetie pie?"

I started coughing again. This usually only happened when I was around cleaning products or fragrances with strong chemicals.

"Oh, sorry," Steven said. "We just came from the groomers and they put perfume on Buttercup."

Perfume. "Buttercup, you're a genius!" I gave her a big hug despite the coughing. "Steven, I know who killed Clive Trenton."

JANICE WAS THROWING a suitcase in her trunk when I pulled in front of Clive's house. She went around the back of the house, returning a few minutes later with more suitcases. It was now or never.

I walked up the drive, startling her.

"What are you doing here, Grace?"

"I just came to thank you for calling for help and saving my life. You're right that I could have been killed, especially with my asthma problems."

"Oh!" Janice looked stricken. "I'm glad you're okay. Sam should pay for what he did to you."

"And to Clive, right? But I don't think Sam killed him or attacked me, do you?" I moved closer to Janice's car. "Clive was a scumbag. All those women victimized. I can understand why you'd kill him. Why you left him the cupcakes laced with peanuts, knowing he'd gobble up any treats when he didn't think you were there to tell him no. Then you placed the evidence and Anna's card to be found nearby. Did you make sure no EpiPens were available too?"

Her face crumpled. "You don't understand! Do you *know* what he did to me all these years? All of that misogynistic abuse day in and day out."

"Why didn't you just quit?"

"Because no one has testified against him. Ever. I was just waiting for the right time to kill him."

A bark and the scent of canine perfume came from behind me.

"Janice Underhill, you're under arrest for the murder of Clive Trenton." Two Castleton Park police officers cuffed Janice and led her away.

"Goodness, Grace, I'm glad you're okay," Steven said. "You should really stop being such a nosy Parker."

"Probably." I reached down to give Princess Buttercup a pat, ignoring my cough. "One of these days, it's going to get me into trouble."

WOMEN'S INTUITION

DONNELL ANN BELL

DR. CASSIDY BLAKE

"Dr. Blake," a wide-eyed patrol officer called over his shoulder, "this is a surprise."

Nodding, I shut the van's passenger door and left Norman, my driver, who doubled as my assistant, to remove the gurney. I knew I should remember the name of the red-faced cop who greeted me. He'd been in my autopsy room a few weeks ago, days after his graduation from the Academy. He'd taken one look at the dissected body on the table and fainted. Now here he was, hands splayed, protecting the scene from a crowd of curious onlookers.

I zipped my windbreaker to ward off a breezy April morning and surveyed my surroundings. Two Colorado Springs patrol cars, a fire truck, and an ambulance flanked the curb of a beautifully landscaped home. If the dispatch operator had relayed the correct information, that ambulance wouldn't be needed. Ambulances didn't transport the dead.

I approached the cop, locating Renfro on his nametag. "Crazy day." I flinched at the understatement.

Seemed like my whole staff had deserted me. I was missing my deputy coroner, my admin, and what I could have really used about now were my ME investigators. One was on a homicide call; his counterpart was attending a seminar in Denver. We were so short-staffed I'd left my autopsy tech to man the office. "What've we got?"

"Looks like a natural," Renfro replied. "Neighbor found the victim an hour ago."

"A natural, Officer Renfro?"

The cop stiffened. "Sorry. Make that an *unattended death*."

"Much better." An unattended death meant that there was no evident cause of death and the victim died alone. My job was to discover if that category would remain on the death certificate. In my fifteen-year pathology career, I'd found loved ones disliked uncertainty as much as I did. "Where's the neighbor?" I asked.

"Officer Ellison's taking her statement next door . . . ma'am."

"Thanks. Would you ask the officer to see me before she leaves?"

Poor Renfro was red-faced again and I was tempted to lessen the sting. My significant other, Ben Davenport, called me a softie and didn't mean it as a compliment. Ben reminded me that as the newly elected Coroner of El Paso County, I shouldn't show weakness, particularly around law enforcement. Who was I to argue with the Chief of Police?

Seeing Norman struggle with the gurney, I rushed to help the man I laughingly called my assistant. Dr. Norman Betz was a retired odontologist who'd worked numerous natural disasters, comparing victims' remains with their dental records. Now a paid consultant for El Paso County, with forty years' experience to my fifteen, he was also my dad's closest friend before he passed. Norman had dropped by as I was leaving the office, discovered my predicament and offered to drive.

I caught the wrought iron storm door and propped it open with my hip. "Need some help, Doctor?"

He huffed. "I thought you'd never ask, Cassidy."

Inside, another officer apprised us further, then directed us upstairs to view the body of Miriam Gowan, age sixty-two. Clothed in jeans and a crewneck cardigan, a trim middle-aged woman lay on the carpeted floor feet away from the still-made bed.

Norman and I donned gloves and shoe coverings, then I opened my bag to perform the particulars. Rigor and livor mortis had set in, indicating she'd been dead at least eight hours. Norman, always a teacher in my case, rarely offered opinions without my coaxing. He squatted beside me. "Thoughts, Doctor?"

"She wasn't ready for bed." *Or to die,* I speculated, glancing at the treadmill and yoga mat in plain view. "No obvious sign of foul play." By the time people reached sixty, most had some blockage in their arteries. As I eyed the body and my surroundings, experience told me that unless there was something congenital, she was too young. "Let's see what else we can find."

With Norman checking elsewhere, I strode to the master bathroom. Inside the medicine cabinet, I found no prescription drugs, but there was a plethora of vitamin supplements, many of them expired.

When Norman and I rendezvoused again, he waved me into the kitchen. "It would appear Ms. Gowan entertained recently." He indicated the empty wine bottles in the recycle bin. On the counter, wrapped in plastic, was a nearly full plate of sugar cookies and a three-quarters-eaten chocolate cake. My rumbling stomach agreed it would've gone for the chocolate, too. I opened the refrigerator and found several containers of leftovers.

Norman, who'd disappeared again, returned carrying two trash bags. "There's a car in the garage with a handbag on the passenger seat."

He'd struck evidentiary gold with this discovery. Gowan's wallet contained her insurance card and listed her primary care physician. From conversations with him, Officer Ellison, and the next-door neighbor, I learned Miriam Gowan was widowed, in good health, her parents were in their eighties, she had a close circle of friends, and with her teaching pension, husband's 401K and death benefits, had recently retired.

So far, nothing sinister stood out regarding the woman now cocooned in a body bag. Still, she'd had company in the hours before she died, and I wasn't prepared to label the death certificate "undetermined."

"Let's get her to the morgue," I said.

I called Ben that afternoon, truthfully to fish for whatever information had traveled up the chain to the busy man's desk.

My partner in crime and romance could be abrupt when I called him at work. Today, he was downright chatty. He said that because of my reticence to list the cause of death, the CSPD had assigned a detective. I jotted the name Detective Emma Marsh and learned the deceased had hosted an afternoon potluck the day she succumbed. Ben also mentioned the contents of the food and drink were now in the custody of the crime lab.

"Detective Marsh interviewed everyone who attended, Cass. Like the deceased, they were teachers. Marsh ran background checks and spoke to each one separately. The four were longtime friends and no one appeared anything but devastated. What's more, they all ate and drank the same thing. No one got sick, much less died."

I was mulling over Ben's comments when he added, "Look, your staff's swamped, you have other cases, including today's *confirmed* homicide with suspects with *actual* felony records. The women Marsh interviewed don't even have parking tickets. Are you sure you want to autopsy this woman?"

I appreciated Ben coaching me on my professional demeanor; he'd been in the public eye much longer than me. But to tell me how to do my job?

I'd run for office after the former El Paso County Coroner resigned in disgrace. I was working to rebuild the public trust on a closely watched budget given me by the county commissioners. Ben endured even more scrutiny, not only for *his* actions but the actions of his officers. What was going on, and why was he suddenly giving me a blow-by-blow of the case?

My soft side disintegrated. "If Miriam Gowan had been three years younger, an autopsy would have been required. Am I sure? Not one hundred percent, no. But I'd bet my medical license something's not right here, and it's my decision, Ben."

"You're right, it is." He moved on to a safer subject, then offered to take me to dinner. I accepted.

———

I DIDN'T SLEEP well that night. Because questions remained, I decided to autopsy Gowan's body the next morning. After notifying my staff, I donned scrubs and entered Autopsy Room Two. As expected, tech Jimmie Richmond had prepped the body and laid out instruments. What I didn't expect was the noise blasting from the overhead speakers.

I dictated while I autopsied and didn't appreciate the gibberish I was hearing. *What was I hearing*? I paused to listen. "The 'something bad' Wendy Bilbersteen thought was going to happen was that she might say something extremely sarcastic when she introduced Doctor Dictionary. Outside chance she might stick out her foot and trip him."

"No podcasts, Jimmie. You know better than that."

"But, Doctor, it's not a podcast. It's an ongoing news story."

Matt Attia, my ME investigator, stood in the doorway. "My bad, Doc. You weren't here yet, and I asked Jimmie to switch on the radio. The murder of Doctor Dictionary was the talk of my seminar—and Denver. It's straight out of a cozy mystery. I was curious if they'd caught the killer yet."

My glare informed Matt we had our own killers to catch. He disappeared, Jimmie silenced the radio, and I raised my mask. "Let's get to work."

The El Paso County Coroner's Office had its own lab. Miriam Gowen's autopsy had shown typical age-related degeneration and plaque buildup, but nothing that could have brought on an early death. I was hopeful the bloodwork and tissue samples would reveal more, but that evening when I checked my email, I stared at the results. Other than alcohol impairment, which was expected, the screen was negative for toxins.

My only recourse now was to await the crime lab results, which could be days to weeks away. Meanwhile, Miriam's parents awaited answers, I hadn't released the body, and I was further behind. Ben's words came back to haunt me. "*Are you sure you want to autopsy this woman?*"

Disheartened, I considered letting his call go to voicemail the next time he called. When the phone rang, however, I pushed my ego aside and told him of my findings.

"You had to be certain," he said. "Now you know."

Two more days passed and although I already worked hard, I worked harder. I pulled into my reserved parking spot, expecting to be the first to arrive. A tan unmarked sedan two spaces down had beaten me to it. I left my vehicle at the same time a freckled-faced redhead in a sports coat and slacks exited her own.

"Dr. Blake?" She held out a badge. "Detective Emma Marsh. Spare me a few minutes?"

"For you, Detective, absolutely. Shall we—"

"I'm squeezed for time. Could we talk here? Privately?" She waved between our vehicles. "Your car or mine?"

Intrigued, I clicked the unlock button on my key fob.

"I was told the autopsy results were inconclusive," she

began as we settled into adjoining seats. "I'm here because I may have found something."

"Something indicating foul play?"

"I think so." Marsh's features took on a harsh sheen. "I made detective four months ago. Since then, I've been patted on the head and handed Major Crimes' bottom feeder jobs. Still, after interviewing everyone connected with the deceased and coming up empty, I went back to my notes. Because there was so much food and libations, I'd asked the teachers to detail what each of them had brought. I even created a spreadsheet." She handed me a copy. "See if you recognize anything off."

I scanned, noting Marsh had been thorough. Every item was categorized, and not five seconds later, the single entry of chocolate cake stood out like a castaway lighting a bonfire. "The sugar cookies, they're not listed."

Marsh beamed. "Correct. I re-interviewed every attendee. Each swears the only dessert at the potluck was the chocolate cake." She rolled her eyes. "Everybody's dieting!"

My mind raced as my heart picked up speed. "So, who brought them? The neighbor?"

"Negative. She'd agreed to babysit her grandchildren and couldn't make it. I spoke to my sergeant. He called the crime lab and asked the supervisor to put a rush analysis on the sugar cookies." Detective Marsh's freckled face brightened, and if she weren't in such a confined space, she might have jumped up and down. Rather, she blurted, "A laboratory technician discovered digitalis in the batch!"

"Shades of Sherlock Holmes," I breathed. Digitalis wasn't among the drugs tested during autopsy.

"Just to ensure there wasn't an error," Marsh continued, "the lab supervisor delivered the cookies to the Denver Crime Laboratory personally. Without divulging to her colleagues what they were looking for, she asked them to run a separate test."

"And they found?"

"Digitalis."

I white-knuckled the steering wheel. "So where are we now?"

"I just finished writing my first official warrant and subpoena to search Gowan's home and to access her computer and phone."

"Well done, Detective." I gave her a high five. "Something tells me your bottom feeder days are over."

EMMA MARSH

When Emma Marsh transferred to Major Crimes, no one in her new department had rolled out the welcome mat. In fact, one cantankerous detective had muttered so loudly, Emma was sure he'd intended for her to hear. "Couldn't they have stashed her in Evidence where she belongs?"

Two females were in the division. They'd welcomed her but kept their distance.

Fine. She had a job to do, and she would do it. With renewed determination, Emma checked email, finding the judge had signed off on the search warrant and subpoena she had written earlier. She rose to alert her sergeant. She couldn't wait to access Gowan's files and electronic devices.

DR. CASSIDY BLAKE

After a long day involving a four-hour autopsy, I was ready for a quick shower at the morgue and a longer soak at home. My admin interrupted those plans, buzzing me on the autopsy room's intercom. "Yes, Ruth?"

"Detective Marsh is on line three, Doctor."

"Thanks." I pushed three. "That was fast. Any news, Detective?"

"Just that accessing Miriam Gowan's computer has been enormously helpful. Six months ago, the victim registered on a dating site called *Something in Common*. From what I gathered from her profile, she was lonely after her husband's death and decided to try online dating.

"She didn't provide too much information, but she gave enough: widow, education, soon-to-be-retired, a list of her likes and dislikes, along with a very attractive photo."

I cringed. Some said online dating services screened better and were safer than social media. To me, there wasn't much difference. "And none of her friends or family knew about this site?"

"Asked and re-asked. Allegedly, no one knew. What I heard repeatedly was that Miriam Gowan liked her privacy."

"Can you tell if she met anyone?"

"There were eight immediate responses that seemed to go nowhere, evidently because the victim cut off communication. But there was one individual, a Roger Kaye, with whom she appeared to connect. They corresponded for months before Miriam agreed to meet him in person."

"Do you have a picture?"

"Several," Marsh replied. "Silver hair, nice tan, not extraordinarily handsome, but pleasant enough. Kaye claims he's an avid golfer—listed all the courses he's played. Miriam and her husband used to schedule golf trips so that might have sparked her interest in him. They've moved on from the dating site and have been emailing and texting since.

"I have reading to wade through tonight, but I'm not alone. The IT department's been authorized overtime."

"Call if you find anything." I gave Marsh my cell number.

At eleven-fifteen, Marsh called again, and I answered immediately.

"You want the good news or the bad news?" she said, not sounding as upbeat as her earlier call.

"Surprise me." I tightened my jaw.

"We're certain our killer is Roger Kaye—if that's his real name. I found an email where Gowan decided they'd waited long enough and begged him to meet her friends at the potluck. He said he wouldn't miss it. However, he texted later that he'd been delayed. To make it up to her, he was having a delivery service drop off a surprise. *Your favorite,* he'd texted. *My mother's secret recipe."*

I squeezed my eyes closed. Just what everybody loves—cookies sprinkled with digitalis.

"We performed a more exhaustive search today and crime scene techs found the courier receipt in a kitchen drawer. Some detective I am," Marsh lamented. "It was delivered the same day as the potluck and I missed it."

"You simply had too much evidence heaped on you at once. Have you run Roger Kaye through the FBI's database?"

The detective sighed. "There are several Roger Kayes in the National Crime Information Center." Marsh hesitated. "My sergeant's adding another detective to the case."

"Emma." I gentled my voice. "This is no reflection on you. An unattended death just exploded into something one detective can't handle alone. Trust me, you deserve credit for the lion's share of the work. Make that *lioness's* share of the work," I teased.

"Thanks, Doctor."

I thought I heard a smile in the young woman's voice.

EMMA MARSH

Emma disconnected, happier than she'd been moments ago. She'd heard people say Dr. Cassidy Blake could be difficult. That hadn't been Emma's experience. Still, she'd never crossed the woman and hoped she never would.

She was out the door by six the next morning. Today, she planned to track down the courier who'd delivered the cookies. Meanwhile, she'd check in with the detective her sergeant had assigned to Gowen's murder—something she dreaded. Lars Bingham was the crusty old buzzard who'd hinted she should have started on a lower rung as a detective.

Inside Major Crimes, Emma found Bingham engaged in

conversation with the IT tech with whom she'd been working. "What'd I miss?" she asked.

Bingham handed her a sheaf of papers. "Bad news, kid. Your dead murder vic's financial accounts have been drained. Seen this a hundred times. Lonely lady trusts the wrong guy, he bilks her for everything she's worth. Don't get your hopes up we'll ever catch this guy."

Emma's stomach dropped as Bingham stalked off. She could only hope her own tenure as a detective didn't balloon into such cynicism.

The courier service didn't open until eight. That gave Emma time to check social media and *The Gazette*. So far, Miriam Gowan's death hadn't been well publicized. She spent the early morning scrolling through the victim's phone and computer. Her frustration grew. No photo of a man other than her deceased husband appeared anywhere.

She arrived at Constant Couriers just as the courier was clocking in for his shift. Yes, he remembered a delivery to Gowan's address; no, he wasn't aware of its contents.

"When you picked up the package, did anybody sign for it?" Emma asked.

"After I pounded on the door." The courier shook his head. "A signature's required before we take possession. This dude opens the door a fraction, claims he's not decent, sticks out an arm, and asks for my pen and tablet. Afterward, he makes an X, hands it back and slams the door in my face."

Emma sighed inwardly. "So, you didn't see his face?"

"Not then," the courier replied. "But this guy had suspicious written all over him. I worked security in the military."

"You saw him later?"

"Sure did. I parked down the street and waited. Not long after, this bald white guy in a Hawaiian shirt leaves the house rolling his suitcase toward his BMW."

Recalling Roger Kay's silver hair on the dating app, Emma squeaked, "Bald?"

"As a bowling ball." The courier removed his phone.

"Don't know if it'll help, but I was so ticked off, I snapped pictures." He enlarged a photo. "Got pics of him, his car, even his license plate. Check this out."

Emma did, then called her sergeant.

DR. CASSIDY BLAKE

Ben and I were at lunch when he got the phone call. He studied the caller ID, apologized, then left the table. We'd been through this a time or two. I signaled the waiter and asked for the check.

Ben had just pocketed his cell when I stepped outside. "That was Detective Marsh's sergeant," Ben said. "She located a witness who photographed a possible suspect in the Gowan murder. He also got the make of his vehicle along with his plates."

"That's a great witness," I said.

"Even better, the CSPD put out a BOLO. The State Patrol pulled over the suspect. Search of his vehicle netted a suitcase filled with wigs and other disguises. No digitalis in his effects but the sergeant believes there's a strong possibility he's Gowan's killer."

I couldn't contain the grin spreading across my face.

Ben noticed and linked his arm through mine. "Pretty pleased with yourself, aren't you, Doctor?"

"That, and I'm happy for Detective Marsh. Like me, she didn't accept the foregone conclusion Ms. Gowan died a natural death. This is Emma's first big case, and she doubled down to solve it—in five days, no less."

"Impressive," Ben said. "I'd say you two women have incredible instincts."

I raised an eyebrow. "Instincts, Ben?"

"All right. Make that education and experience."

"Much better," I said.

THE PURGATORY OF EMILY GRAY

FLEUR BRADLEY VISSCHER

"Who is your missing person?" I click my pen and hold it over a clean notebook, the kind kids take to school at the beginning of the school year. It's a ritual for me. New case, clean notebook.

The man (named Lewison Ward—yes, *that* Ward family, the one with the eight gazillion grocery stores) who sits across from me looks like he has money. Expensive golf pants and polo shirt. Good shoes—you can tell a lot about a person by what shoes they wear. He can afford to pay me.

I hate to think like this, but the electric bill is a month past due, the water bill two. River, my nephew who I'm responsible for, has a camping trip that costs sixty bucks.

Mr. Ward huffs. "I don't know who can help me at this point!" A frazzled rich guy. This one feels iffy.

I smile, though, thinking of how my fee can cover those three bills. Maybe there'll even be enough money left over to get donuts for breakfast. Lou, my grandfather who founded his PI agency Lost & Found, he loves donuts.

I say, "Why don't you start with who is missing, Mr. Ward."

My private investigations focus on finding missing people. I have a nose for it, although sometimes I think I should branch out. Especially when I get the mail and there are two past due bills, and I sit across from a client like Mr. Ward.

We're at his house, a fake lodge-looking affair with a view of the valley of Aspen Springs, a Colorado mountain town. The house sits inside a gated community within its own gate, because when you're really rich, one gate is not enough. The house is decorated in tacky-lodge style, complete with a bear hide nailed to the wall. Some sort of muzak that annoys my ear is playing from an invisible stereo system.

Mr. Ward sighs. He leans forward on the leather couch. "She's haunting me. Emily Gray—she was my assistant twenty years ago." He is wringing his hands on his lap. I see now that he's older than I originally thought. Definitely in his sixties.

"The missing often haunt us all," I say, cringing at my own platitude. I'm hoping my calm, Zen-like demeanor will mellow Mr. Ward out. "I understand."

He shakes his head. "No, you don't. Emily is dead. She was murdered, and she's been haunting me ever since. She's in purgatory!"

Normally, I don't do hauntings. I don't believe in the after-life, and I'm not a psychic. But the bills …

I click my pen. "Tell me more, Mr. Ward."

CASE NUMBER 855. Friday, April 11th. Emily Gray, the twenty-two-year-old intern-slash-assistant to Mr. Ward, had been let go and was escorted outside the company building, which was located in a Denver tech center. She was going to take the bus, but for some reason had decided to walk instead. The company's cameras followed her until she disappeared from view. Mr. Ward was kind enough to have his security team forward the footage.

I watch it several times, but can't find any clues, other

than feeling a kinship to Emily. I had been unceremoniously fired myself, from a well-paying job as a journalist in Seattle. That same day, my boyfriend dumped me and told me to move out. I was a walking, talking country song. But the heartbreaking thing came when my grandpa Lou called to tell me my sister Tori had gone missing.

Finding my sister was my very first case as a PI. I have since solved more than a dozen cases, all while running the family cabin rental business (it makes sense somehow) with my grandpa. It was strange to think back to my early days, and how it felt to move to Colorado after being gone for a decade.

Back to the case. Mr. Ward tells me Emily was found a few days after she disappeared, stabbed and left for dead in an alleyway near her Denver apartment. He hands me a folded-up newspaper clipping about Emily's murder that's practically turning to dust in my hands. The ink is barely legible and the image of Emily (a school picture) too pixelated to be of any help.

Mr. Ward knows little about her, other than that Emily was from the East Coast and only had a handful of friends at the time of her death. Twenty years ago. This case is as cold as the knife she was stabbed with.

But Mr. Ward writes a check for three times my normal fee, so of course I take the job. "Please, solve this murder and help Emily cross over, so she won't haunt me anymore." He describes typical paranormal events: voices in the night, cold air out of nowhere, the smell of rose-scented perfume wafting in. I resist the urge to roll my eyes, because I don't believe in ghosts.

As I leave the Ward house, I catch a whiff of roses.

"You smell that, right?" Mr. Ward clutches my arm. Outside, there are freshly pruned rosebushes. That's obviously what's causing the floral smell.

"Leave it to me," I say to Mr. Ward in my most reassuring PI voice. "Lost & Found is on the case."

I RETURN to my office (a tiny house in our resort), cash the check, pay the bills, and regret the whole thing instantly. This case isn't just cold; it's frozen. I need help if I'm going to get anywhere.

The check clears, so I procrastinate by buying Lou some donuts and bringing them to his tiny house. He's like a kid, picking his favorite out of the box. He loves the kind with custard inside.

"Thank you, Mr. Ward," he mutters as he sinks his teeth in. Lou is having a good day. Sometimes, he gets confused or forgetful. Dementia is a cruel house guest. "Emily, huh. Never heard about this case." Lou was a Denver PD detective for thirty years before retiring and moving to Aspen Springs. He would've been on the job at the time of Emily's murder.

I'm on my third donut with no regrets. I use my sticky fingers to do a quick internet search on Emily's murder. Nothing comes up.

"You should call Petey." Lou gives me a sideways grin.

Peter Smith, a Denver PD detective, is my best source. He's also my childhood friend; there are several pictures of us splashing in kiddie pools and eating birthday cake. Only now, Peter is a grown and very attractive man with a big stick up his—

Lou interrupts my thoughts. "You don't have anything else to go on in this case."

He's right. I groan and eat another donut. My gut is already protesting, partly because of the donuts and partly because of the dread of calling Peter.

I step outside Lou's cabin. It's spring; soon the cabins will be booked solid, kids playing in the park, s'mores at the firepit in the center of it all. Right now, it's still calm, and I enjoy the quiet and the breeze on the porch steps for just a minute.

Then I pull up Peter's number on my phone. I'm secretly hoping he won't answer.

He does, on the second ring. "Isa. How are things in PI Land?"

"Great, business couldn't be better," I lie. I pause.

"Just tell me what you need." His tone is soft. He must be having a good day. "I know you're not calling to chat."

"What if I was?" I say before I can think better of it. We flirt. It's our thing.

Peter is silent on the other end of the line, because he knows I'm just calling him for information. That's also our thing.

"Fine, you're right." I sigh. "Emily Gray. Missing, found stabbed." I give him the location and her full name and age.

I can hear keyboard keys clacking. "Nope."

I spell her name, again.

"Still a no, Isa."

I feel a headache coming on and regret the sugary donuts. I've already spent my fee on overdue bills. I have to deliver Emily Gray's killer. "Not even missing?" A girl can hope.

Peter doesn't bother to answer. "You still owe me that green chili dinner you promised the last time."

"Yeah, yeah." I hang up, feeling stumped.

What happened to Emily Gray?

MY NEPHEW RIVER ends up eating the rest of the donuts, and since none of us are hungry, we graze leftovers for dinner. I really have to work on cooking, or at least making it to the grocery store for healthier options.

The donuts are tumbling in my stomach when I make the hour-long drive to Denver, where Emily disappeared.

"Who killed you, Emily?" I mutter as I sit in my old truck. There was the building. And the bus stop. I'm parked across the street, trying to imagine what it would've been like back in 2005. Could she have walked home? But then why take the bus in the first place? Was there snow? I didn't see any on the security footage Mr. Ward sent me, but that didn't mean there wasn't any coming that day. I really don't feel like looking up the weather from twenty years ago.

I'm about to drive away when I hear a chime. Bells, the kind a tourist trolley uses to get people to move out of the way.

Maybe Emily decided to take the trolley instead, if it was in operation back then. I watch it pick up a few tourists. I think of following it, but then realize it's still too wide of a net to cast. There's no murder case, no missing persons file, nothing to go on.

I hate to admit it, but I'll have to tell Mr. Ward I can't solve Emily's murder. It's impossible.

I'M NOW DRAGGING my feet on the case. The next day, I drive River to school. He's drawing in his sketchbook, the page turned away from me so I can't see. I don't mind. He's a good kid, and besides, he's entitled to have his secrets.

River has high-functioning autism, I found out last year. There are only some moments I notice it, like now when he is hunched over his notebook with his earmuffs on. After my sister disappeared and River's dad was out of the picture, I became his legal guardian. I'm still adjusting.

While we're waiting at a light, I flip through the radio stations.

"It is now known that Olivia Twist, suspect in the Doctor Dictionary murder, knew about Doctor Dic's allergy to marijuana, although he was never public about it with his fans, especially the kids. Everyone remembers his famous sign-off: *Don't do drugs and be sure to wear your sunscreen!*"

River has one ear out of his earmuffs and listens. "This

case is all anyone is talking about. What dude would even want to be known as Doctor Dic?"

I laugh. Hanging out with River always makes me feel better. He puts everything in perspective.

The newscaster continues, "Doctor Dic's allergy was common knowledge, though. Anonymous tipsters tell us that Wendy Bilbersteen was seen by many people popping gummy edibles. Did she dose Doctor Dictionary?"

I turn the radio off. "You're right, it's stupid." The next left gets us to the middle school. "Do you need lunch money?"

River shakes his head. "Nah. Stuff's garbage."

He's right. Of course, I'm about to stop by my favorite food truck for a breakfast burrito. The kid is healthier than I am.

"What's the case today?" River drops his earmuffs and closes his sketchbook. He tucks the pencil behind his ear like an old man.

I tell him about Emily Gray and how I'm stuck. We inch our way down the drop-off line at his school. I don't tell him about the bills. I'm not about to burden the kid with stuff like that. I grew up not knowing if I was going to have a meal that day or a roof over my head. I don't want that for River. "Anyway, I'll just have to do some digging, see if maybe the case is out of the metro jurisdiction." I sound more optimistic than I actually am.

River tucks his notebook inside his flannel shirt's front pocket. "Maybe she isn't dead."

I'm about to scoff when I realize he's right: Emily Gray is probably alive. If she was murdered, I would've gotten case information from Peter. I smile. "You're a genius, River."

He gets out of the truck. "I know."

———

IT DOESN'T TAKE me long to get back to my office and run Emily's full name through our database. It takes a little digging, but I eventually find a county record. Emily Gray changed her name. For the past twenty years, she's been living as Rose McGuire. She owns a landscaping company, Rose Landscaping. I bring up her address.

Rose lives in the Aspen Springs mobile home park that's right at the base of Mr. Ward's neighborhood. Outside the double gates, of course. I grab my coat and drive over there, hoping I can catch her at home.

I'm lucky. She's just unlocking her trailer when I get there. She's wearing overalls and a sunhat, the kind hikers wear.

"Rose?" I ask, putting on my best smile.

"Who wants to know?" She turns to me, and I wish I had something other than that grainy newspaper article's photo to go on. But I'm betting it's her. She has very blue eyes and a hard stare.

"Do you provide landscaping services at the Ward house?" I say as the pieces fall into place.

Rose shrugs. "Maybe." She holds the door cracked but doesn't go inside or invite me in. I can't blame her. She doesn't know me.

But I have to get the truth.

"I know you weren't *always* Rose," I say softly.

She closes the door and backs away from me a half-step, until she's wedged against her front door. "Who sent you?"

I shake my head. "Look, I won't tell anyone that you live here. And especially not Mr. Ward. I just want to hear your side of the story." I hand her my card, which she takes as enough proof to let me inside.

The place is clean and decorated with vintage furniture. A designer might call it eclectic. My place is similarly outfitted, so I know it's as much about budget as it is about style. Rose gets me a glass of water and guides me toward her living room.

I lean forward in the overstuffed chair. "Tell me about Lewison Ward."

She exhales. "It started out innocent," Rose says, as she

sits in the chair across from me. She holds my card and turns it between her index fingers. "Ward was just flirting with the intern, you know. It was gross, but pretty typical. He was the boss, so I wasn't about to complain to HR." She pauses. "But he started waiting for me after work and walking me to the bus. Then he showed up at my front door with a bottle of wine."

"A stalker," I say, because that's what he was.

Rose nods. "I was able to get him to leave but he drank that bottle of wine and came back. And he broke into my apartment."

The silence is heavy.

I don't want to ask her if she reported the assault to the police, because I know it's not that easy. Guys like Ward get charges dropped so easily, or the police turn the victim into a suspect. Not everyone wants to travel that road.

"I got pregnant. And then I lost the baby a month in." She shakes her head and bites her lip. "I took a week off after the attack. Then the company fired me. But he still called my house, showed up at the grocery store when I was there—it just didn't end."

I wait for her to find the words, my notebook still closed and in my bag. This is off the record.

"There was no other way to get rid of him but to disappear." She looks at me, her eyes brimming with tears but her face angry. "I faked a murder and had a friend send him the mocked-up newspaper article. I changed my name, changed my look, and moved in with my cousin in Illinois for a while. But then I thought, why does he get to live his life like nothing happened?"

"So you started haunting him."

Rose nods and half-grins. "I opened my business and worked hard to get that contract. With my different hair, glasses, and a hat, Ward doesn't even recognize me. It's so easy. You're just invisible to rich guys like that, unless they want something from you."

I know the feeling all too well.

The grin turns devious. "It has been a lot of fun, to watch him think he's lost his mind."

I nod. "He thinks you're dead. In purgatory."

"Emily Gray *is* dead." Her eyes are fierce. "And she's one vengeful freakin' ghost."

I WAIT out the rest of the week, contemplating what I'll tell Mr. Ward. Do I give him a fake killer's name? Do I report Ward's assault to the police? But that was Rose's choice, not mine.

In the end, I drive up to the Ward house and meet with him. He did pay me to do a job. I'll just have to get a little creative when it comes to considering the case closed.

Lewison Ward is so eager to hear what I have to say, his hands are shaking. We sit in his faux lodge living room, the smell of roses lingering in the air. I resist the urge to smile.

"Tell me, tell me," he says, leaning forward in his chair.

I pull out the fake report and hand it to him. "I talked to some of her known associates," I lie. I don't feel guilty about it. "There was a man who'd been stalking her, apparently. So bad, she feared for her safety."

"Did he kill her? What's his name?" Ward adjusts his seat as I look at him. The information finally clicks. He freezes.

I take a beat. I want him to know that *I* know that this stalker was him.

"This man stalked her at your office, apparently." I pause. "There may still be footage at Ward Enterprises—evidence of this stalker following her. Like that footage of her leaving the building when she was fired."

"*Let g*o," he says quickly. "Emily was *let go*; it was normal for an internship to end."

I don't say anything. I leave the implication of the possibility of evidence hanging in the air. Evidence that Ward stalked Emily Gray.

He folds the report. Twice.

"Emily Gray is dead," I say. Now I'm not lying. "You'll just have to make peace with that."

I hear the sound of a hedge trimmer coming from outside and I smile—to myself, of course. Rose's secret is safe with me.

Ward shows me out, his shoulders slumped like he's carrying the weight of the world on them. A guilty man.

At the door, I say, "Sometimes, a spirit is pleased if you make good on their suffering." Oh brother, I'm full of it. "There are plenty of women's shelters in Denver that could use a donation."

Ward is pale and nods. He closes the door.

He's the one in purgatory now.

MRS. T

FRANCELIA BELTON

"If you leave now, you get nothing."

Lonnie's words followed Curtis as he stormed out the back door of Mrs. Thompson's old Victorian house. *And if you tell anyone what happened, I'll kill you* was the implied threat behind those words.

Curtis swallowed the lump of guilt and fury lodged in his throat as he trudged across the dew wet yard. Head down, hands in jacket pockets, he stalked down the block to where he and Lonnie left his car. Screw Lonnie! Curtis knew they would be breaking into one of the big homes in Park Hill tonight, he just didn't know it was going to be Mrs. T's. He didn't remember until the moment Lonnie stopped in front of her house that Mrs. T was on a week-long cruise. The cruise she didn't go on ten years ago with her husband to celebrate their 50th anniversary, because he had died on their way to the airport.

So here it was, ten years later on April 12th. On what would have been their 60th year together, Mrs. Regina Thompson at long last was able to let go of her grief and tour the country she and her beloved Abraham always wanted to visit. Shirley, her longtime housekeeper, accompanied her. Was it Italy? France? Curtis couldn't remember.

It didn't matter.

If he had known it was going to be her house they were hitting tonight, he would have never gone along. And yet … Lonnie was able to talk him into going into the house—*it'll be in and out, just grab a couple of things*—and like a fool, he went along. It wasn't worth it to beef with Lonnie over a couple of things Mrs. T probably wouldn't miss. However, when it came right down to it, Curtis couldn't do it. *He* would know. And he couldn't steal from Mrs. T. Not after what she had done for him. Not after being so nice to him. Not after believing in him.

Curtis's Pontiac G5 Coupe was parked under the canopy of a large American elm that blocked the streetlight from shining on the car. He opened the driver's door and got behind the wheel. Then he shut the door, being careful not to slam it, and turned the key in the ignition. The engine turned over, but instead of pulling away from the curb, Curtis stared down the block toward Mrs. T's house. He didn't like that someone was wandering through her home, invading her space, poking through her house of memories.

The warm air from the dash vents started fogging the windshield, obscuring his view. He knew he should drive away and pretend like he didn't know about any of this. Go home, get back in his warm bed, and don't think about how devastated Mrs. T will be when she gets back from her trip to find that her home had been broken into. But worse, that her treasured family heirlooms were gone. Why didn't she ever put an alarm on her house? Or why didn't her husband, back when he was alive? Why didn't they think to protect their possessions? Just because they lived in Park Hill didn't mean they were exempt from being targeted.

Curtis fiddled with the knobs on the dash and turned on the radio. "According to reports, Charlotte Webb was seen arguing with a guy in a tuxedo skulking around with a large trash bag." He turned the knobs some more looking for music, but all he got was country, jazz, or commentary, so he went back to the original station. "The kitchen staff couldn't make out anything they said, except the words, *Doctor Dictionary* and *I told you not to!*"

Curtis clicked off the radio and slammed his fist on the dash. Man, why did it have to be Mrs. T's house? Why couldn't it have been one of the neighbors? *Because she was the one out of the country for a week,* he chided to himself. How did Lonnie even know about that in the first place? Curtis hadn't told him.

Working for Mrs. T was a side job, something Curtis did on his own time. He wouldn't even let her pay him anymore. She was the one who gave him his first job when he got out of juvie for stealing seven years ago. The only one who trusted him and had faith in him. Because of her, he finished his vocational classes at Denver Community College and got a job as a mechanic. She was sweet. She was trusting. And she didn't deserve to be robbed. Not after she had finally found the courage to leave her house and truly live her life again. Curtis hated to think what something like this would do to her failing heart. He couldn't do it. He couldn't let Lonnie do it.

Lonnie would have to find another payday.

Curtis' hands gripped the steering wheel, moving back and forth over the imitation leather. He swore and slapped the top curve of the wheel. He had to go back in there and tell Lonnie to get out.

There were plenty of other houses to hit in Park Hill.

CURTIS CREPT through the back door of Mrs. T's house. The kitchen was dark, except for one of those plug-in night lights which illuminated Mrs. T's hot water kettle on the counter. "Lonnie," he stage-whispered. He wasn't sure why he did that, not like anyone could hear him. These old houses were built with bricks and plaster.

Overhead, the floor groaned under the weight of someone

walking above. Curtis' heart revved into overdrive. Lonnie was upstairs. Could be in Mrs. T's bedroom. Curtis gave up any semblance of quiet or caution. "Lonnie!" His voice boomed through the empty house. He darted out the kitchen, through the hallway to the foot of the stairs. Then, bounding up, taking them two steps at a time, not caring about the noise anymore. "Lonnie, stop!"

Lonnie stepped from Mrs. T's bedroom and into the hallway, a 9mm pistol in his hand.

Curtis pulled up short and lost his footing, almost falling back. He grabbed the stair railing. "Lonnie, what the—?"

"What are you doing back here? I thought you chickened out."

"I ain't scared. I just don't think this is the house we need to be hitting tonight."

"Oh? And why is that? It's perfect. Nobody's home, and no one's about to be anytime soon."

Lonnie was right. This was usually how they chose the houses they hit. They made sure the house would be empty for at least a few hours, but in an ideal situation, nobody would be home for days.

Curtis took a lungful of air. There was nothing to do but come clean. "Look, man, okay, here's the truth." He stepped forward so he wouldn't be inches from tumbling back down the stairs. "I know the old lady. I sometimes help her around the house, shovel her walks when it snows, change a light bulb, bring her groceries. Those sorts of things. I've known her for a few years, and I just don't feel right about it."

Lonnie nodded as he took in what Curtis just told him, then a slow, devious smile spread across his face. "I was wondering when you were gonna fess up."

Curtis slumped against the hallway wall. "Wait, you knew?"

"Yeah, my girl, Latonya, is Shirley's niece. And the old lady's always bragging to anyone who'll listen about her sweet, reformed Curtis. And know this … I'm not here just for some knickknacks and trinkets. I'm here for one specific reason." Lonnis's smile spread, showing teeth. "You've been holding out on me, buddy."

"I don't know what you're talking about."

"Still gonna pretend like you don't know anything? Shame on you. I thought we were like brothers." Lonnie pressed his lips tight and shook his head in mock disappointment.

"We are, but come on, man, not the old lady I work for."

"I know about the pocket watch."

"What?"

"The old watch that's worth a lot of money. We're talking like a hundred Gs, man. Think of the ride I could get with that."

Curtis felt like he was sucker punched below the belt. He remembered a few months back an estate lawyer came by the house and met with Mrs. T. Later, she had told Shirley and him that she wanted to settle her affairs. She and her husband had no children, so to make sure her estate didn't end up in probate court, she wanted it drawn up so that the proceeds from the sale of her assets went to various charities, most especially domestic abuse and foster care shelters. She knew Curtis had come from the system and believed everyone should have a second chance at life.

But she most definitely didn't mention anything about an old expensive watch, and Curtis wanted to believe that even if she had, he would not have wanted to steal it. No matter how much it was worth. No matter how much he could have used the money.

"Lonnie, listen, I'll help you hit whatever house you want, but I'm begging you, not Mrs. T. She's a nice old lady that's never hurt anyone. She doesn't deserve this." Curtis reached for his phone in his pocket.

"I wouldn't do that if I were you." Lonnie gestured with the gun.

"You're actually going to shoot me?"

"I will if I have to. But I'd rather you help me find the watch. Then, we can part ways now and forever. Needless to say, the terms of our friendship have expired. Now, give me your phone." He held out his hand.

Curtis handed it over. "I can't believe you'd shoot me, man."

Lonnie slid Curtis' phone in his back pocket. "Was never the plan. But if you think I'm going to stand here and watch you call the cops, then you're dumber than I thought." He shook his head. "I don't know what to think about you anymore. You gone soft or something. Doing gigs like this has always been our bread and butter. But nah, you gotta go to college, get a job, act like you're better than everyone else. But you ain't. You're still that l'il punk from the system ain't nobody cares about. So either you help me, or the old lady is not only going to come home to find out she's been ripped off, but she's going to come home to a familiar dead body lying at the foot of her stairs."

"Okay." Curtis held up his hands. "Okay."

"Look at the bright side, as long as we straighten up behind ourselves, she'll never know she was hit. It'll be like no one was ever here. Now, does she have a safe? Latonya didn't know that. Her aunt never told her."

"I don't know. Not that I ever saw. I've never been upstairs."

Lonnie narrowed his eyes.

"Man, I'm telling you the truth. I've never been up here. This is like her private space or whatever."

"Okay, then. We'll have to do this the hard way. I already checked her bedroom. I didn't see anything."

Curtis' stomach tightened. That wasn't cool, Lonnie going through Mrs. T's personal things.

But Lonnie took a step back and gestured for Curtis to precede him as they went into the second bedroom. The guest room. They looked behind the paintings hanging on the wall, opened the drawers of the nightstand and dresser, and checked under the mattress and bed frame. Nothing that indicated a hidey-hole or secret compartment. They even searched the bathrooms, though Curtis doubted Mrs. T would hide a watch in there.

"I think you're holding out on me, man. You know, I could just pay a return visit to grandma when she gets back and interrogate her point blank for the watch. And I'll be sure to tell her that I'm here because of you."

"Look, I told you I didn't know about any watch."

"Man, you're testing my patience. Mrs. T is about to come home to a dead body." Lonnie held up the gun and pointed it straight at Curtis' face.

"Wait! Her husband had a study downstairs. That's where Mrs. T always met with her lawyer. Maybe it's in there."

"You could have started with that."

"How was I supposed to know? I don't hang around listening to her business."

They headed downstairs. It felt like a death march to Curtis. He couldn't delay, he couldn't stall any longer. The study would be the most logical place she would keep a very expensive watch. The room was filled with bookshelves and had a desk and credenza that held papers and journals, and books, tons of books. Curtis would sometimes sit at the desk tinkering with household appliances and various other items that needed repair, while she sat in the easy chair, reading a passage or two from her favorite book to pass the time. She liked to read to him the old classics. Books from her childhood, but ones that he might like himself. Curtis wasn't much for reading, but he always indulged her. In many ways, she was like the grandmother he never had and a part of him knew he should treasure it.

He opened the double doors to the study, and they went inside. Lonnie immediately went to the desk and started rummaging through the drawers.

Curtis walked up and saw some of the half-finished projects strewn across the desk blotter. There was her second pair of reading glasses that needed another screw in the frame to keep the lens from popping out. The vintage toaster that needed a new spring. Hidden among the broken and disassembled items was a black one-button fob. Mrs. T's back-up medical alert. He was supposed to put a new battery in it.

There was only one thing he could do.

He stepped away from the desk and started pulling items from the shelves. "I bet there is something hidden behind one of these panels."

Lonnie dropped the Montblanc pen he was holding into the open drawer and came over.

On the top shelf, Curtis pulled down an ornate wooden box with a lock on it. There were intricate designs carved in the wood. Lonnie came over and seized it from his hands. "I bet this is it." There was a little lock on it, but it didn't take much for Lonnie to pry it open with the letter opener he grabbed from the desk.

Curtis wandered away, knowing he didn't have much time. He went back to the desk and scrounged around for the coin cell battery that he hoped he left on the desk next to the fob. Sure enough, it was there. Sweat beaded on his brow as he used the tiny flathead screwdriver next to the broken glasses to pry off the back of the alert. With trembling fingers, he popped the battery in and pushed the button.

Nothing. The red light didn't come on.

He cursed under his breath. Did he put the old battery back in? He pressed the button again.

"Got it!" Lonnie's shout nearly had Curtis jumping out of his skin. "We found it, brother! We got the mother lode."

The look of triumph and exhilaration on Lonnie's face almost made Curtis forget where he was and filled him with the same excitement they both would get when they hit pay dirt. Until he saw what Lonnie held in his hands. The strikingly ornate gold pocket watch twirling on the chain.

Curtis couldn't deny it. It was a thing of beauty. It was

almost a shame it was locked up and hidden away. It needed to be seen.

In the distance, the sound of sirens blasted through the early morning air. Lonnie peeled his gaze from the watch and glared at Curtis, lifting the gun from his side and brandishing it in Curtis' face. "Man, what did you do?"

Curtis held up his hands. "I didn't do anything."

Lonnie set the watch back in the box and shut the lid. "Doesn't matter. I got what I came for. I'm outta here."

But before Lonnie could leave the room, on impulse, Curtis picked up the old broken toaster on the desk and hurled it at Lonnie. It slammed into the back of his head with an audible clunk and Lonnie fell to the carpeted floor. The wooden box's lid broke open and out tumbled the watch.

The sirens approached the house and the red and white lights strobed through the windows. Curtis stepped outside with his hands above his head.

Firemen and paramedics raced up the paved walk. "Where's the medical emergency?"

"Inside the study."

The medical personnel rushed past, but the police officer who accompanied them asked who he was.

Curtis replied, "I'm the guy that's supposed to help take care of the place while Mrs. Thompson is away."

"Curtis Chambers, you have a visitor." Curtis shuffled behind the sheriff's deputy to the visiting room, expecting to see his court-appointed attorney. Instead, Mrs. T sat behind the plexiglass barrier, a patient smile engulfing her wrinkle-lined face.

"I heard what happened."

Curtis hung his head in shame. "I'm really sorry, Mrs. T. I know I must be a disappointment to you."

She tapped on the plexiglass and waited until Curtis

looked her in the eye. "No. I am not disappointed. I'm proud of you. I know what you had to do that night wasn't easy."

No, it wasn't. Curtis knew Lonnie would never forgive him. Curtis wasn't sure he could forgive himself. But he also knew he couldn't live with himself if he had done otherwise.

"They're saying this is your third strike. That you're not getting out."

Curtis nodded.

"But there were extenuating circumstances. You turned yourself in."

He shrugged. It didn't matter, three was three.

"Well, I happen to know a really good estate lawyer whose daughter went into criminal law. Turns out we can file an appeal to petition the court to have you re-sentenced with a penalty that reflects your second strike, rather than the mandatory twenty-five years. But we're going to work to have the case dismissed."

Mrs. T placed her palm on the plexiglass. "You're a good boy, Curtis. I'm not going to give up on you and I expect you to do the same."

She kept her hand up on the scratched and grimy plastic. After a moment, Curtis lifted his hand and placed his palm opposite hers. Mrs. T was his family, and she showed she would do anything for him and he for her, and there was nothing more he could want.

VIGGO'S PRIZE

G.P. GOTTLIEB

Ginny Grasso shuffled into the activity room and bristled at the sight of someone slouched in a wheelchair in front of the television, blocking the screen. After a few more steps, Ginny recognized Melvin Figa, whom she liked. He was the only man on the third floor who had a full head of silver hair and some personality still intact.

He was friendly, about her age, and had introduced her to his friends among the residents. He'd also amused her with a stream of quips and sly remarks about their surroundings. She'd have considered pursuing him as husband number four if they were a decade or so younger, less decrepit, and weren't already counting down their remaining days at Denver's posh Alameda Arms Senior Residences.

Ginny's mind was sharp, and she was ambulatory, unlike many of the other residents, but she had chronic lung disease, rheumatoid arthritis, and vestibular balance problems. After her last tumble, while she was high on painkillers, her daughter Margo had moved her to what Ginny saw as death's waiting room, despite the posh furniture and spectacular views.

The well-heeled residents at the Alameda Arms spent their final months entertained by visiting performers and perky activity directors. They were sustained by flavorless meals and easily digestible but tasteless desserts. It was worse than prison food and yet another indignity of getting old.

In addition to her other health problems, Ginny's hearing was precarious, so the television lounge was a cacophony of sound. Hearing aids helped her get through one-on-one conversations, but they were useless in a crowded room, and according to three different doctors, she wasn't a candidate for cochlear implants. Silence would have been better than the constant buzzing punctuated by sporadic barking, usually from an attendant yelling at someone who'd tried to get up without their walker.

"Hello, Mel," she said to the slouching gentleman, "mind if I join you to watch the news?"

She was dying to sit down. It had been a tiring day, what with getting her hair cut in the morning and an hour spent on the phone closing the one final bank account that neither the IRS nor her daughter had found. Then, her grandson Viggo paid a visit in the afternoon.

Melvin smiled like she was the best thing to happen all day and said, "Don't you look nice today." Ginny was eighty-five, her face was a river of wrinkles, and her hips were disintegrating so that she limped like a wounded animal, but it felt good to be the recipient of a man's attention.

"I'd be delighted for you sit by me," Melvin added in his Texas drawl. "You know, Ginny, it was a pleasure to meet your grandson today. It's so nice that he comes to see you every week. None of my grandchildren even bother calling." He shook his large head. "And my sons stopped being interested once I signed everything over to them."

Ginny returned Melvin's smile. She'd felt much cheerier since changing her will so that her beloved grandson would inherit everything as soon as he turned thirty. Unlike his mother, Viggo had always been interested in Ginny's stories about her family and her once exciting life. She saw herself in him and couldn't imagine him ever becoming critical and disapproving like his mother.

She paid both her own and Margo's rent and expenses, and she'd made it clear that her continued good health was in Margo's best interest, but Margo had moved her into the Alameda Arms when she'd been too weak to protest. Their relationship had been fraught for years and Ginny thought it was too late to do anything about it.

Everyone on the third floor had met Viggo, because he'd already come three times since Margo moved her in a few weeks before. He'd brought a box of fresh strawberries with him, which she appreciated, because the seemingly ritzy Alameda Arms served a lot of canned fruit.

During his visit, Viggo had talked about his post-college plan to travel over the summer, and Ginny told him about a fabulous trip she'd had in Italy in the 1980s, but as she spoke, she wondered if she was recalling a movie or her real life. After a pleasant chat in her room, Viggo had walked her to the lounge, greeted everyone, asked how they were doing, and generously flashed his impish grin.

"Viggo is a delightful kid," she said to Melvin, "and he's going to be on the five o'clock news today. He's getting a prize from the University of Denver. I need to sit close so I can see and hear him."

It was ten minutes to five. Ginny had probably told every single person on the third floor about Viggo's prize and his television appearance.

"I'd be happy to move so you have a better view, if someone would help me," Melvin said as he gazed out the big front western-facing windows. "You know, I'd be looking out at the mountains if it wasn't such a foggy day." He chuckled at his non-joke and scanned the room for one of the attendants.

Ginny looked out the window on the other side of the room. The mountains were frosted with snow in the distance and glistened in the bright sun, but Melvin was plagued by macular degeneration, in addition to his immobility. What a match they'd make, she thought. He could barely see, and Ginny could barely hear.

She watched him struggle to move his electric wheelchair. Shouldn't there be an attendant in the room in case of exactly this situation? She checked her watch – seven minutes before the news began. A staff member sauntered in, and Melvin raised his hand to ask for help.

Ginny settled on the chair next to Melvin, close to the television, as the newscasters appeared on the screen. The man wore a dark jacket and tie and had the chiseled good looks of Ginny's third husband, the one she'd been saddest to leave. The woman was a beautiful brunette in a tight red blouse who reminded Ginny of her sister Rose, whose motto had been, *if you've got it, flaunt it.*

The male newscaster said it was in the low sixties and blustery. He read local stories about a tree that had damaged a roof in West Washington Park, a fire in the Five Points neighborhood, and a thwarted robbery at a store on South Colorado Boulevard. A picture of a suspect running, holding a gun, appeared on the screen.

The tiny, fussy woman sitting to the left of Melvin's wheelchair, who dressed like she was expecting to be 'wined and dined' at one of the fancy new restaurants near Union Station, pointed at the television and bellowed, "Isn't that Ginny's grandson with the red hair and freckles? He's wearing the same blue shirt he wore when he was here today."

Ginny knew Elsbeth Turner's booming voice and froze for a second before repeating the "pft" sound that her father, the first Viggo, used to make whenever he thought something was absurd. The robbery suspect in the picture might have had red hair, and might have worn a blue sweatshirt, but Ginny's grandson did not need to commit armed robberies.

"That was not Viggo," she said, pointing to the screen, now showing an ad for hemorrhoid cream. She heard increased buzzing in the room but as usual couldn't decipher what anyone else was saying. "That was definitely not my grandson."

Elsbeth shouted, "You told everyone that he was going to be on the television today."

Melvin came to Ginny's aid, saying, "He's getting a prize from the University of Denver, for goodness' sake. Now that's a good kid."

Ginny could have kissed him, but she couldn't risk moving quickly. She should have known better than to brag about Viggo. After a lifetime of keeping family stories to herself, she'd turned into the kind of person who boasted, like all of them, about their grandchildren. Ginny only had Viggo.

Someone sitting behind Ginny said, "Congratulations."

Elsbeth said, "I think that suspect looked exactly like Ginny's grandson."

"Well, none of us have the clear vision we used to have," said Melvin, still on Ginny's side.

Ginny felt herself prickling. "My grandson is getting an award for volunteering at homeless shelters all through college," she said, matching Elsbeth's volume. "Did someone in your family get honored today?"

She was glad when the sleek newscaster in the tight red dress changed the subject.

"We've just received more details about the murder we've been covering at the Twelve Mooses Ballroom here in Denver. Beloved television host Leo Linder, AKA Doctor Dictionary, is dead of a suspected drug overdose. Suspect Wendy Bilbersteen has claimed that her gummy worms were to feed her sugar habit and were not marijuana-laced."

The male newscaster interrupted to say, "I'm a big fan of those gummy worms, but what I'd like to know, Dana, is how possible is it to overdose on marijuana?"

"That's an interesting question, Dave," said the female newscaster, without answering. "The Denver Police confiscated the candy earlier and we are waiting for confirmation of the suspect's claim. In a deepening twist, also discovered on the scene were marijuana-laced brownies. Suspect Lois LaLanne brought them to the Twelve Mooses Ballroom. Reports of her shouting, 'Not him! Not him!' are being investigated to clarify whether the brownies weren't meant for Doctor Dictionary, or whether she was in disbelief he had died. We'll keep you updated as this story develops."

Ginny heard the part about gummy worms, which had always been Viggo's favorite candy, and felt a little teary. When the camera again focused on the male reporter, Elsbeth yelled, "I wouldn't mind him warming my feet at night."

Melvin said, "How do you think he feels about bunions?" He winked at Ginny, who stifled a smile. Mel was funny when she could hear him.

"How can you be sure that the robber on Colorado Boulevard wasn't your grandson, Ginny?" Elsbeth asked in her meddling voice. "It's only a six- or seven-minute drive from that neighborhood to the DU campus."

"Because I'm not an idiot," Ginny whispered to herself so that nobody else heard. She held her head high and said, "I'm quite sure that my grandson has plenty of his own money. There's no reason for him to steal anyone else's."

Elsbeth kept speculating about Viggo through the commercials, and Melvin kept trying to shut her up in his gentle way. Ginny hadn't liked Elsbeth from the start. The woman was always complaining about her knees as if she were the only one in any discomfort. Or she stuck her nose into other people's business. She'd continuously chatted during the last two movie nights, making it impossible for Ginny to follow the plot, and she wore a cheap perfume that made the place smell like a bordello.

Nobody responded to Elsbeth, and when the show came back on, the female announcer reported that an anonymous donor had given two million dollars to the University of Denver. It was to be awarded to a graduating DU student who'd done substantial volunteer work in the city.

When she heard Viggo's name and saw his picture, Ginny

lifted her arms as if she'd won the gold, although her arms didn't go that high anymore. It had been her accountant who'd come up with the plan to give Viggo enough to live on until his inheritance came through.

"That's what I'm talking about," she said as they showed Viggo standing outside one of the university buildings, handsome in his navy blazer, wearing the light blue tie Ginny had sent him for his birthday.

"That adorable young man," she said to Melvin and anyone else who could hear, "is my grandson."

"Handsome kid," Melvin said.

"Being at that ceremony doesn't prove anything," said Elsbeth, who'd risen and was walking over to the doorway. "He had time to go home and change after robbing that store."

It would be better to be completely deaf, thought Ginny, so that she couldn't hear this woman. "I'm telling you for the last time," she said in a steely voice. "My grandson would never commit a crime like that."

She rose from her seat, and without wishing anyone a good evening, headed out of the lounge. Everyone already knew about her balance issues, so nobody was too surprised when she teetered into Elsbeth, who screamed and fell.

Attendants came running, and Ginny heard the wail of an ambulance as she slowly made her way to her room. Later, when an attendant came to help her get to dinner, Ginny learned that Elsbeth had broken her hip.

"What a shame," Ginny said, tsking. "We should all be more careful."

She was glad to know that she still had what it took to survive. Viggo would never learn who'd made the anonymous donation to the university or forwarded his name as the recipient of the "prize." If the rest of the residents avoided aggravating Ginny, they could expect to live their final days in peace.

THE NORTH PASTURE

HOLLY HARRIS

Wylene and I were gathering strays in the north pasture when three sheriff's department SUVs pulled off the highway near our gate. The day was breezy but warm. Our young geldings had started to sweat, and they could use a breather. I trotted over to greet sheriff Ed Hensley as he stepped out of the first SUV. We were friends and had a running weekly card game with our spouses.

"Good morning, Sheriff."

"Shayna." The sheriff tipped his hat.

"What brings you out this morning?"

Ed removed his hat, wiped his brow, and put it back on. He shook his head and said, "You're not going to believe this, but we got a tip that there's a body buried here in your pasture. The caller said it had been there almost thirty years."

"A body! No kidding. Did this tipster say who it was?" I thought about it for a moment. It *was* a little hard to believe. Nothing like this ever happened in our little town of Angus, Colorado. "Who went missing thirty years ago?"

"You know, I can't talk about any of this, Shayna. Listen, I know you love a good mystery, but you need to stay out of this one and leave it to us professionals."

I looked off across the prairie. A coyote was sneaking up

on a pronghorn, as if he thought he had a chance. "All right, I hear you," I said, fingers crossed down where he couldn't see them. "You don't have to tell me twice."

"Do I have your permission to conduct a search and excavate?"

I agreed, and he gave me an acknowledgement form to sign. If I didn't, Ed would have to get a search warrant and why make him go to all the effort? I also knew my husband, Cody, would agree to it. I felt an urgent need to return home and talk to Cody. Maybe he remembered something about someone going missing thirty years ago.

They drove through the gate and parked. One of the SUVs was a K-9 unit with a cadaver dog. The dog's handler clipped a lead to his harness, and they began working a grid by the windmill and a lone cottonwood tree where lightning had struck some years back. The other deputies stayed behind the dog and his handler. I imagined this would avoid contaminating any scent which might still be around. They seemed to know exactly where to look.

I figured it would take a while to find a body, if it was there. So, I trotted back over to Wylene, who had been waiting patiently.

"What's going on, boss?"

"Someone called the sheriff and said there's a dead body buried out here. I imagine they're going to find a lot of nothing."

"That's a weird one." Wylene shrugged. "Some heifers are behind that hill." She pointed at a scrubby knob nearby. "I could bring them around to this side on my own. They're a small group."

"Sounds good," I replied. While waiting, I soaked up the view. Highlighted by a brilliant blue sky, storm clouds built above the mountains to the west. This time of year, they could bring either snow or rain. Snow seemed unlikely, given the pleasant morning, but one never knew about the April weather in Colorado.

We spent the rest of the morning gathering cattle, then penned them in the corral with the solar water tank. I was still anxious to return home and talk to Cody. We had grown up together here in Angus on the plains of northeastern Colorado. We both would have been in high school thirty years ago. I didn't remember hearing about anyone missing back then. Of course, I was in my own world of horses, music, and Cody.

BACK HOME, we unsaddled the horses, groomed them, and turned them out in the paddock by the barn. They walked to the middle, plopped down and rolled, then groaned as they shook off the dirt.

I have always enjoyed working with horses. They made me smile and lightened my heart no matter what else was going on. My father left us when I was a baby and my mother raised me on her own. After the day's ranch chores, she worked a job in town to make ends meet. Her brother, my Uncle Joe, helped with ranch work as much as he could, but he lived off the ranch with his family. So, I was often on my own after school. The daily responsibility of owning and caring for horses provided me with a certain steadiness I don't think I would have found otherwise.

Cody was underneath the tractor in the equipment shed. I told him what was going on out in the north pasture.

He sat up and banged his head.

"Ouch! That's crazy! Thirty years ago? I don't have any idea who it might be, do you?"

I shrugged. "Can't think of anyone. Ed said I wasn't supposed to talk about it except with you."

"And you won't either, right? Let them do their job."

I love my husband. He's my guy and the only one for me, but he has never understood this part of me, this desire to solve mysteries. To my way of thinking, puzzling through this one was completely justified since the body was supposedly buried on *our* property. My property, specifically, since my family had owned it for four generations.

I HAD some errands in town after lunch. One was a stop at the post office, ostensibly to drop off mail. My real reason was to see Susie McKinney, my mom's long-time friend, who had worked there since I was a girl. Maybe she remembered something.

Susie was busy with a customer when I walked in, so I read a newspaper left on the counter. On the front page, there was an update on a story I was following about a murder in Denver. The headline read, "Olivia Twist Was Lying." The article said, "Twist had lied when she said Doctor Dictionary's allergy to marijuana was common knowledge. She only knew Doctor Dictionary had an allergy to marijuana because she had the allergy, too. She recognized it from his telltale red ears. Furthermore, Olivia's doctor had warned her she could die from too much pot." What an interesting update, I thought. I wondered why she might lie about this. Perhaps she was involved in his death?

One mystery at a time, I thought. Susie finished her business and walked over to me, bringing my focus back to the present.

We talked for a few minutes about the weather and happenings around town.

Susie asked, "How's Lila doing after Joe's passing?"

"She's alright. Honestly, most days, Mom doesn't remember he's gone. I miss him, though. I wish I'd seen more of him before he was gone. Isn't that always the way it is?" We were both silent for a moment.

"Susie, do you remember anyone around here going missing thirty years ago?"

"What's that about? Why are you asking?" She seemed to

stop herself from saying something and gave me a questioning look.

I tried to act casual, like it was unimportant. Ed would be upset if he found out I was asking around town. "It's no big deal. I heard someone was missing from back then and never been found, so I wondered about it. You know me. I don't let things drop."

Susie laughed and said, "Yes, you are that way." We talked a bit more, but something had shifted, and our conversation became stilted and awkward. I told her I had other errands and said goodbye.

I WENT OUT to my truck and started it, then sat there, staring at nothing. It seemed as if Susie had wanted to say more but had stopped herself. What was it? Something was playing at the edge of my awareness. It was like a thought or memory I couldn't quite retrieve. I shook my head to clear it, put both hands on the steering wheel, and drove to the hardware store for some tractor parts Cody needed. Distracted and lost in thought, I did a terrible job of parking. I bumped up on the curb and rolled back. Then a memory came to me. It felt more like a dream.

I was sixteen and a new driver. Mom asked me to go to the hardware store for parts to repair a leaky kitchen faucet. I was excited to drive to town by myself and felt grown up. As I drove up to the store, I saw a man entering who seemed familiar, yet I couldn't place him. How did I know this man, a stranger? Then, I saw or remembered my Uncle Joe, my mother's brother, rush up the sidewalk, shove this man and start yelling at him. Why would Uncle Joe do this? It was so unlike him. How did he know this man? How did I know him?

I was startled by a knock on my truck window. Jeremiah, who owned the hardware store, stood next to my truck. I rolled down the window.

Jeremiah said, "You okay in there? You've been staring at nothing for the last ten minutes. Thought I better come check on you."

I said, "I'm fine," although I wasn't. I was far from fine. I tried for a reassuring smile and asked, "Jeremiah, do you remember someone from here going missing about thirty years ago?"

"Thirty years! That's a long—" He stopped mid-sentence and looked at me. "Why are you asking?"

"I just heard something, is all." I got out of the truck and walked inside with Jeremiah. "I need some parts for Cody. He's working on the old tractor again."

AFTER LEAVING THE HARDWARE STORE, I had another stop to make. Angus's one nursing home was situated at the crest of a hill, affording its residents unceasing views of rolling prairie in all directions. I found it calming to stand on the home's front porch and gaze out toward the distant mountains. Springtime was the best, when the tall grasses undulate in the wind. Now, the storm clouds I had seen earlier had drawn closer and threatened rain. I steeled myself to go inside and ask the hard questions I needed to ask.

On the way over, Ed called. They had found the body of a man. The coroner was there and would take the body for autopsy and identification. Ed suggested I go home to be with Cody. They had also found a wallet in the same area. It was possible the person they found was related to me.

"Say again?" I asked. "To me?"

"It's too early to confirm. We will have to wait for dental records if we can locate them."

"So, you're saying this body you found in my pasture is one of my long-lost relatives? Why would he be there? What happened to him?"

"Shayna, go home. Be with Cody. I will be there as soon as I can."

"What are you not saying, Ed?" Then, I knew. I knew who he was.

———

I PUSHED OPEN the glass front doors of the home and was greeted by all the familiar sights and sounds. The pulsing of bedside alarms sounding from open doors, the coughs from someone struggling with respiratory disease, the background noise of the television in the common room, an aide laughing with one of the residents she wheeled down the hall. The residents' rooms lined the west side of the building so every resident could see the plains and mountains. My mother was in the farthest room. I passed the nursing station along the way.

"How is Mom today?" I asked Thelma, the day nurse.

"Same as yesterday, Shayna. She's been mumbling in her sleep, calling out. Sometimes when I'm taking care of her, she starts to talk to me as if I'm one of her old friends. She thought I was Susie yesterday. And she talks of long-ago things." Thelma seemed to want to say more but didn't.

"I hope she remembers me today. I have some questions for her."

Thelma gave me a quizzical look and said, "I hope she does, Shayna. I'm going off shift now. You take care of yourself, you hear?"

I smiled and walked toward Mom's room. My heart pounded. The hallway felt like a tunnel closing in on me. Black spots began at the edge of my vision, and I thought I might faint. I stopped, took a few deep breaths to steady myself, and felt better, stronger. I pushed open the door.

Mom was in bed, propped on pillows, looking out the window. I was grateful to the home's architect for this view. It was a gift. She was wearing nasal cannulas and there was the hiss of the tank expelling oxygen.

"Hi, Mom, it's Shayna. How are you today?"

She slowly turned her gaze to me. "Oh, it is you. I thought it was the nurse. Bernice? Never can remember her name."

"Yes, it's me, Shayna." I walked over to the chair by her bed, sat, and took her hand. She smiled at me. Mom was only in her late sixties, but after a stroke, then a bout of cancer, and now Alzheimer's, she had aged considerably. Her once signature dark red hair had gone snow white. Deep wrinkles from years of smoking lined her face.

I stopped by to see her every few days. Each time, I didn't know whether she would recognize me. When she didn't, she often became argumentative and wanted me to leave. I always did. I wanted her to have as peaceful a life as possible. Today, though, I had some hard questions for her. Questions I was afraid to ask but knew I must. A big secret had haunted our lives, and it was time to bring it to light.

"Mom," I faltered, then had to begin again. "Mom, where did my father go when he left us? What caused him to leave?"

She narrowed her eyes. "Why are you asking about him? He was no good. He ran out on us when you were little. He was no good, that man."

"Yes, Mom. But where did he go? What happened to him?"

"I don't know. I only wanted him gone. He was no good." She began crying. "He beat me, Shayna. You were in the crib, crying. He kept saying, 'Shut that baby up.' I went to get you, to protect you. I was afraid he would hurt you. But he grabbed me and threw me against the wall. I will never forget it. He beat me and I kept screaming for him to stop. I thought I would stop breathing before he stopped. Then he was gone. And I crawled over to you. You were just a little thing. You couldn't help crying. You couldn't help it."

"Mom, don't cry. I'm fine and I'm right here with you now. You took care of me. You raised me by yourself, and you did such a good job, Mom. You were the best mother a girl could ever hope for."

She looked at me so sweetly then, her cheeks wet with tears. I brought her hand up to my cheek and held it there. After a few minutes, I laid her hand back down. "Mom, I have another question for you. Did my father ever return to Angus? Maybe when I was in high school? I have this memory and I'm not sure it's real."

She drew back and sucked in a deep breath. "Why? Why do you ask these things now? I don't want to talk about this. I'm tired. Can you come back tomorrow?" She looked away out the window.

"Mom, I must ask. Please tell me the truth. Did my father ever return? I saw him, I think, with Uncle Joe."

Mom started sobbing again. I held her hand. "I know this is tough, Mom. I think we should talk about it. Get it out in the open. Please tell me."

She dabbed her eyes with a tissue and the long-held story poured out of her. "Your father was a mean, cruel man. You're right. When you had just turned sixteen, he came by the house looking for you. He said he wanted to see his daughter. He shoved his way in and started going through the house, calling for you. I told him you were out running errands. He grew angry and pushed me down, then laughed, saying I had always been clumsy. He banged out of the house and drove off looking for you. I was afraid he might find you. I didn't know what he might do if he did. I called your Uncle Joe to go find you or him first. He found your father in front of the hardware store. They argued and began shoving each other. But Joe didn't want to fight him there in the street. So, he said, let's go for a drive. And they did. I don't know exactly what happened, but they drove out to our land, to the north pasture, and Joe came back alone, without him. He said your father had fallen when they were fighting and hit his head on a rock and died. Joe buried him right there, where they had fought. He said he didn't expect anyone would be looking for him." She stopped talking, looked down at her hands, and then up at me. "Don't hate me for keeping this from you. You were only sixteen and it wouldn't have done you any good to hear it."

"Mom, that was my fuzzy memory. I saw him and Uncle Joe at the hardware store. I saw the two of them and they were arguing, but I never told you. He was a stranger. I didn't know he was my father. Mom, there is nothing you could ever do that would make me hate you. I love you. I'm sure you did what you thought you needed to do."

I was crying, too. We hugged. I told her to get some rest. When I left the room, she was gazing out the window. I was again thankful for her view.

As I pulled her door closed, Susie stepped forward from the edge of the hall.

"Susie, what are you doing here?"

"Thelma called me. She told me how Lila had been talking with her, thinking she was me. Thelma asked me about your father and Joe and what had happened. Lila told me about it when it happened. She was so distraught about the fight and your father's death she had to talk to someone. She was a mess, and so was Joe. I don't think he was ever the same after. Today, when you stopped by and asked about someone going missing, I knew then that Thelma had decided to call the sheriff about it. I think she cares about your mom a great deal, but she thought it was time for the secret to come out now that Joe had passed."

I was stunned. So much had been revealed to me in such a short time. I found a chair and sat down, speechless. Susie brought me a cup of water from the nurse's station. The act of sipping water and holding the cup seemed to ground me. I looked up at Susie. "You knew all this time?"

"Yes. And I promised your mother to keep it a secret. Maybe Joe's death brought it all back for her and that's why she mistook Thelma for me and talked about it."

"I wish I had known, though. I guess, from Mom's perspective, there was never a good time or reason to tell me."

I finished the water and stood on shaky legs. Susie grabbed my elbow to steady me. We walked down the hall and out into the spring sunshine.

"It's time to tell the sheriff the rest of the story," I said. "Joe's not with us anymore. I suppose Mom's Alzheimer's will keep her from being a credible witness and not likely to face any charges."

"You're probably right," Susie said.

I retrieved my phone from my pocket and made the call.

MAKEOVER MY DAY

JENNA LINCOLN

As I exited the train from the concourse to the main terminal in Denver and pushed my way onto the escalator, all I could think about was drinking a cold margarita with my best friend after a brutally long travel day and a worse year. I didn't have a plan for tomorrow or the day after. For eighteen months, I'd lived only for this moment.

At first, I didn't recognize Mercedes with her dark hair piled into a fancy up-do and wearing what looked suspiciously like the bridesmaid dress from my ill-fated wedding. In one hand she held a bouquet and in the other a sign. "WELCOME HOME FROM PRISON, MARINA! HE DESERVED IT!!"

Yup, that was my ride.

Cheeks hot because all these strangers were looking at us, I hurried up to her and grabbed the sign as I gave her a huge hug. She smelled like expensive perfume and sunless tanner and my eyes watered a little. It had been a long time since someone hugged me and meant it.

Mercedes pulled back and held out the bouquet. "For you! Also, do you love the sign?"

"Is that the bridesmaid dress from my wedding?" I asked, dodging the question.

"It's so cute," she said, twirling to flare the ruffled raspberry skirt. "Today is going to be a new beginning for you, and this dress needs a new beginning too. Now it's going to be my *Marina gets a new life* dress instead of a bridesmaid dress." Mercedes beamed.

"Still looks great on you," I said with an appreciative glance at her long legs.

"Aww, go on." Mercedes made a partial catwalk turn before leading us to a pearl white Lexus, an upgrade since I'd gone to prison. In her chatty emails, she'd mentioned that her business was growing, but I hadn't realized how much.

"Wow, the indoor plant business must be treating you well," I said, sliding into the buttery leather passenger seat.

Mercedes started the engine and gave me a saucy wink. "I design and maintain interior landscapes, darling. I'm not just the plant lady anymore."

"Tell me everything!" I probably overdid the enthusiasm, but Mercedes loved an audience, and I did want to hear more.

When we pulled into a strip mall twenty minutes later, I gave her a quizzical look. "I thought we were going to happy hour."

"My favorite hole-in-the-wall is next to the salon. You're getting a new look while you enjoy that margarita I promised you."

HOURS LATER AT MERCEDES' luxury townhouse, she handed me an ice cream sundae. "Here's to your new look and new life!"

I clinked my glass bowl against hers, still feeling the after-effects of three prickly pear margaritas. "Maybe I'll have more fun as a blonde," I said, hoping if nothing else, my luck would change for the better.

Mercedes took a big bite and gave me an approving nod.

"Down to business. I know you're a planner. What's next and how can I help?"

I licked my dry lips and swallowed. I had thoughts, but nothing cohesive. "Okay," I began. "A few of the other victims wrote me while I was in jail and—"

"I knew it! I knew there were others. Why didn't they speak up during your trial?"

"Intimidation, mostly. A few had signed NDAs. A few had someone encouraging them to keep quiet, so they didn't lose the hush money."

"Ugh," Mercedes said.

"Yeah, but here's the interesting part. It wasn't just Ramsey's clients. Some of the people who wrote to me had worked with other lawyers in the firm."

"What?!" She shot me an incredulous look. "So the jerks who came forward as character witnesses for Ken Ramsey are also preying on vulnerable newly divorced women?"

"Yeah, pretty much."

"People are terrible. What are you going to do?"

It was the million-dollar question. I lost my license as a school counselor after my manslaughter conviction and most employers wouldn't hire someone with a felony.

After the fifth email from a person claiming to have been assaulted by one of the lawyers from Navish and Lyle, I'd looked into getting a private investigator's license. As a PI, I'd be my own boss which solved the hiring-a-felon problem.

Based on my own case and the emails I'd received, the pattern was to invite attractive female clients out for coffee or drinks to celebrate the successful end to divorce proceedings, drug their drink, pose them in a compromising position, take a photo, send it to their frat-bro partners, then dump the women at their homes.

If I could somehow get those photos and files into the right hands, they'd lose their rights to practice law and their access to vulnerable women. Maybe I could get my conviction overturned, though without the testimony of the security guard and photographic evidence, my self-defense case was weakened.

Before I could stop it, my mind wandered backward.

IT WAS the sound of the Polaroid camera that had roused me out of my stupor enough to realize something wasn't right. I'd already had a ton of coffee that day, so when I met my lawyer for yet another cup of coffee, maybe whatever he'd slipped into it wasn't strong enough to knock me out very long.

The moment I realized I was in his car with my shirt unbuttoned and bra unhooked, my adrenaline spiked. I snatched the taser out of my bag and shot him, hitting him squarely over the heart. He dropped the camera and spasmed.

I bolted out of the car and waved my arms at the first visible security camera. My head was pounding, and I staggered over to a concrete wall to throw up. I buttoned my shirt and ran a shaky hand over my hair, trying desperately to recall how I'd gotten from a local coffee shop to this parking garage.

Less than five minutes later, a security guard bolted out of the elevator. "What's happening?"

Throwing up had cleared my head, though I still felt woozy. I gave a very short version of the story and said we needed to call the police.

"Yeah, ok," the security guard said. "I'll check on Mr. Ramsey."

I propped myself against a large SUV and watched the security guard as she opened the car door. After a moment, she peered at me over the roof.

"This just happen?"

"Yes," I said, my tone sharper and higher than I intended. "Why?"

"He's dead," she said, resting a hand on her holster. "Police are on their way."

I STIRRED MY SUNDAE. "Right now, I need to get back on my feet, find a job and a place to live."

"I've got you covered. Seriously, no rush, Mar. The guest room is yours and one of my people quit last week, so I need help. It's not the highest salary in Denver, but it should keep you from having to use your savings."

A WEEK later I leaned over Mercedes' shoulder as she scrolled through her spreadsheet of clients. "Wait, go back a few rows," I squinted at the screen of her laptop. "Does that say Donald Dross?

"Yeah. Don Dross left corporate law to found a non-profit to help families going through divorces."

"That's him," I said. "He was the head of Navish and Lyle."

"No way." Mercedes brought a hand to her mouth. "I didn't put that together. I shouldn't have taken him as a client."

"You wouldn't have known. He didn't testify, but he was the managing partner of that firm."

"Do you think he was a part of Team Creeper?"

"Someone had to push to get my trial moving so quickly. Someone had to pay off the security guard, who quit the next day. Someone had to make the polaroid disappear, along with the garage security camera footage. And someone had to buy the drugs that were nearly undetectable in my system by the time they tested me. Maybe he's not that guy, but I'd love to get into his computer and find out."

Mercedes opened the file on Phoenix Legal Advocates and scanned it. "A guy like that might be too smart to keep records of his dirty deeds, but I happen to know their new front desk person. She's super cute."

"Did you date her?"

"Nothing serious. We have a regular appointment there tomorrow. You should go."

"Are there plants, I mean *interior landscapes* in all the offices?"

"In the corner offices, conference rooms, and reception."

"What about security cameras?"

"Only on the front door, I think."

THE APPOINTMENT at Phoenix Legal Advocates was for two in the afternoon. I drove the company van and wore the company polo shirt with khaki pants. I skimmed the instructions for maintaining Marina's landscapes, feeling nervous. I didn't want to go back to jail, but I desperately needed to find proof that I was the victim, not the perpetrator, as Ramsey's colleagues had convinced the jury.

My career and reputation were ruined. I wasn't sure I'd find anything there, but I knew I had to try.

The lobby was generic fancy with black stone floors, tall chrome framed windows, and a TV in the corner playing a local news channel on mute. Someone was being interviewed. The closed-captioning scrolled the dialogue: *Wendy Bilbersteen's beef with Doctor Dictionary was an open secret. If she'd been upset enough to kill him, she would have done it long before now.*

Soft scents wafted through the air and one of Mercedes's interior landscapes stretched between two leather couches.

"Hi, welcome to Phoenix Legal Advocates, you must be Maura." The pretty woman at the front desk greeted me with a friendly smile.

I had completely forgotten my alias. "Yeah, I'm … Maura."

"I'm Katie." She stood and smoothed her miniskirt. "I'll show you around."

Katie's black miniskirt was topped by an oversized white

sweater that matched her white patent leather ankle boots. Her long hair was half up and half down showing three different earrings in each ear.

Despite my makeover, next to Katie I felt as frumpy and unstylish as I had in my former life as a high school counselor.

Katie raised her eyebrows at me, and I flushed, realizing I'd been staring. "Uh, I really like your boots," I said. "Makes me wish I'd picked cuter footwear to style my uniform."

She grinned. "Totally get it. This is my first job without a uniform, and I've been having maybe a little too much fun." She stepped toward me. "Let me show you the rest of the landscapes. Mercedes does such a great job. Our clients comment on our plants all the time." She walked us to a glass door and tugged it open. Beyond the doorway was a gray carpeted hallway with cream-colored walls.

Along the hallway were frosted glass doors with small brass signs affixed to the wall. Some signs had labels like "south conference room" and others had people's names. As we continued to walk nearly the length of the building, I asked, "How many people work here?"

At the far end of the hall, Katie opened a door and the overhead lights blinked on. "Full time? Four. The three attorneys who started this place and me. We have another ten to twelve who work part time or rotate through to do pro bono work."

"Oh," I said, gesturing back down the hall. "That's why some of these are—"

I was going to say empty, but Katie said, "Flexible workspaces." She rolled her eyes. "That's what the boss calls them. The plants help, but I still think they're kind of ..."

"Impersonal?" I offered. The smaller plain offices reminded me of the shabbier but otherwise very similar offices at the prison and the courthouse where I'd met with my public defender.

"Yeah, exactly." Katie's immaculate brows drew closer

together as she glanced up and down the hall, then checked her watch. "You know what? Let's start in the boss's office. He won't be here for another thirty minutes or so. He has some of that old school 'I'm the managing partner' attitude and treats anyone who's not a lawyer like the help."

I wrinkled my nose in sympathy, but my brain sparked. If this guy was the missing puzzle piece, it was in my best interest that he was old school because that might mean he kept things on his computer that he shouldn't. "Ew, that's terrible," I said and wiped a sweaty palm on my khakis.

The large corner office had a light airy feeling with floor-to-ceiling windows overlooking a park. The interior landscape included a quietly bubbling fountain and many varieties of plants in a range of heights.

"Wow. That is gorgeous."

"I know, right?" Katie took a step back and bumped into a corner of the desk. The computer monitor lit up behind her. "Oops, well, I'll leave you to it."

"Thanks so much." I willed my expression to remain neutral when all I wanted to do was rush to the computer and start clicking.

As soon as Katie left, I turned in a slow circle looking for obvious security cameras. I didn't see any, but I took the spray bottle out of my satchel and did a cursory job of misting the plants while checking for hidden cameras.

When I was as certain as I could be, I casually moved to the computer and jiggled the mouse. Just as it had a moment ago, the monitor lit up, showing the desktop without a login window or any password prompt.

Either this guy was supremely confident that no one would touch his computer, or he was just plain dumb. Based on my research, I was going with arrogance over stupidity.

I opened the first drive and started clicking into files. Yes, I was looking at confidential information, but my entire job as a counselor had been dealing with confidential information. It was weak justification, but at least it allowed me to skim the cases with slightly less guilt. After several dozen files, I'd only found a few photos, mostly police images of women's injuries from their spouses, totally upsetting and sad, but not what I was looking for.

Minutes were slipping by, and Katie would eventually come searching for me if I didn't move on to the other landscapes.

I was about to give up when inspiration struck. A few years before, I'd been helping my dad figure out if he needed to buy cloud storage to back up his stuff. When I opened his trash, I'd found hundreds of files, many of them large. He explained that he filed things in the trash.

At the time, I'd shrugged off the interaction as *weird things my dad does*, but, well, Don Dross was basically the same age as my dad.

I clicked the trash and was prompted for a password.

Bingo. I opened the top desk drawer looking for something that might contain this guy's passwords. I found mints, pens, notepads, an address book, and a few files with some of the same case names I'd found on his hard drive.

I opened the address book to 'P' and under the written entry 'Passwords' was a single note: COSMOPOL1TAN. I carefully typed the password and a list of files appeared organized alphabetically by name.

Halfway down the list was Ken Ramsey, my former, now deceased, lawyer. My hands shook with adrenaline as I clicked and scanned for my name. I held my breath and opened the first photo, but it had been taken in the divorce lawyer's office. The second photo was me, slumping into my coffee and the third was me in the backseat of Ramsey's car.

"Gotcha," I muttered and inserted my drive to copy all the files.

"I thought I recognized you."

Startled, I snapped up my head to see Katie in the doorway holding a gun.

"Someone gave you a great makeover after you got out of prison, but you're Marina Taylor-Hernandez."

"Uh," I stalled, glancing at the files copying onto my drive. "Yeah, that's me. Just trying to get my life together working for my friend—"

"You came here to find me," Katie said, gun still raised.

"No," I said, drawing out the word. "I don't know you. I'm just—"

"Rummaging around in Dross's files so you can find me." The pitch of Katie's voice was rising as she glanced at her watch. "And he's going to be here in five minutes."

The files were sixty percent copied. I had no idea who this woman was or why she was pointing a gun at me. Luckily, I'd taken many de-escalation courses and had lots of practice calming distraught teenagers. "Look Katie, I can tell you're upset," I said in my best counselor voice. "But this is a misunderstanding. I work for Mercedes now—"

She rushed around the desk and shoved me with her free hand. "What are you doing on his computer then? Move."

Katie scanned the open files and photos and gave me a puzzled stare. "These are old client files."

"Not exactly." I gently reached past her and began clicking through the series of pictures of drugged women.

Katie's eyes widened. "You weren't the only one? I mean, I should've known, but I was so scared. They offered me money and when I wouldn't take it, they called in a favor with the police department and ruined my chances of getting into the Denver police academy."

I stared at Katie's profile as she took the mouse and opened more files. Cold sweat pooled under my arms, but my face was hot. "You were the security guard on duty that night. The one they couldn't find for the trial." Frustration laced with anger flooded my mind as I searched my memory for her true name. "Without your testimony or the photos, they painted me as a crazed divorcee who attacked her attorney."

"They fired me and threatened my family. I couldn't go to

the police because they'd already called them. Said I'd been fired for attempted blackmail and couldn't be trusted." Katie's tense tone matched mine, but she slowly put the gun on the desk.

"I didn't come here to find you," I said. I took a deep breath and let it out, trying to release some of the tension in my chest. "I came here to find this." I gestured to the screen. "Some of these women reached out to me when I was in prison, and I want to make things right."

The text box showed the files were now one hundred percent copied. I ejected my drive and slipped it into my pocket.

Katie tucked the gun under her sweater and pushed in the heavy leather chair. She glanced around, checking that everything was in place, then opened a different drawer and took out a package of wipes. She handed one to me and said, "Quick, wipe the keyboard and I'll wipe the mouse and the chair."

Less than ninety seconds later, a tall man with a mane of silver-black hair passed us in the hallway as we headed into the next conference room with an interior landscape. Dross nodded but didn't say anything.

"He knew," I said under my breath.

"He orchestrated the whole thing," Katie said, pulling the door shut. "One of the partners admitted as much when I got him drunk. That's why I changed my whole look and my name and applied for this job. I've been in his computer, but I never thought to look in the trash."

I squeezed my eyes shut, reeling from that news. Of course. Every group had a leader, and here he was, working at his nonprofit and probably sleeping great at night.

Despite threats and intimidation from Navish and Lyle, Katie had been working along a parallel track to mine, trying to find the apex predator. Trusting my gut I said, "I'm still not sure about my post prison makeover, but your new look is fantastic. You're Katja, right?"

She nodded. "People only see the uniform when you're a security guard and now, some of these guys, especially him, only see the miniskirt. Either way, they don't care about my name."

"A predator like Dross should be in jail," I said, picturing him in an orange jumpsuit.

"Maybe he should have to try his luck in the court of public opinion," Katja said. "My cousin works at Nine News. I bet she could get that drive into the right hands."

I searched her face, glad her fierce expression matched mine. "I like the sound of that." I stuck out my hand to shake. "Here's to a terrible man getting the new look and new life he deserves."

AS THE OIL FLOWS

KERRY HAMMOND

Travis took off his cowboy hat and ran his fingers through his wavy hair, a habit that drove women absolutely wild. "But Sara, I thought you loved me." They sat on a leather sofa in the grand living room of the Colorado ranch, a fire burning in the fireplace, an open bottle of wine on the coffee table. The dog, a beautiful border collie named Champ, slept at their feet.

"Get real Travis, I was just using you to get to your older brother and his oil fortune," said Sara. She swept her hand across the room dramatically, as if to itemize that fortune in each and every piece of furniture. "Not that I didn't have fun doing it." She looked past Travis and gave a toothy smile somewhere over his shoulder, her teeth so white they looked like they might glow in the dark. She stood and turned her back to him. "Now that your brother is going to divorce that horrid wife of his and marry me, I have no use for you," she said.

"Sara, please. Is there anything I can say or do to make you change your mind?" Travis walked to her and put his arms around her waist, awkwardly hunching his back as he did so. His six-and-a-half-foot frame towered above her petite form. The top of her head barely reached his collarbone. "Sara, darlin', we had so many … so many, um."

"Cut," yelled a voice off to the side of the living room. "Geez, Tony, why can't you learn your lines? It's not rocket science! We already dumbed them down as much as we could for your little pea brain to comprehend. And Susan, for the last time, stop smiling into the camera. This is a soap opera, not a game show." Kent Cooper tore the headphones from his head, threw them to the ground and stomped toward the back of the studio. "Take five everyone, while Tony looks up what the heck he's supposed to say and Susan admires herself in the mirror for the hundredth time." Everyone froze as he passed them, like an adult game of Red Light, Green Light. "Stupid cowboy hicks. Why am I in this godforsaken town working on this godforsaken show?"

The godforsaken town was Dawson, Colorado, eighty miles from Denver. The godforsaken show was *As the Oil Flows*, a daytime soap opera following a wealthy family of Colorado ranchers who had recently struck black gold. Kent Cooper was a New Yorker and recent Colorado transplant, a move that was precipitated by a fall from grace six months ago, involving a married woman, her studio executive husband, a weekend in Barbados, and a bottle of Johnny Walker Blue. The footage ended up on the internet and Kent ended up in Dawson.

"I'm sorry Sara, I really did study my lines," said Tony, looking sheepish.

"It's Susan, Tony. My real name is Susan." She shook her head. "Oh, never mind." It was lucky for him that he was so good looking because he really didn't have a brain in that pretty head of his.

Susan turned away from her co-star and checked her hair in the mirror she kept hidden under the plant pot on the set's end table. Remembering what Kent said, she quickly returned the mirror to the table and scanned the room to make sure no one had seen her. She reminded herself that Kent's rampage had been mostly directed at Tony and his trouble remembering his lines.

For the most part, Kent was an indiscriminate jerk, but he had recently started aiming the bulk of his anger in Tony's direction. Susan suspected it had something to do with Pam, the soap's makeup artist. Pam had been dating Kent for about five months but had recently started to gaze just a little too long at Tony after she'd buffed the shine off his nose. She also laughed a bit too loudly at his corny jokes. Everyone had noticed. More importantly, Kent had noticed.

The director's mood was not improved by the fact that their ratings had been slipping and the studio had been coming down hard on him to turn things around. He was the hotshot director from New York, after all.

Kent walked back into the room, trailed by Eddie, his assistant and all-around studio gofer. "Eddie, I swear, if you get my coffee wrong one more time, I'm going to make sure it's scalding hot, pour it over your head, and then fire you. What is so hard about two creams and two sugars?"

Eddie bowed his head and took the coffee Kent handed him, scurrying off to get a new cup and muttering "Sorry, Kent" over his shoulder. It seemed that those words were the only two in Eddie's vocabulary these days.

Eddie wasn't an idiot and he didn't have a bad memory. The problem was, he was a dreamer and easily distracted. As he had stood waiting for the coffee machine to brew, he was daydreaming that he asked Susan out on a date and she said yes. By the time Eddie realized that the coffee had finished brewing, it had started to cool and Kent had already shouted his name twice. He had quickly run after his boss, failing to add both cream and sugar to the tepid brew.

"I don't know what you're looking so smug about, Susan, you're just as replaceable. Getting a bit long in the tooth if you ask me. Might be time to bring in a younger model," Kent chuckled. He was so pleased with himself, he didn't even notice the constipated look on Susan's face. She was going for angry, but she was notorious for getting her facial expressions wrong, even in real life.

Susan had been on the show for nearly a year. Her character, Sara, had wormed her way onto the scene after seducing Travis. She frequently wandered outside of his cabin in nothing but a t-shirt, showing just about everything that the network would allow. Her character's plan was to catch the eye of Travis' brother, the ranch owner. Mission accomplished. The scene they were filming today was the big reveal; she was telling Travis that she had planned the whole thing and was dumping him for his brother.

"Take it from the point where Sara tells Travis she was using him," said Kent. "Let's see if we can get this scene finished. Some of us have a life and plans for the evening." He shot a glance at Pam, who was cleaning her makeup brushes, and gave her a wink.

Pam's blank look might have been taken for shyness. She was a well-known introvert. But today, her look meant something else entirely. It was her poker face. Tonight, Pam was going to let Kent buy her dinner and then dump him over dessert. She had confided in Susan because Susan had been trying to get her to dump Kent for weeks. She needed a friend to talk it over with and there was no one else on set that she even remotely liked. Well, except maybe Tony.

It took another forty-five minutes, but they finished filming the breakup scene as well as two others. They were just about to break for the evening when Kent called an all-hands-on-deck meeting. The crew stood in a circle around the director and waited to hear what he had to say. His bad mood seemed to improve after Tony got his lines right, so they were at a loss as to what his latest complaint might be.

"Eddie, are we keeping you from something?" Kent asked. Everyone looked over at the gofer, who was glued to the screen of his phone.

"Oh, sorry, Kent," Eddie stammered. "It's just that, well there's been breaking news with that murder in Denver. It says that there was a tuxedoed man skulking around the venue and they just learned his name was Jack Como. By the time they caught up with him he was in a daze and told a reporter that Charlotte Webb seemed to really admire Doctor Dictionary. He said she even had a dartboard with his picture on it." Eddie, who loved to follow local murder cases, looked proud of himself for having the scoop before anyone else.

"I don't give a fig about a dead guy in Denver. I've got a sinking ship here in Dawson to deal with." Kent turned away from Eddie to address the crew. "As you all know, the ratings have taken a hit lately," Kent said, looking from each actor to the next, as if accusing them of contributing to the sinking of the ship. "The network is losing advertising dollars because of the drop and is forcing us to cut back on costs to make up for it. Since we film on set for the most part, in this sad studio, in this one-horse town, there just isn't anywhere else we can cut back. Our costs are already as low as they can be." He took a pause and drew it out, like he was about to announce the winner of *American Idol*. He clearly enjoyed their discomfort. "The only way we can cut back is on salaries."

You could have heard a pin drop. "I'm sure you're wondering who's getting the axe," he continued with a smirk on his face—the man really was a sadist. "Well, you're just going to have to wonder for the night. I have a conference call scheduled this evening with the top brass and they're going to ask my opinion on who should stay and who should go. Trust me, I've got just the answer for them." If Kent was prone to evil laughter, he would have inserted it here.

Several of the crew members shuffled their feet.

Eddie just knew he would be the first to go. It was much cheaper to get your own coffee and donuts than to hire someone to do it for you.

Susan couldn't imagine it would be her; she was too pretty. She stood there looking pleased, but she wasn't actually pleased, she was shocked. Again, the proper facial expression eluded her.

Tony wasn't sure what to think, so he decided to conserve energy and not think at all.

Pam wasn't surprised about the announcement. Kent had told her about the cutbacks. He had also told her that her job was safe. "Don't worry babe, they can't let you go. Those actors look like tree frogs until you paint faces on them. You're indispensable." She wondered how indispensable she'd be once she dumped him.

"So go home, get some sleep, and reflect on what it might mean to make a career change," Kent said. "Everyone needs to be back here at nine o'clock sharp. I'll make the announcement then. Sweet dreams." The sarcasm was thick, but everyone was so stunned about the prospect of being out of work that they didn't even register it.

THE NEXT MORNING at nine o'clock on the dot, the same cast and crew were standing around in a circle, drinking bad studio coffee and looking tired. Eddie stood there with a coffee in his hand, two creams and two sugars. Tony had his script and was attempting to memorize his lines. Susan was, of course, checking her hair in the mirror. Pam was standing next to Susan, looking sheepish.

"How did it go last night?" Susan asked. "Did you do it? Did you dump him?"

"I couldn't," Pam said.

"Lost your nerve?"

"No. I couldn't because he never showed up. He stood me up."

It was nine-fifteen and the crew was getting fidgety, but no one wanted to attempt to find Kent. As a group they seemed to have decided it was better to delay the inevitable. At nine-twenty it was too much to bear and Susan finally spoke up. "Eddie, why don't you go and find him. You're his assistant."

Eddie, who couldn't argue with her logic, turned on his

heel and headed to Kent's office. The door was closed, so he knocked and called out, "Kent?"

When there was no answer, he tried again. "Kent, we're waiting for you to start the meeting." When there was still no answer, Eddie had to make a decision. Try the door handle or give up. The last time he entered Kent's office without an invitation he was berated by the director for interrupting a private phone call.

Eddie finally decided. What did he have to lose? He would probably be out of a job in the next few minutes anyway. He reached down and twisted the knob. It was unlocked and as he pushed it open, he announced himself. "Kent, it's Eddie, we're ready to start the meeting now, and we're just waiting for—"

His last words caught in his throat and he froze, his eyes fixed on Kent's body lying in a heap on the floor in front of the sofa. The director's face was contorted into a sneer and his skin was pale. His laptop sat on the coffee table, the lid closed. An empty coffee cup lay next to the body.

Eddie scanned the room and saw no one lurking in any corners. He slowly backed up, reversing his steps and exiting the office the way he entered. He closed the door and when he heard the latch click, he paused, turned, and reached into his pocket for his cell phone.

———

THE 911 CALL summoned the local police. Unlike Denver, the town of Dawson had to make do with one detective. He was on the wrong side of fifty, balding, and wore a tan raincoat over his short, stout body even though it hadn't rained in over a week. His mustache was in need of a trim and hadn't been stylish since the '70s. When he introduced himself as Detective Palumbo, everyone but Tony saw the irony. Eddie went as far as to wonder if the raincoat was intentional, quickly deciding it probably was.

The interviews dragged out like a bad courtroom drama. Detective Palumbo, 'not to be confused with Columbo'—yes, he actually said that—had an interesting way of interrogating his suspects. His idea of questioning was to accuse each person of murdering their boss. Instead of having a reason to back up his accusation, he turned it on them, asking why they wanted the director dead. No one was dumb enough to give an accurate answer, but most were willing to find the nearest bus and throw one or more of their co-workers under it to get Palumbo's eye off their own hide.

Susan implicated Pam, the make-up artist and girlfriend, claiming she killed her boyfriend to be rid of him and his bad temper. Pam implicated Eddie, the assistant, who knew he would be out of a job if Kent lived to bring down the hammer. Eddie implicated Gus, the cameraman, for no reason other than that Gus never said good morning to him. Gus blamed Tony but admitted he might be too dumb to actually pull off a murder. Tony refused to implicate anyone, but acknowledged he had no fondness for the cameraman, who had once called him a hick when he thought Tony was out of earshot.

It was amazing what you could get people to reveal while they were busy trying to put the blame on someone else. Palumbo questioned every crew member at the small studio. He made the lighting operator cry, the electrician blush, and the maintenance worker curse. He managed to fill his little notebook with all kinds of dirt on each person.

He found out that Pam was going to dump Kent, that Tony was constantly berated for being too dumb to learn his lines, that Kent had refused to give Susan a break in her shooting schedule to audition for a movie, that Eddie was scared of his own shadow because of the verbal abuse he received, that the catering crew had been replaced three times because the food wasn't up to Kent's standards, and that the cameraman had been caught peeking into Susan's dressing room once when she was changing for a scene.

After all of his questioning, Palumbo was still no closer to figuring out which of them had actually done it.

Susan sat next to Tony on the same leather couch where her character dumped him the day before. "Seems weird that just yesterday our biggest problem was learning our lines. Now we're suspects in a murder." Tony gave her one of his signature blank stares. She again wondered what was going on in that head of his.

"Do you think that arrogant police detective will actually solve Kent's murder?" she said, continuing the one-sided conversation. The silence on the set was killing her. It was usually so lively and full of noise. She considered going to her dressing room to check her hair and makeup.

Tony finally spoke. "I think it's downright possible," he said, as he patted her knee like an older brother. "Don't you worry yourself over it, though. I'm sure they don't think you have anything to do with it."

"I heard them talking about poison and Palumbo had them take away all the food and drink on the set so they could analyze it and find out if any of it contained poison. I mean, who would do such a thing?" She adjusted her face, trying for quizzical but only pulling off confused.

"You're caught." The words were spoken with such vehemence and at such a high volume that the speaker's voice was unrecognizable. Everyone turned to see that it was none other than Detective Palumbo. Like ants to a picnic, they were drawn to the scene playing out and they found a red-faced Palumbo pointing at the cameraman. His arm was outstretched and he pointed a long finger in the cameraman's face.

"I knew you were guilty as soon as I questioned you," Palumbo said, preening a bit now that he had an audience.

The scene could have been any number of scenes the writers used for the show. The cameraman sputtered and spit, but no distinguishable words came out of his mouth. Not that he could get a word in edgewise, for Palumbo had gone off on a monologue that rivaled any ever spoken in *As the Oil Flows*.

A search of the crew lockers had turned up a white powder residue in a duffle bag belonging to the cameraman. Preliminary testing had concluded that the powder was rat poison: the same substance that had caused the death of Kent Cooper.

The cameraman, whose name everyone finally learned was Rick, was read his rights and handcuffed. Palumbo ordered one of the uniformed police officers to 'get him out of my sight' and he was led away.

Palumbo only stayed long enough to fluff his feathers and congratulate himself in front of the rest of the actors and crew. He patted himself on the back for closing the case so quickly, for being such an asset to the Dawson Police Department, and even, it seemed, for the sunshine they were experiencing that week.

After he had run out of things to praise himself for, he told everyone they were free to go and walked out of the building. It only took about two seconds for it to sink in and the crew slowly filtered out of the studio.

Prior to Palumbo's performance, the cast and crew learned that an interim director was flying into Denver and was due to arrive in the morning. They had the green light to continue filming the show and everyone seemed to think that the real-life murder of the director would be ratings gold.

Tony was the only person left in the studio and he stood, script in hand, next to the fireplace gazing up at the painting above the mantle. He'd always admired the print. He knew it wasn't valuable, but he liked the way the cowboy sat on his horse, tall and powerful. The cattle in the background grazed in an open field. It was everything he loved about Colorado.

He set the script down on the mantle and took off his hat to run his fingers through his wavy hair. Before he replaced the hat on his head, he turned it over and peered inside. He reached in and pulled out a small, clear bag containing a white powder. It had been secured behind the band that wrapped around the inside of the hat.

With a smile on his face, he picked up his script, turned the page and continued to memorize his lines for tomorrow's big scene.

SINS OF THE PAST

LEANNE KALE SPARKS

Waiting is the hardest part.

Truer words were never spoken. And crouching behind this bush, waiting for him to come up the trail, it's excruciating.

I'm anxious. And exhilarated—today I finally get retribution.

Footsteps approach. Any reservations I've had about my next steps dissipate, like the morning chill as the sun rises. I step onto the trail.

He halts. Our eyes lock. He takes half a step back.

My stomach is tight, my heart racing. No one ever suspects a guy like him of the atrocities he's committed. It's how he's been able to get away with so much for so long.

But not anymore.

"It's you?" he stutters, surprisingly. Are those tears in his eyes? Why is he pulling this act?

I raise the gun, aim center mass, and pull the trigger. His hands clasp his cold heart. Blood seeps between his fingers. His mouth gapes, eyes bulge. He stumbles and falls to the ground, hands outstretched, eyes pleading. *Help.*

I shove the gun into my pocket, and stand over him. "Go to hell."

"911, WHAT'S YOUR EMERGENCY?"

The voice snaps me back to reality. But my eyes stay fixed on the body splayed across the trail in front of me.

"Yes, sorry," I say, trying to get my mind straight. "I-I'm at the Garden of the Gods, and there's a man—he's bleeding."

The words rush out. I thought I'd be able to handle something like this. I watch crime shows all the time, harshly judging others for the same *deer-in-the-headlights* I'm displaying now.

"What happened?" the dispatcher asks.

"I was walking up the trail," I answer, "and he's just lying here—bleeding all over the place—"

"Yes, ma'am. I meant do you know what happened to him?"

"Oh. No."

"Did he fall?"

"I don't think so."

"Can you tell me where he's bleeding from?"

"From the hole in his chest?"

There's a pause. "Is he breathing?"

I shake my head.

"Ma'am?"

"Sorry, no."

"Do you know CPR?"

There is absolutely no way I'm placing my mouth on his. "I don't think that will help."

"Why?"

I stare at his pale face, blue lips, and vacant eyes. "He's dead."

IT'S true what they say on crime shows: innocent or guilty, the police department is intimidating.

I take a sip of coffee and my mouth fills with bitter dishwater. I guess the nasty police coffee cliché is true. I set the cup down and turn my attention to the TV, mounted on the wall. The news blares, all the newscasters bright-eyed and happy.

A picture of a woman flashes on the TV screen. "Wendy Bilbersteen's alibi? She states she was very busy at Doctor Dictionary's event and in sight of people the entire time. Interestingly, notable online prankster Ryan Rizzuto—known as The RizzBizz—was also sighted at the fundraiser. When asked, the police stated the investigation is ongoing as to his activities at the event—"

"Ms. Bailey?"

An impossibly slim man with a bald head and piercing dark eyes steps in front of me. "Detective Johnson," he says, hand out. "I hear you've had an exciting morning?"

I stand and shake his hand. "Yeah, you could say that."

"How about we go down the hall and you can tell me about it?"

Relief flows over me. Thank goodness he's not giving off that *everyone is a suspect* vibe. I'm nervous enough as it is.

"Do you want to grab your coffee?" He points to the abandoned Styrofoam cup.

I shake my head, perhaps more forcefully than necessary.

"Yeah, it's pretty bad," he chuckles.

We enter a blindingly white room with a small table and plastic chairs on faded linoleum. In the upper corner I spot a camera, with a blinking red light. Any sense of comfort I had drains away.

Detective Johnson has a file—already quite thick—which he opens and proceeds to look through.

His smile disappears. His face is stern, his brows tightly knit.

"Tell me what happened this morning," Detective Johnson says. He lifts his head and the smile returns, albeit a bit more forced.

"I was on the trail and found the guy. There was blood all around him."

He nods. "When did you get to the park?"

"Around five-fifteen. I didn't look so I don't know the exact time, but that's when I normally get there."

"This a routine for you?"

"Yes."

He stares at me for a moment. I don't tell him I need to hike in the mountains for my mental health. Communing with nature helps relieve my PTSD.

"Okay, you get to the parking lot just after five this morning. What did you do when you got there?"

"Grabbed my water bottle, my phone, and my pack. Locked the doors and headed for the trail."

"Which trail do you hike?"

"Scotsman."

"Every day?"

I nod. "When you find what works, you stick with it."

It's his turn to nod. "Anything unusual about the hike?"

"Other than the dead body?"

"Touché," he says. "Before that."

"No."

He stares at me for a long moment, which is unnerving. It's like he's searching my soul for an answer to a question he hasn't asked. But I know what the question is—

Did you have something to do with this?

KATE BAILEY IS INTERESTING. Judging by the way she didn't want to talk about her reasons for getting up before the sun to hike, I'd say she has a past that would make for a fascinating story. I get the feeling she wants to be helpful, but there's a limit. Not sure what it is, but I'm game to find out. Even if it has nothing to do with this case, I'm intrigued by the incongruity.

"So, you're hiking—how far did you get before you found the man?"

"Not far, just before you get to the start of the loop."

I nod, *go on.*

She takes a deep breath and looks down at the table. "I came around the bend and saw him. At first, I thought he'd fallen or had a heart attack or something." She looks up at me. "A lot of people have heart attacks while hiking. They don't realize how much work it takes this far above sea level."

I remain silent, maintaining eye contact. It's a good trick. People hate the silent void and run their mouths to fill it.

"So, anyway, I was calling out to him, but he didn't answer. I wasn't sure what to do. I was nervous about approaching him."

I understand her hesitation. Too many years on the job. Countless women try to help men who then help themselves to the women. The world is a savage place.

Kate's gaze returns to the table. "I didn't see the blood at first. When he didn't move, I got closer. That's when I called 911."

"Did you check to see if he was breathing?"

She pauses. "Yes." Another pause. "But he wasn't. And he was staring at me without blinking for a while. I figured he was already dead."

"But you didn't check?"

A longer pause, her eyes hardening. "I didn't need to. I could see he was dead."

"And you didn't hear anything? No gunshots?"

"No, I had my headphones in." She pauses. "I like to listen to music."

If you're afraid of being attacked, why would you wear headphones?

She must see the question in my eyes, because she says, "Classical music gets me into the right frame of mind."

Plausible. I do that on my way into work, especially in the

middle of a heinous investigation. "See anyone else? Run into any other hikers?"

"No. I rarely do. That's why I like to go so early. It's like I have my own personal park." She glances down at her hands. "The air is pure that time of the morning. Like anything is possible." She raises her head, her smile lights up her eyes. "And life is good."

"Did you know the man? Ever seen him before?" I ask.

Her voice is soft, but her eye twitches. "No." Her head tilts to the side. "Who was he?"

I pull out a picture of the dead man's driver's license.

She squints for a minute. "Joseph Farris." She looks at me. "Is he visiting?"

"Why would you ask that?"

"Maryland license."

Good catch. "Yes, seems he's been here a couple of days."

She nods, a grim smile on her face. "That's too bad."

THERE's a knock at the door. I've never been so happy for an interruption. Detective Johnson has a creepy staring problem.

A police officer steps into the room and motions for the detective.

"Excuse me," Johnson says, getting up.

The door closes behind him. I glance up at the camera. It's mesmerizing and unnerving. I'm starting to understand how people falsely confess to the police. It's intimidating here. I'm considering selling out my grandmother just to get out of here.

Speaking of, I should really let Grandma know what's going on. She's been through so much in her life, yet she opened her heart and home to me when I needed it most. I retrieve my phone and receive a response as soon as I send the text.

Do you need help?

I glance at the door and start typing.

No. Just getting questioned. Hopefully not for much longer.

Have they identified him?

Yes.

Do they know who he is?

They know his name and that he is from Maryland. But it doesn't appear they know what he's doing here. I think they assume he was on vacation.

A smiley face appears on the screen followed by a heart.

I love this woman more than my own life. Her arms are always open, always warm, always protective. Now that her age is showing more with each passing year, I'm the protector.

And there is nothing I wouldn't do for her.

"WE FOUND a man lurking around the south entrance of the park," Officer Garcia says. "He has some outstanding warrants, so they brought him in. Do you want to question him before he's booked?"

"What're the warrants?" I ask.

"Failure to appear on speeding tickets. Bench warrant issued. Also has past assault charges he pled out."

"I'll talk to him." I glance back at the room where Kate Bailey sits. There's really no reason to keep her here. I find her engrossing yet guarded, but that doesn't mean she had anything to do with the murder. People don't always want to talk about their lives. Doesn't make them guilty of anything.

"Let Ms. Bailey go but tell her we may need to ask her more questions. Let's get more background on her, though."

Garcia nods.

I enter the interview room. "Mr. Holman, I'm Detective Johnson."

"Rusty," he says.

I pull out the chair across the table from him and sit, dropping the file onto the table. "I understand you were in Garden of the Gods this morning. Can you tell me what you were doing there?"

"Walking," he says, sliding down in his chair, legs wide, arms across his chest. "Is that a crime?"

"It can be, since technically you were there when the park was closed." I look up at him. "What made you decide to walk around the park so early in the morning?"

He shrugs.

I squint. "Were you drinking last night, Rusty?"

"I had a couple of drinks. Decided to get some fresh air. Didn't know the park was closed."

"Did you see or hear anything while you were in the park?"

He stares at me for a moment. I can practically see the wheels spinning. "No."

"Really? There was quite a bit of commotion during the time you were there. Didn't see anyone? Hear anything?"

"Nope." He runs his hand through his hair, tossing the long strands off his face. "Something happen?"

"A man was shot in the chest."

He looks up at the ceiling. "Don't know nothin' 'bout it."

I slide a picture of the victim across the table. "Do you know this man?"

There's a slight glimmer in his eyes. He pushes the photo back. "No."

"Is this your backpack?" I ask, sliding another photo across the table.

He shrugs. "I have one sorta like it."

"Did you sorta toss this into some bushes when the police approached you?" I flash another picture at him. "How about this gun that was found in the backpack? Is this sorta yours, too?"

He stares at the photo but says nothing.

"Look, Rusty, this little back-and-forth has been amusing, but I'm done with this dance. I have a man shot to death in a park you were illegally trespassing in. A backpack that I would bet my paycheck on is yours, with a gun inside that—and I may be going out on a limb here, but—I'm certain is the murder weapon. How about you and I agree this will go a lot smoother if you cooperate. Otherwise, I'm going to gather my stuff, leave this room, and have you arrested for first degree murder."

He shrugs. "Didn't kill no one."

"Then why did you run from the cops—and toss your backpack with a gun—if you're innocent?"

"Got some weed in there. I didn't want to get caught with it."

I quickly stand to leave, which catches Rusty off guard. Best to let him sit and stew for a bit. Maybe he'll have a *come-to-Jesus* moment and confess.

Garcia meets me in my office. "Seems our victim Mr. Farris has had some trouble in the past. About thirteen years ago, his child was kidnapped in the middle of the night."

"Kidnapped?" I ask, then use air quotes. "Or '*kidnapped*'?"

"Not clear, but there wasn't evidence to charge him. He was also a suspect in his wife's death a couple of years later."

"How did she die?"

"Slipped in the shower, hit her head. He explained the bruising around her upper arms was because she was a drinker after the kid disappeared, and often had episodes where she was unsteady on her feet, and he would grasp her to stop her from falling. Family and friends corroborate his story, so the coroner marked it as an accidental death."

"Any idea what he was doing here? Any friends or family in the area?"

"Trying to break into his phone to see if there are any text messages or calls that will answer that question."

"Let me know what you find out. Anything interesting on Kate Bailey?"

Garcia shuffles through papers. "Not really. Moved here when she was twelve. Lived with her grandmother. Graduated high school in 2017. Associate's degree in paralegal studies. Works for a local attorney."

"No legal trouble?"

"Nothing. Not even a speeding ticket."

"Impressively squeaky clean. Where did she move from?"

"Haven't been able to figure that out. I'll keep digging, if you want."

"I don't see any reason to. Sounds like she was in the wrong place at the wrong time." I reach for my water, wishing it was a double espresso. "See if we can get any other information about Farris's missing kid. Picture. Specifics. Anything."

"You think it has something to do with why he was here?"

"Not out of the realm of possibility." I toss the water bottle into the trash and watch it bounce off the rim. "What about Rusty?"

"Only his prints on the gun, but no gunshot residue on him or his clothing."

Odd. If he shot the gun, left his prints behind, there should be residue on him somewhere.

A young female cop appears at the door. "Detective, Rusty Holman wants to talk to you."

———

"I UNDERSTAND your memory lapses have cleared," I say, entering the interrogation room.

Rusty draws in his eyebrows. "Huh?"

The lack of sarcasm understanding is extraordinarily low in youth today. It makes me weep for the future.

I sit. "You wanted to talk to me about something?"

His foot is tapping a thousand miles a minute, and he's continuously running his fingers through his hair and pushing it back. "So, the gun—it's not mine. I didn't kill anyone. I found it."

I pull my notepad closer. "Where?"

"In a crevice at Cathedral Spires."

"A crevice?"

He nods but his gaze is on the table.

"And you—*what*—randomly reached your hand into a crevice and, low and behold, find a gun there?"

He inhales through his nose and releases a long breath. "No. I saw someone put it there."

"Who?"

"I don't know. I was walking and saw them put something in the rocks, so I waited for them to leave, and I went to see what it was."

"Can you describe this person?"

"Not really." He squints his eyes. "My eyesight ain't the best."

"I'm sure. Well, if you can't provide actual details about this mystery person who hides guns in rocks, I'm going to have to conclude you're lying. And that you shot and killed this man."

"It wasn't me!" He pounds the table. "I swear."

"As much as I'm sure you're an upstanding guy who doesn't lie, I'm finding it hard to believe you."

"It was the person who shot that dude."

The air stills, instantly stagnant. My mind is spinning, trying to comprehend what he's saying. "You're telling me you witnessed the murder? Why wouldn't you lead with that?"

He shrugs. "I have issues talking to cops. I've been jacked up a couple of times."

Not sure I believe him, and at this point, I don't care. "Start from the beginning. I promise not to jack you up."

He nods. "I was walking around the park, that's no lie. I heard someone talking on a cell phone."

"What were they saying?"

"I don't know, I couldn't hear. But they ended the call as soon as the guy walked up. It seemed like they might know each other."

"Okay. Did he say anything?"

"Yeah, but I don't know what. Then all of a sudden—*bam!*—the woman pulled out a gun and shot him."

"What woman?"

"Don't know, but she stood over him for a minute just watching him bleed out. Then called you guys."

"Are you telling me the woman who called 911 killed the man?"

"Shot him point blank in the chest. Then walked over to the spires, shoved the gun in, and walked away. By the time I got the gun, and was walking back, she was on the phone, acting all upset."

My heart is racing and I'm sweating. *How is it possible Kate Bailey killed Farris? And why?*

"I have a picture of her on my phone."

I could blow an aneurysm, but I don't have time. "I'm going to have an officer come in here and get your statement. Tell them everything you just told me."

I dart from the room, wondering where this all fell apart. I got cocky, jinxed myself thinking I was going to close this case easily, and get on with my day. I should've known it was going too smoothly. And now there is a real potential I have let a killer con me into thinking she was just unlucky, stumbling on a dead body.

Garcia comes around the corner. "You're not going to believe this." He shoves a piece of paper into my hand. "The age progression came back on Farris's missing child—missing *daughter*."

A death drum pounds in my ears. There's no denying it's Kate Bailey.

"Get someone over to her place."

Garcia's phone rings. "What?" He's quiet while he listens. A grim smile crosses his face, and he closes his eyes. "Get a crime scene unit over there, and get it processed. We'll be there soon." He ends the call and turns to me. "Kate Bailey is gone."

MURDER IS WRONG.

But so is abuse. And after a lifetime of getting beaten at the hands of my father—murder is also sometimes justified.

I'm not sure how he found me. For thirteen years, I was safe. The bruises disappeared. The injuries healed. But the scars remain.

A few years ago, I decided I was not going to be a victim anymore. If he was going to come for me, I was going to be ready.

That's when my grandmother and I started putting together another escape plan. I was hoping we were never going to need to use it. Life rarely goes the way you want.

The server places two more piña coladas on the table between our chaises, blocking the bright sun. "Anything else for you?"

I shake my head. My grandmother does the same.

All I want to do now is sink into our new life in Mexico. New names, new home, new lives.

The murder of Joseph Farris was a mercy killing. And the memory of his death warms me more than the hot sun.

THE WRONG LINDA

LINDA SOLAYA

If Linda Kiczla had checked her mailbox as she regularly did, and if a teenager hadn't been frustrated with his life, then events the evening of April 13th might not have taken such an alarming turn.

But one day Linda Kiczla *did* forget to walk to her mailbox, hence her bank statement sat unguarded when Justin, the frustrated teenager, came shuffling down the rural Colorado road headed toward town and his stocking job at Arnold's Rite Price Market. Ahead of him, he watched a mail carrier in a rusted Datsun stop at each mailbox. Suddenly, he considered the possibility that the contents of these lonely receptacles could be a source of financial reward.

Although Justin had never stolen anything in his life, frustration overwhelmed him. As usual, his mother had confiscated his paycheck, claiming the need to buy food for him. At last check, the refrigerator contained a package of American cheese, a bottle of ketchup, and the decaying remnants of an Arnold's Rite Price rotisserie chicken. Justin weighed 135 pounds. His mother was considerably larger.

Desperate, Justin reached into the next box he passed and quickly grabbed its contents. Fortunately, his cargo pants were wide enough to fit a prize-winning dairy cow, and he stuffed the mail into an ample pocket. His trousers slid downward, a common occurrence, which he quickly corrected with a heft of his belt. He kept his eye on the mail carrier, but she was at the end of her route and focused on reaching town at the end of a long day.

Back at home that night, the enterprising Justin, not aware he had committed a federal felony, was stunned to learn that a woman named Linda Kiczla had $158,209.83 in her checking account. He thought back over the familiar road and tried to think which of the houses he passed could be hiding the owner of such wealth.

Justin thought and thought, but his brain was currently in a state of decline due to lack of proper nutrition and the hours spent watching reruns of The Brady Bunch. He decided to consult his older cousin Def, more experienced by virtue of his habitation in Denver, as to how he could liberate Linda Kiczla's riches for his own benefit. Def was so named because ninety percent of his wardrobe consisted of Def Leppard t-shirts offered by his parents as compensation for abandoning him to his grandparents the year they attended every Def Leppard concert in the United States and Canada.

On the fateful night, four women gathered in Linda K's dining room. These women loved papercrafting, from creating greeting cards to scrapbooking to origami to the obscure art of quilling, which involved even more folding than origami. Their once-a-month meetings had become a safe haven for the women overwhelmed with the various tribulations of being women in their sixties – grandchildren; elderly parents; spouses in denial about aging who could no longer bench press one hundred pounds, much less a small grandchild; and jobs that after three or four decades had lost their allure. Two of the women had countdown charts to their Medicare eligibility date, which they carried with them and pulled out when their jobs became too despairing. A much more inspiring and less fattening fix than chocolate.

In attendance were two Lindas (Linda being the most

popular baby name for the years between 1947 and 1952), along with a Susan (quite popular in the 1950s), and the inevitable Mary (the runaway most popular name for the century). Surprisingly, there were no Patricias in attendance. Another Linda had bowed out in favor of attending a grandchild's basketball game. The others commiserated about the demanding schedule of being a dutiful grandparent.

As the ladies enjoyed the soothing pleasure of creative activity, the soon-to-be federal offenders sat outside Linda K's house in an aging minivan, reviewing the plan Def had hatched.

Justin, only a junior in high school, wanted the approval of his older cousin but was now feeling remorse and concern for what his Pop-pop would say about this slip into immorality.

"How are you going to get her to give us the money? It's in a bank."

Def snorted. "Look, she's an old lady. I checked her out. She walks to her mailbox with a cane." In this, the hopeful criminal was wrong. Linda K walked to her mailbox with a trekking pole, a tool that allowed her to walk faster on her daily three-mile walk. "She'll be scared and she'll do whatever we tell her to do."

"And what will we tell her to do?"

"We'll drive her to the ATM and make her take out all her money and give it to us."

"They have cameras at those places."

"We'll wear disguises." The optimistic criminal had thought of everything. However, he didn't know that every ATM in the country, in the world, had limits on how much you could withdraw from your account, and those limits in no way approached $158,000. If Def had paid more attention to the personal finance course mandated in his senior year of high school, he would have known this.

In their haven of creative bliss, the four crafters had taken up the topic of a murder in Denver.

"Doctor Dictionary. You remember him."

"Oh, yes. Personally, I didn't like him. Seemed a little sleazy to me."

"He was murdered at a dinner in his honor."

"Those entertainment folks do like to give themselves awards, don't they?"

"Anyway, the news showed his assistant Olivia Twist crying and saying, "I wanted a relationship with my dad, not to kill him!'"

"It's always something with those entertainment types."

The women, content with the evening's production of assorted paper creations, opened the newest catalogs and began tagging additional items to purchase in order to augment their arsenals of papercrafting paraphernalia.

Ever fearful of driving in the dark, Linda B was first to pack her bag. She opened the front door and light spilled onto the dark driveway. From within, a voice called out.

"Linda, you forgot your trekking pole."

Linda B, also a devotee of the trekking pole, turned back. More goodbyes and Linda B began the dark walk to her truck.

"That's her," Def said. Justin shuffled backwards, but Def grabbed his arm. The front door closed, and Def pushed his cousin forward.

Linda B stopped at the sound of scrabbling feet on gravel, then wondered at the unfamiliar vehicle parked behind her truck. The fact that the intended victim was leaving the property where she supposedly lived was a detail the criminal duo failed to evaluate. They heard the name Linda, saw an old woman with a cane and, therefore, acted.

They pulled Linda B kicking and screaming toward the minivan. She was a tough old broad, still strong from years tending to chickens, goats, children, and the subsequent grandchildren, but an old woman is no match for two teenage boys even if their most physical activity was walking from a recliner to a refrigerator.

As the two wannabe criminals shoved Linda B into the

minivan, the other women gathered at the front door, confused by the noise and the sight of two men hitching up their pants before jumping into an old minivan. The vehicle backed up, made a tight turn, then rocketed down the long driveway to County Road 12.

Susan's car being closest, the three women walked toward it, running not being an option. Of the many cliches about old people, the one that they are always in pain is true. This evening Susan hobbled on her left ankle, Linda K babied a bum knee, and Mary felt the strain of a stiff neck. Despite these limitations, the women piled into Susan's car.

The two criminal masterminds, squinting through the windshield at the barely discernible road, had not noticed Linda B reach into the side pocket of her leggings for her ever-present cell phone. Of the many cliches about old people, the one that they don't know how to use technology is not true.

As Susan turned to follow the lights of the fleeing minivan, Linda K's phone rang. Seeing that it was Linda B, Linda K answered the call, hit mute, and jacked up the sound.

"Stop this vehicle!" Linda B's voice came through loud and clear.

Def almost stopped the minivan. Linda B was a retired teacher, and her voice carried with it the weight of thirty-five years managing classrooms packed with students in infinite need of guidance.

"You're driving too fast for these roads, and you should really turn on your brights."

Def heard a strange clicking sound. Linda B was ratcheting down her trekking pole into a short, sturdy baton worthy of a 1950s Soviet prison guard and, in similar fashion to a 1950s Soviet prison guard, she began to beat Def's head and shoulders.

"What the—? Get her!" Def shouted as he tried to squirm away, swerving and speeding down the road.

Justin twisted and grabbed, but Linda B fell out of reach as the minivan hit a bad stretch of washboard. Def cursed and pulled the minivan straight.

"What are you boys thinking, grabbing me like this? Do you want to spend the rest of your lives in jail? Kidnapping is a federal crime."

"Shut up," Def said as he switched on the brights, grateful for the wider spread of light that illuminated the ditches on either side of the crushed limestone road.

"My mother never let us say 'shut up.' It's such a disrespectful way to talk to another person," Linda B instructed.

Justin recognized that tone of voice and turned to get a better look at the woman. "Mrs. Braun?"

"Yes?" Linda B leaned forward.

"It's me, Justin Hauser. From third grade."

"Oh my, Justin Hauser." Linda B smiled at the memory of a quiet student eager for approval.

For the benefit of her friends, Linda B said, "I hope no one calls the sheriff about what you boys have done." If Justin was still salvageable, she wanted a chance to help.

The minivan reached an intersection.

"Which way, Justin? Which way?" Def pounded the steering wheel.

"If you turn left, you'll be headed toward my house and can drop me off, and we can forget this whole mess."

Def turned right. "And what's this way?" He laughed because ahead lay a low, heavy darkness. "Man, how do people live out here?"

"Why did you turn right onto County Road T?" Linda B asked for the benefit of her listening friends.

At the intersection, Susan stopped, her knuckles white on the steering wheel. "I can't drive without the headlights on."

Mary, being the youngest at 63 and still with no evidence of cataracts, switched places with Susan. Mary turned onto the road of light-colored limestone that gave her some hope of visibility.

"Justin, I don't know how you got involved in this, but I

can help. My brother owns a small garage in Fort Morgan. He could train you to be a mechanic."

"Mechanic?" Def crowed. "You don't want to be a mechanic."

"Why not?" Justin asked. "I helped my Pop-pop work on a tractor once. It was interesting."

"We're going to make more money tonight than you'll make being a mechanic," Def replied.

"Maybe not," Linda B continued. "Mechanics are in big demand these days. You should also think about robotics. One of my former students went into robotics, and he's making ninety thousand a year."

"Ninety thousand?" Justin turned in his seat. "And you get to work with robots?"

Def slapped at Justin. "Are you kidding me? We're going to make $158,000 tonight."

"Uh oh," Linda K said from the back seat of the geriatric chase car.

"What?" Mary leaned forward and squinted at the road.

"They've got the wrong Linda."

"The wrong Linda?" Susan swiveled in her seat.

"I had about $158,000 in my checking account last month, the life insurance from my father. I've since moved it into a CD."

Meanwhile in the minivan, Linda B was explaining the economics of one-time payments versus habitual employ-ment. "First of all, if you split fifty-fifty, you only get $79,000 each, which won't last long in today's economy. Then what will you do?"

"We'll find another old geezer to rip off."

"To equal the annual income of a $90,000 robotics mechanic and, by the way, that's a starting wage with benefits which you will not get while ripping off old geezers, you'd have to rip off at least one old geezer every year. Is that a sustainable occupation?"

"Would you shut up!" Def checked his rearview mirror. "Someone's back there."

"Probably the sheriff." Linda B continued her financial tutorial. "There's really no guarantee of income if your plan is to rip off old geezers. Contrary to the many advertisements on television, most old people do not live on golf courses and do not have million-dollar retirement funds. And you'll have a lot of expenses trying to find enough old geezers to rip off."

"Shut up!"

"No, wait a minute, listen to her, she's got a point," Justin said.

Def glared at him. "Are you kidding me? What's this old bag know?"

"Excuse me, I don't appreciate being called an old bag. I am old, but you shouldn't make that word into a pejorative."

"A what?" Justin turned and looked at Mrs. Braun.

"A pejorative. It means a word that has negative connotations."

"I always enjoyed learning new words with you, Mrs. Braun."

"Shut up!" Def slapped at his cousin.

"Don't hit me!" Justin yelled as he cowered against the door.

"Now, boys. You shouldn't fight. You are, after all, business partners."

"Shut up!" Def screamed.

In the other car, Linda K began laughing. "I swear, I'm going to wet my pants."

"I guess they don't know that old doesn't mean stupid." Mary braced herself as the car shimmied through another washboard section of road. They could barely see the tail-lights ahead for the dust.

Def took his foot off the gas. "What is that?"

Ahead a giant shape loomed in the darkness, a row of lights highlighting the dust rolling forward as the minivan crawled to a halt.

Justin, seeing a chance out of prison for kidnapping his third grade teacher, said, "It looks like a spaceship." Which indeed it did, but Justin knew that the apparition before them was a John Deere 8R250 with a row of lights three feet above the road, leaving the tires invisible in the hovering dust.

"No way! I've heard about this. Alien spaceships always land in the sticks." Def began to panic.

Behind the wheel of the tractor sat a farmer named Bill, known affectionately as Big Bill, not for his size which was indeed formidable, but for his charitable nature. Big Bill had once given a hundred-dollar bill to a ten-year-old faking his way onto a crew hand-picking pigweed from Big Bill's beet field. To a friend's argument that he was spoiling the kid, Big Bill simply replied, "You gotta reward that kind of work ethic."

After another twelve-hour day, however, Big Bill was not in a charitable mood. He wanted to get home in time to watch his eldest daughter play basketball. He couldn't imagine who would be on the road since every parent, grandparent, aunt, uncle, sister, brother, and miscellaneous cousin or friend within a 60-mile radius was at the middle school gym. No one supported sports-playing kids like a farming community.

Big Bill had moved over when he saw the approaching vehicle, his right tractor wheels into the soft shoulder. He was irritated that the other vehicle did not cooperatively move to its right where there was a dry ditch and a barbed wire fence. Big Bill put the tractor in neutral and cracked open the door, reaching behind him for a protective ratchet wrench when he heard the screaming.

"It's a spaceship! I swear I'm never leaving Denver again."

"What do we do? What do we do?" Justin yelled in unconvincing mock horror.

From the cab of his tractor, Big Bill grinned then flipped the switch for the spotlights above the tractor cab.

"It's going to attack!"

Big Bill heard a woman laughing, then the side door of the minivan rolled open, and a woman hobbled away.

"You boys better run before it beams you up," Linda B shouted as she extended her trekking pole to its full length and descended into the dry ditch.

Big Bill revved the tractor engine, creating a high-pitched whine, like a spaceship powering up to transport unwilling humans.

The minivan shot backward, the open door rolling shut as the vehicle fishtailed. Finally, the van swung around and headed back the way it had come, leaving a dust plume shimmering in the lights of the tractor.

Big Bill climbed down the tractor steps, landing lightly for such a big man on the limestone road.

"Is that you, Mrs. Braun?"

"Is that you, Billy?"

Big Bill reached down a hand and helped Linda B out of the ditch. "What is going on?"

Linda B swiped at the dry grass and stickers clinging to her leggings. "If you can believe it, I was kidnapped."

Big Bill reached for his cell, but Linda B put a hand on his arm. "No, don't call the sheriff. We need to handle this ourselves."

"Whatever you say, Mrs. Braun."

Linda B's listening friends had figured out her intentions and turned their car sideways across the road in anticipation of the kidnappers' return.

"Typical Linda. Always thinking she can save a kid," Mary commented.

Susan nodded. "Her students loved her, no matter how hard she was on them."

In the distance they could see the headlights of the kidnappers' returning minivan.

"Perhaps," Linda K suggested, "we should get out of the car in case these guys do something stupid."

"In case?" Susan laughed. "Good thing I have insurance."

The women stepped cautiously down into the dry ditch.

"Watch out," Mary warned. "Big patch of goatheads down here."

Grateful for sturdy shoes, the women stepped over the matted mass of dry puncturevine and its clusters of spiked seedheads that resembled demon-like goats. They assisted each other in stumbling between the strands of barbed wire and took protective cover in the density of winter wheat. Beyond the lights of the kidnappers' minivan, they could see the threatening beams of Big Bill's tractor in rumbling pursuit.

"Can't you get this thing to go any faster?" Linda B complained.

"I'm maxed out at thirty miles per hour," Big Bill explained. "And I've got to be able to stop because those boys have run out of road." He nodded toward Susan's car.

"It's following us," Def screamed, staring into his rearview mirror at the lights of the spaceship. His mind had gone to that dark thought of the alien inclination to probe humans. Def did not want to be probed.

"Look out!" Justin screamed.

Def's eyes returned to the road, and he slammed on the brakes. Not remembering the irrigation ditch on the right, he let the van slide until the back end fell into the water.

The tractor began to slow, its big engine rumbling. Def crawled out his window, fell into the ditch, and came up howling with streamers of ditch grass clinging to his face.

Big Bill revved the engine.

Def clambered out of the irrigation ditch and ran across the road into the dry ditch. He stumbled, fell, then screamed in pain.

"Darn goatheads," Mary whispered.

Def rose and pitched forward into the barbed wire fence. He screamed again, twisting and pulling, causing the barbed wire to dig deeper into his baggy pants until his only recourse was to leave the pants behind.

"Oh, my," Linda K whispered at the sight of Def's brightly-colored Sponge Bob Square Pants boxer briefs. "He seems a bit old for that."

Free of the barbed wire, Def whirled, surveying his options for flight.

Linda K stood, causing Def to fall into another patch of goatheads. He screamed a third time.

"Can I help you, young man?"

"Which way to Denver?" Def shouted at the apparition standing before him.

Linda K, tempted to point east, took pity on the young man and pointed west. Def began to run.

"He's going to have a long trip home," Susan commented.

Linda K sighed. "We may be seeing him again. I have a feeling that boy can't walk a straight line."

With two Linda's, a Susan, and a Mary on site, it didn't take long to get Big Bill on the way to his daughter's basketball game and to corral Justin's future into the care of Linda B. By the time Def inevitably circled back, his van had been retrieved from the ditch. He never traveled east of Denver again.

The women left Def's pants entangled in the barbed wire as a warning and continued to meet for evenings of papercrafting, their trekking poles at the ready.

FOR THE FIRST TIME

MARIE SUTRO

The brown bits on the floor could have been anything. Whether remnants of broken twigs, carcasses of deceased insects, clumps of soil from the flower bed just outside, or something altogether worse, I didn't want to know. Without looking too closely, I vacuumed the mess off the driftwood gray floors.

"You're stalling again," Trent called out from the kitchen.

A strong Colorado wind was having its way on the other side of the front door. Ignoring Trent, I made a mental note to get the weatherstripping replaced and shoved the hand-woven rug against the gap under the door.

"You know I'm right, Delores," Trent taunted.

"I know you spend more time here than at your place," I fired back. "You could at least help out once in a while."

With the vacuum returned to its nook by the hall closet, I made my way back toward the kitchen. Selling the grand house in Hilltop had been a huge help. The newly built condo on the outskirts of Denver had a manageable open plan and far less square footage. More important, it was mercifully free of old memories—or at least some of them.

Sitting primly at the oak table, Trent pinned me with his

signature stare. Chin settled against his throat, his vivid blue eyes betrayed nothing from under his perfect brow.

At the risk of sounding shallow, Trent's brow wasn't as perfect as it had been when I'd first spotted him mulling over Tony Bennett albums at the local record store four decades ago. Back then he'd exuded a confidence that could turn even the most jaded divorcee's head.

Don't get me wrong. It's not as if I'd pried the fountain of youth out of Ponce de Leon's hands. Of the two of us, Trent had definitely fared better in the aging looks department.

Tossing a soiled paper towel in the trash, I made my way to the stove, turned off the burner, and tipped the kettle over my mug. Chocolatey goodness mushroomed into the air as scratchy jazz danced in from the speakers in the living area—sensory perfection.

"Delores … you're going to have to address it," he pressed again.

Plunging a spoon into the brown sludge, I turned back to the table. Trent eyed my cocoa. If he took affront to the fact that I hadn't offered him one, he didn't show it. The subtext about his taste for heavier-hitting drinks wasn't worth rehashing, nor was the devastation that had been wrought by their excessive consumption.

"You have to do something about it. Ignoring it won't make it go away."

The right side of my mouth lifted in a wry salute. "Any chance I can make *you* go away?"

A flicker of frustration in those impossibly blue eyes. "I'll leave, once you've taken care of it."

That same relentless mindset had once earned him some of the highest retainers in Denver. Sadly, Trent's position as the city's top corporate attorney had eventually been stolen from him by one tragic accident. He'd been drifting ever since.

I rubbed my forehead harder than necessary. "You know

what you're asking. And you know what it could cost me at this point in my life."

His features softened. "I do, but I also know you want to do the right thing. Besides, you don't have to tell her everything."

"Don't be ridiculous! She's bound to have millions of questions. It's not my fault that you … what's that expression … *ghosted* her mom all those years ago."

He held up his hands. "I had no idea she was pregnant, I swear!"

Post-accident Trent would never have walked out on a pregnant girlfriend, but pre-accident Trent was entirely capable of it. Still, the woman who had emailed me deserved a response.

"Why did I ever agree to keep talking to you after our marriage ended?" I grumbled as I picked up my cup and headed for the sofa.

"You know exactly why." His smile fell, carrying the weight of our combined failures with it.

Sitting on the couch, I set down my drink and opened the laptop. Pulling up Jesse Saenz's email, I typed a quick reply confirming I was the Delores Fairhaven who had been married to her father.

"Tell her I didn't know." Trent prodded as he dropped down beside me.

I did as instructed. Buoyed by a wave of sympathy, I sputtered, "I'll do you one better." Trent watched as I typed out my certainty that he would have loved being there for her if he'd had the chance. A few more niceties followed, then a kind closing before I hit send.

"You are pretty fantastic when you want to be." He reached out to rub my shoulder, something he used to do before the accident. It was his ineffectual way of making me feel better about things that never should have happened.

A chirp from the computer. "Oh no," I groaned.

He spotted the new email. "She responded? That's great!"

"No, it's not!"

"Oh, come on. Just open it!" Hope swam in his eyes.

I'd barely finished reading the email before Trent slapped his left knee. "She wants to meet you. This is fantastic!"

"Are you insane?"

"Come on."

"What if she asks about the accident?"

The joy faded from his face. "Use the same line."

"To your daughter?"

The word fell between us like a bloodied meat cleaver. His daughter. Not mine.

Thanks to Trent, I could never have children. Thanks to Trent, my home had never rung with the squeal of tiny tots, nor had it been ravaged by the taciturn temper of teens.

"It worked with everyone else," he countered. "The cops, the reporters, my family. They all believed it was an accident. Why wouldn't she?"

"For crying out loud, Trent!" I screeched over the dulcet jazz tones. "How many times do I have to lie about killing you?"

THE PLACID LLAMA'S smile was an odd match for the ferocious feline body. I peered at the mismatched logo emblazoned on my cup, trying to ignore the fact that Trent's left leg was doing its best impersonation of the Titanic's distress call beneath the bistro table.

Despite the rush of wind blasting downtown Denver, the air in the hipster coffee shop was warm and thick with the acrid smell of espresso. Pushing the cup away, I flashed him a sour look. "Would you stop that?" I hissed under my breath.

Trent's gaze slid across the table. "Sorry, babe. I'm just so excited!"

"That makes one of us," I mumbled. "And you know how I feel about you calling me babe."

Guilt blossomed between us, flowing over the table and stilling his bouncing leg. I opened my mouth to account for my share of it when the espresso machine roared to life on the counter. Hair pulled back in a total of six separate ponytails, the thirty-something barista went on about her duties as if my future freedom wasn't hanging in the balance.

Fighting the urge to run, I picked up my phone and checked the screen.

"Is it her?" Trent asked.

"She's parking," I murmured.

Trent checked his overpriced watch—a leftover from days of abundance. "She's on time. That's a good sign."

I lifted the cup to my lips, counting on it to mute the emotion in my voice. "There's nothing good about it. This woman just tracked down her dead father's widow. Emphasis on the word *dead* because for the past forty years, the entire world has believed you were. You shouldn't even be here."

"But—"

"Shocking her is a recipe for disaster. You always do this! You push too hard and things break."

Seeing his pained expression, I sighed and tried again. "I'm not saying it can't happen one day." I reached for my purse. "But, if you really insist on staying, I'll go. You can wreck this train on your own."

Trent's eyes locked on the front door. I could almost see the wheels turning in his head. Finally, he let out a gust of air. "Okay. You're right. I don't want to overwhelm her, and I'd never want to do anything to hurt you. This is a great first step and I need to be happy with it. Promise me you'll be careful not to say too much about what happened." Another squeeze of my shoulder before he headed for the back door.

He left just as the front door opened. A slim brunette entered. Long chestnut hair danced on the burst of wind accompanying her.

Jesse looked exactly like the picture I'd found on Facebook. Copies of Trent's arresting blue eyes set off rich caramel-colored skin in a face that likely attracted more than its fair share of interest.

Spotting me, she smiled wide. Like her father's, it was the kind of smile you couldn't help but return. Placing her luxury leather bag on the table, she stuck out her hand.

Callouses were unexpected for Trent's offspring, but not for the owner of a national chain of classic car repair shops. According to the five-star online reviews for Keep it Humming Auto Repair, Jesse was a hands-on proprietor who certainly knew her way around a wrench set.

The fact had tickled post-accident Trent. The pre-accident version would have been mortified.

"Thank you so much for doing this," she gushed. Her tone was as warm and full of hope as a summer sunrise over the Rockies.

"You're welcome." I hazarded a glance at the front window fully expecting to see Trent, but he had kept his word.

"I know this must be awkward for you. I read the news-paper reports about the accident."

She took the seat across from me, seemingly unaware of the concussive effects of the verbal bomb. Her brows pulled into a knot. "I want to say how sorry I am that you had to go through that."

"Not as sorry as I am," I managed.

The barista appeared. An angel of mercy bearing a notepad. "What can I get ya?" She peered at the new arrival.

"Decaf coffee, black please."

"How about a Dirt Digger Donut with that?" She motioned to the nearby counter where a stack of chocolate donuts sat under a glass dome. Each of the deadly delights was laden with colorful gummy worms.

"Thanks, but those are more my daughter's speed," Jesse demurred.

"I hate even having 'em here. Every time I look at 'em, I think about that murder."

The m-word drained all the blood from my face.

"The kid's TV show host, you mean?" Jesse asked, wide-eyed.

"Yeah! That Wendy woman was on my favorite podcast last night. Claims she was there when it happened, but she sure didn't mind throwing the senator under the bus."

"How so?"

"Something about needing gummies for anxiety. Claimed sugar calms her, but we all know what *optional* ingredient in gummies calms you." The last words were punctuated with an eye roll. "Anyway, she claims she asked the senator for some and he wouldn't give her any. Odd, huh?"

A voice called out from the open door behind the counter.

"Gotta go! I'll have the coffee for ya in a second." With a toothy grin and a wild whip of strawberry-scented hair, we were left alone.

"Murder is so horrific!" Jesse exclaimed. "I can't imagine how anyone could do that, can you?"

"No, I ... I can't." It wasn't a lie. I still couldn't understand how I'd done it.

Sitting back, she searched my features before finally recalling her manners. "I'm sorry for staring! As I explained, my father's family is gone and since my mother's passing, you're the only one left who can tell me about him."

"I understand." Another sip to try to cover the fact that I didn't understand at all. "You found out about Trent when you went through your mother's things?"

"Yes. I'd always believed he died before I was born." She shook her head. "My mom was a wonderful person who did her best for me. I guess she wanted me to believe I would've been loved and wanted. Can't fault her for that."

Recalling how post-accident Trent had pestered me nonstop since Jesse's original email arrived, I figured she would have been both loved and wanted. Pre-accident Trent was another story.

THE VICE-LIKE GRIP had become so habitual that the Tyrannosaurus Rex's neck no longer bore the weight of its head. Three-year-old Isabella nuzzled against the misshapen pink reptile. Marveling at her long, dark lashes, I basked in the now familiar warmth spreading over me as I watched her little chest rise and fall.

"Amazing that little terror could sleep so soundly," Trent mused from the doorway to the guest bedroom.

Carefully wiping a stray curl from her brow, I straightened and joined him where he leaned against the moulding.

"She's not that bad," I whispered. "In fact, she's pretty darn good for a toddler."

He donned his trademark stare. "You're just saying that because she's started calling you Dee Dee. And now you're sweet on her."

It turned out Jesse had wanted more than the prepared overview of Trent I'd offered at the coffee shop. Somehow, I had ended up agreeing to a second visit at my place. Little did I know that her sitter would cancel at the last minute. Jesse had arrived at my door with the little tyke peeking at me from behind her mother's skirt.

Upon entry, Isabella had carefully inspected every inch of my home. Considering every object at a thoughtful distance, she'd shown uncharacteristic restraint for her age.

During that visit, one thing had led to another, including Jesse's revelation that she had a huge collection of jazz music on her phone. I can't even recall how or why the next visit was scheduled, but Isabella and her mother had returned.

By the third meeting, I had to plunge deeper into who Trent was. Instead of regaling her with stories of the pre-accident Trent who had dumped Jesse's pregnant mother, I told the same stories with post-accident Trent.

Eventually, the stories had run out. But Jesse and Isabella

had kept coming over. Now, I was Dee Dee and the guest room had been redecorated with dinosaurs.

Trent put his hand on my shoulder, gently leading me down the hall to the couch. A growing sense of anticipation grew with each step. Electricity hummed between us. By the time I sat down, dread had begun to well up from the place where the truth had been locked away for so very long.

Trent dropped to a knee in front of me, taking both my hands in his. The decades fell away. There he was again with that ridiculously large diamond ring, asking me to make him the happiest man alive.

"It's time, babe," he said, drawing me back to the present with a note of wistfulness.

"Time? You don't want me to tell Jesse …"

Jagged memories chewed away at the warmth between us, rending our shared memories with serrated teeth. That first weekend away together after the honeymoon. The black eye, the bruised ribs. Flashes of a host of hospital visits over the following two years of marriage.

And then the night it all stopped. The night of the accident.

"No, Delores, you don't have to tell her. There's no point in that."

Memories came in fits and starts, flooding in and out of sequence. The scream of the ambulance as it pulled into the driveway, the smell of blood, the all-consuming need to … just … make … him … stop.

The knife from the butcher block. The questions from the police. The version I had told them … the version they'd believed.

It had helped when they saw the nursery. They had nodded sympathetically when they heard I'd lost the baby the week before. I left out the part about one of Trent's alcohol-fueled rages being the cause.

I had told them Trent was away on a business trip. That part was true. I also said I had no idea it was him coming through the bedroom door, that I had no way of knowing he'd called to say he was coming home early. That part wasn't true.

There'd been a string of break-ins in the area. I was alone and distraught, mourning my lost child. It was easy to believe paranoia had gained more than a foothold in the swirl of devastating emotion. Totally understandable that I'd brought the knife to the bedroom just in case.

It had also helped that the light was still blinking on my answering machine when they inspected it. The police believed me when I said I wasn't home when the call came in. They believed I hadn't been standing in the front hallway when his voice echoed through the house as the call was recording, my heart dropping as I heard the telltale slur in his words.

All so easy to swallow. Especially since I had doggedly hidden it all from family and friends. Everyone had accepted the lies because the alternative was too difficult.

In all honesty, I had never planned to kill Trent. I'd merely grabbed the knife in desperation. I'd been trying to make it back to our bedroom, hoping I could barricade myself in. But he'd been undaunted by the blade. He had grabbed me. I'd lashed out against what was coming. It had ended in a heartbeat.

So many years had gone by since. So many years of hiding the secret. Worried I might someday slip, I had pulled away from everyone. It was merely a process of finishing what had started after the first black eye and broken ribs. When it was time to retire from the phone company, I was well and truly alone … except for Trent.

Leaning in, he planted a chaste kiss on my forehead. "Don't ever think of it again, Delores. I never should have put you in that position. It's all over and done with now."

Tears welled in my eyes. I could feel what was coming.

"And you have Jesse and Isabella—everything you should

have had all those years ago. Everything you could have had if I hadn't been so messed up."

In the next moment, he vanished.

The minutes passed by slowly, each one punctuated by the tick of the grandfather clock in the corner. Swiping away at the last of the tears, I rose and drifted back to the doorway of the guest room.

The dinosaur was suffocating under the weight of the little girl's abdomen. How she could possibly sleep in that position was beyond my comprehension.

In hindsight, it was all beyond my comprehension. I had spent decades trying to make sense of something that could never make sense. Trent was right. It was enough to acknowledge it had happened and to move on.

Lids heavy, I crept over to the bed. Isabella barely moved as I cuddled up beside her.

The warmth of her little body against mine melted away the last of the sadness. For the first time since I'd killed Trent, I was finally capable of letting him rest in peace.

TIME WOUNDS ALL HEELS

MARY BIRK

Pearl peered out her front window at the house across the street, hoping to get a glimpse of her neighbors. Neighbor watching and soap operas were Pearl's favorite activities since she'd retired. For a bunch of old folks, she thought, her neighbors were pretty interesting. The woman next door was a retired state senator with a tattooed twenty-something boyfriend, and the couple on the other side of her had made a fortune selling their patent for using recycled plastics for military applications. The string of visitors to their door looked like a John Wick movie.

She'd moved into the gated retirement community last month, a year to the date she'd lost her Pete. The two-bedroom ranch was perfect for this new phase of her life, and the neighborhood, gated and crime free, a welcome refuge from the city. She wasn't lonely, just alone. Well, except for her little Havanese, Lola.

She had managed to meet most of her neighbors since then, but the wife across the street seemed determined to keep her distance. Pearl's instincts, honed from years as a homicide detective, told her the woman had something to hide. She was sure she'd seen Bernice Reynolds somewhere before. Figuring out where was difficult because Bernice always wore sunglasses, the big, round, movie star kind. She was always in full makeup, hair in a perfect, stiff updo, dressed to the nines, and downright unfriendly. And always with those darn dark glasses.

But Pearl was determined. To that end, she'd installed a doorbell camera, pointed across the street. Sooner or later, she'd catch the woman without her shades.

According to the neighborhood grapevine, Fred Reynolds and Bernice—a flashy looking blonde who had to be twenty years younger than Fred—were practically newlyweds. Pearl had met the husband, a nice silver-haired gentleman, but not his wife, though not for lack of trying.

Pearl let the drapes close. She couldn't sit and neighbor watch all day. The bareroot roses she'd ordered had been sitting in water for a week now. If she didn't get them planted soon, they'd never make it. Soggy roots were no joke.

It was a little chilly, but in April with the Colorado sun, as long as she kept her jacket zipped, she'd be fine. Pearl retrieved the plants from her bathtub, transporting them to the front yard in a plastic bucket, Lola at her side. She put each plant close to where she wanted to install it, then went to the garage to get her shovel and the gardening cart she'd filled with compost and took them out front.

A door slamming across the street caught Pearl's attention. She watched as Bernice stormed out of the house, clearly madder than a wet hen. Bernice wore an obviously expensive black sheath with a red belt, mile-high heels, and of course, the ubiquitous sunglasses. Holding a shiny red cellphone to her ear, Bernice slid into the driver's seat of her ruby red Thunderbird convertible, her lips in a pout so obvious, Pearl could see it from across the street. Why did the woman look so familiar? If only she'd take off her glasses.

Trying to seem uninterested, Pearl grabbed her shovel and considered the exact placement for the roses in her postage-stamp sized yard. Lola flopped down in the sun. Out of the corner of her eye, Pearl watched Fred come out front, holding what looked like a woman's red shoe.

Bernice leaned out of the convertible. "Throw it away. The heel's broken. I'm going shopping for another pair."

"I told you; I'll fix it."

"I'm not wearing a glued-together Jimmy Choo."

"And *I'm* not paying for another pair of thousand-dollar shoes, no matter what color. Your closet is full of shoes. Pick another pair."

"But, sweetie, they're my only red Jimmy Choos," Bernice whined.

What a piece of work.

"No more shoes."

Good, Fred wasn't falling for it.

"Why are you being so stingy?"

"Stingy? You've spent thousands of dollars on shoes since we got married. I'll fix the blasted thing for you. Superglue works miracles. I'll even nail it down."

"No way. I'm getting new ones."

"Not with *my* credit card, you aren't. I just shut it down."

Bernice held out a finger in a rude gesture, backed out of the driveway, and drove away.

Fred put a hand over his eyes to shade them as he watched the convertible disappear. Then he spotted Pearl and waved. Pearl, embarrassed to have been caught spying, waved back then bent her head down to her work.

Fred called out, "Want some help?"

"Sure. Thanks."

He crossed the street, joining her. "What you got there?" He bent down to rub Lola's tummy.

"Roses. Bareroot. Three of the little buggers, and the ground is hard as iron."

He straightened up and took the shovel from her. "I'm good at this."

"You're sure you don't mind?"

"I don't have anything better to do. Well, except fix that shoe."

Pearl barely suppressed her smile. "It looks like a nice shoe."

"It's a ridiculous shoe. Bernice can hardly walk in those things." He tossed the shoe to the ground nearby. "Where do you want the holes and how deep?"

Pearl pointed to the spot she'd selected for the first rose. "About eighteen inches deep." He started to dig, and Pearl went on. "I have the feeling I've seen your wife someplace before. Is she from Denver?"

Fred shook his head, easily lifting the soil out and piling it to the side. "She's from somewhere out west."

"Somewhere out west?" That was a bit vague.

"I'm not sure where exactly. She doesn't like to talk about her past. Is this deep enough?"

"Perfect. What does she do?"

"She was a healthcare aide. That's how we met. She was my wife's caregiver. After Francie died, we just kind of started seeing each other. Now she shops. A lot." He smiled. "Sorry. I shouldn't complain. The stock market's been good to me, and I can afford it."

Pearl smiled back. "Good attitude. None of my business, but is there something wrong with her eyes?"

"Her eyes?"

"Every time I see her, she's wearing dark glasses. Even when there's no sun."

"Oh, that. She's developed some light sensitivity. Started about a month ago."

Interesting, Pearl thought. Just when I moved in. Was there a connection?

Still digging, Fred jerked his head in the direction of her house. "You were smart getting the ranch-style model."

"It's smaller than yours, but then, there's two of you and just one of me. Not counting Lola."

"You're widowed, right?" He added, in explanation, "Neighborhood grapevine."

She nodded. "A year and a month. Pete and I had a big house in the suburbs. Perfect size for raising our family, but once the kids grew up, and Pete died, it was too much for me to deal with. Have you lived here long?"

"This deep enough?"

Pearl gave him a thumbs up and got down to plant the rose.

He stabbed the shovel into the ground to start the next hole. "We bought the place in January right after Bernice and I got married. She picked it out."

"It's nice."

"To be honest, I wanted the ranch model. I didn't want steps. At my age, one fall down that staircase onto that marble floor, and I'm a goner." He shrugged. "But Bernice thinks the staircase is elegant. She loves coming down the stairs in those killer shoes of hers. I tell her not to, but she's stubborn. Not me, I hang on to the handrail for dear life."

"That's smart." Pearl pulled a rose from the bucket, giving it a little shake to straighten the roots. "I had a private caregiver for my Pete for a while. It didn't work out."

"Why not?"

Pearl gave a wry smile. "I caught Portia—that was her name—making advances to my Pete. It was about four years before he died, when his dementia was getting bad. She actually had the audacity to try to get him to divorce me and marry her. She figured out Pete had money—the stock market was good to us, too—and his health wasn't good, so if she got rid of me and married him, she'd be a rich widow soon. I did a background check on her, and it turned out she had a history of cozying up to men for money. Two of the men died under suspicious circumstances. I set her straight real quick. Showed her my badge—I was a cop—and told her where the monkey put the peanut. The girl hightailed it out faster than you could say *gold digger*."

"No fool like an old fool." Fred gave a rueful smile. "Sometimes I think I'm an old fool myself." Pointing to the hole, he asked, "This good?"

"Perfect." She knelt down and arranged the rose bush in a mound of compost and good dirt inside the hole. Patting it down, she said, "Do you mind me asking what your wife died of?"

He started digging the final hole. "It was a fluke thing. We had just gotten back from Australia and were supposed to be going to Canada for my nephew's wedding. She fell and broke her hip when we were about ready to leave. Francie insisted I go to the wedding without her. He's my sister's only kid. We found Bernice from an ad in one of those neighborhood network things and hired her to take care of Francie while I was gone. When I was on the plane coming home, Francie died. Pulmonary embolism. The doctor thought she must have developed a blood clot on our trip, and then with the hip break, and the medications, it was a perfect storm." He jabbed a finger at the hole. "This good?"

"Exactly right." She scooted over to plant the last rose. "Did you and Francie have children?"

Fred shook his head. "We couldn't. Need any more holes?"

"No, that's wonderful. Thank you so much." Pearl stood up, brushing off her clothes. "Let me do something to thank you for all your help. Would you and Bernice like to come over for dinner? Not to brag, but I'm a tolerable cook." Also, she thought, it would be the perfect opportunity to see Bernice without her shades.

He looked embarrassed. "I'd love to, but Bernice doesn't like socializing much. Or cooking. She likes restaurants."

"Oh, okay." Darn, there went that idea.

Fred got the garden hose and washed off the shovel. "To be honest, I'm sick of restaurants, so she mostly goes without me. I usually make myself a sandwich and canned soup."

"What about if I put something homemade together that

you can just heat up when you're hungry? It would give you a change from soup and sandwiches." She picked up his wife's broken shoe and handed it to him. "And if Bernice decides to eat at home, there'll be plenty for her, too. What do you think of meatloaf?"

His eyes lit up. "My favorite."

"I'll bring it over tomorrow. Thanks, again."

Fred waved the shoe in acknowledgment as he crossed the street.

Going back inside her own house, Pearl thought that if she got inside their house to drop off the food, maybe she could catch Bernice bare-eyed. She looked at her watch. Almost time for General Hospital. She poured herself a glass of iced tea, plopped down on the sofa, and turned the TV to the channel with her soap opera. She was a little early, and the news was still on. Oh, well, she could wait.

She groaned when she saw the news story being covered. The Doctor Dictionary murder case again. Pearl had had her fill of murder cases when she was on the job, and now tried to avoid anything even close to the subject. At least it wasn't about politics. That would have been even worse.

Pearl lifted her little dog up onto her lap, listening idly while she waited for General Hospital to begin. The reporter was interviewing a guy named Jack Como. Como told the reporter that he was going to have Doctor Dictionary help him pop the question to his girlfriend, Charlotte Webb, at the same awards banquet where Doctor Dictionary ended up being murdered.

Immediately, Pearl perked up. There was a romance angle to the story? Right up her alley, after all. She had always been a total romance addict, even when she was still on the job. Being a homicide detective had meant immersing herself in all the ugly of life, and she'd needed romance stories to stay sane. She needed the fun, the tender moments, the healthy tears. The happy endings.

She smoothed her hand along Lola's curly fur as she

watched. Como told the police he'd been trying to convince Doctor Dictionary to do a trivia quiz during his acceptance speech that focused on things about Como's relationship with Charlotte Webb. Como planned to pop out after the quiz, unfurling a banner with "Will you marry me?" spelled out in big letters. Seems he'd been lugging it in a trash bag, sneaking around so Charlotte wouldn't see him, but she caught him and figured out what he was up to.

Men, Pearl thought. So clueless sometimes. She was glad this wasn't her case.

It was a relief when General Hospital came on. Watching Willow and Drew dance around their budding romance was much more fun than watching some guy explain his lame proposal idea, or see the cops explain their mistake.

THE NEXT DAY, Pearl took a meatloaf, twice baked potatoes, and cheesy beans over to Fred and Bernice's. She knew someone was home, because the garage door was open and both cars were in the garage, but she'd had to ring the doorbell several times before Bernice, wearing her dark glasses, darn it, finally answered the door. It was beyond obvious that Bernice wasn't glad to see her.

Bernice stood behind the screen door, wrinkling up her nose as if she smelled something stinky. "What's that?" As usual, the woman was fully made up, dressed to kill. She was wearing what looked like red Jimmie Choo five-inch heels. Pearl wondered if they were a new pair or if Fred had fixed the old ones.

"Dinner. Meatloaf, potatoes, beans. A thank you for Fred's help with my rose bushes." She tried to peer around Bernice for any sign of Fred, but the woman blocked her view. "I told him I would bring it by."

Bernice frowned. "He didn't mention that to me."

Pearl's arms were starting to ache with the weight of the food. "Why don't I put this down in your kitchen?"

"I don't think he'll want it. He's not feeling good. He's in bed."

Pearl wanted to push her way in. It was close to two o'clock in the afternoon. "Can I do anything to help? Did you call a doctor?"

"He doesn't need a doctor. It's just a little bug. I'm sure he'll be up and around by morning."

"Then he might want the food later. Let me just bring it in."

Bernice gave an exasperated sigh. "No, that's ok. I'll take it." She opened the screen door just wide enough to take the food box from Pearl. "Thanks."

"I could—" The door shut before Pearl could finish her sentence. She had definitely seen Bernice somewhere before. If she could just see her without the shades, Pearl felt sure she would be able to place her. She hadn't been a detective for thirty years for nothing.

During the next few days, Pearl found excuses to hang out in the front yard, but Fred didn't appear. Nor did Bernice, either in person, or in her car. The place was shut tighter than a pinecone in a downpour. When the mailman mis-delivered some junk mail addressed to Fred to Pearl's mailbox, she took it as a message from the universe.

Holding the fliers, Pearl rang the Reynolds' doorbell, but no one answered. Instead of ringing again, she crept around to the side yard and peeked in a side window to the garage. Both Fred's SUV and the Thunderbird were inside. They had to be home and had to have heard her ringing. Were they just ignoring her, or was something truly wrong?

Channeling her inner detective, Pearl went around to the backyard. The gate was closed, but not locked. Should she go in? What was the worst that could happen? If nothing was wrong, and the couple was simply avoiding her, she'd act like a dotty neighbor wanting to get her dishes back.

She opened the gate, looking around before going in. The backyard was empty—no one in the lounge chairs, no one sitting at the umbrella table, no one tending the flowers. Leaving the gate open, Pearl approached the glass door leading into the house from the patio. Hoping the impact alarm on the door wasn't set, she rapped a few times. No answer, but also no audible alarm. What the heck, she thought, and leaned against the glass, cupping her hands around her eyes, trying to see in. Nothing.

Pearl tested the door handle. Unlocked. Taking a deep breath, she pushed it open, calling out Bernice's name. The kitchen was empty, but Pearl's box of food sat on the counter, untouched. Bad sign.

Pearl called out again, first for Bernice, then for Fred. Was that a sound coming from deeper inside the house? It was so faint, she couldn't be sure. Then she heard it again. This time she could tell it was coming from upstairs.

Moving quickly out of the kitchen, Pearl headed for the stairs. Then she stopped short. On the hard marble floor, right at the bottom of the stairs, Bernice lay sprawled out, her red dress limp now, her red Jimmy Choo sandals still attached to her feet. One heel was broken off. Across the foyer, Bernice's sunglasses sat upside down where they had landed, not far from a bloody hammer.

Pearl looked down into Bernice's unseeing eyes. Bernice was, or had been, Portia, the gold-digging caregiver Pearl had fired five years ago. No wonder she wouldn't let Pearl see her without those dark glasses. Another sound came from upstairs. Fred's voice, faintly calling for help. Pearl took the stairs quickly, holding on to the handrail.

She rushed toward the double doors of what she assumed was the couple's bedroom. Taking a steadying breath, she opened the door carefully, not knowing what she might find. To her surprise, the bed was empty. Then she heard cries coming from across the hall. Following the sounds, she found him in the bed of one of the smaller rooms. He was clearly weak, his arms and legs strapped to the sides of the frame, the gag that must have been on his mouth now down around his chin.

Without hesitation, Pearl worked to free him from the bed. "Are you ok?'

He nodded.

"How long have you been here?"

"Since we planted your roses."

"Four days? What happened?"

"After I got home, when I was glueing Bernice's heel back on, I started thinking about you suspecting you'd seen Bernice before, and what you told me about the caregiver you'd fired. I realized how little I knew about my own wife. It seemed too coincidental that just when you moved in, Bernice started wearing dark glasses anytime she went outside, whether it was sunny or not.

"So, I went through her closet. In one of her purses, I found an ID with her photo but with another name. Portia Sanders. I recognized the unusual first name and got a creepy feeling she might be the same person."

Pearl nodded. "You were right."

"Unfortunately. When she got home, I confronted her. I said I was getting the marriage annulled and she wouldn't get a cent of my money. I said I suspected her of killing Francie. She denied it, but I didn't believe her. I turned my back to call the police, and that's the last thing I remember." He touched the back of his head. "She conked me on the head with something hard."

"Your hammer."

"I left it out to nail the heel after the glue dried. Anyway, when I came to, I was strapped to the bed. That's when she admitted she'd engineered Francie's death. Something about the medication. I didn't understand exactly. She said she was going to kill me, too, as soon as she figured out how to make it look accidental." He looked around. "Where is she?"

"At the bottom of the stairs. Dead." Pearl saw relief in his eyes.

"What happened?"

"She was wearing the red Jimmy Choos. The heel broke off, and she landed on the marble floor. Broke her neck."

Fred closed his eyes, looking tired and old. "I warned her about wearing those shoes on the stairs."

BOOKED FOR MURDER

MEAGAN DALLNER

Three knocks on the door reverberate through my living room just before seven a.m. I hardly have the deadbolt turned when Alice bustles in, full of energy, nerves, and an imperfect white halo of hair.

I pat at my wet tangles that would otherwise frame my frown lines.

"Emma, did you hear?" Alice's eyes are huge with excitement, and she looks twenty years younger.

I brace. "Hear what?"

She goes to my kitchen table, newspaper in hand. I grin at this unexpected visit. Alice is my favorite book-club-lady-turned-friend.

She sits down and flops her paper onto the table. "Gwen called me this morning. She said that author we were supposed to meet at the library last night? The one who stood us up? Turns out he's dead."

"Dead?" My brain short circuits. "How does Gwen know?"

"Her nephew is a police officer, or maybe a paramedic." She waves her bony hand in the air. "That's not all, either."

I raise a brow, not sure anything could top her previous announcement.

"The man was murdered with a garden spade."

"Wow. We shouldn't have been so awful about him not showing. Not a good look for the Murder Sisters Book Club."

"Agreed. I thought maybe it would be in the paper, but I don't see it. The front page is all about that Doctor Dictionary fella in Denver. The article says he had gummy bears stuffed down his throat and they're wondering if that's what choked him." Alice shakes her head. "Oh, to be an investigator on such a case. You know, I've been to Twelve Moo—"

"Did Gwen have any other details? About *our* murder?" I try to get us back on topic, still feeling a little shocked our guest speaker is dead.

Alice pulls her eyes up from the article. "Sorry—"

Barely a knock and my front door opens again for the second time this morning. Savannah. She scurries in, heels clacking and blond hair cascading down her back. She stops when she sees Alice at the table.

"You already know." Savannah is the amateur writer in our book club and always hyper-critical of our book choices and opinions. She also lives three houses down.

"Yes. So tragic." Alice stands and gives her a comforting squeeze, ushering her to a chair. "David Weiber was in your critique group, right? You booked his talk for us."

"Yes. I don't know where else to turn. I can't believe he's gone." She sniffles. Her face, usually glowing with expertly applied makeup is bare and splotchy. She sees Weiber's book on the corner of my table. "I can't even look at that now." Her fists clench at her sides.

"Do the police know who killed him?" I ask.

Savannah gasps, appalled, and I wish I could stuff the words back into my mouth.

"No. It's a real-life mystery." Alice's eyes sparkle with delight. "It's usually the girlfriend/fiancé/lover, isn't it? Did he have one of those?" she asks, and I could hug her. Curiosity loves company.

"I'll google him." I probably shouldn't sound so excited,

but I crave answers. It's why I love mysteries. There's always a resolution.

Savannah scoffs. "He's hardly written or published anything in a decade. I doubt you'll find much on Google."

"Married?" Alice asks her.

"Doubt it," Savannah mumbles.

I read through a few search results before responding. "Divorced."

"Oh, a bitter divorce would give the ex motive—"

"She's living in California with a new guy, and social media says they're on a cruise."

"The plot thickens." Alice drums her nails on the table.

"You know, I came over here for some support, not to play Nancy Drew," Savannah pouts.

Guilt heats my cheeks. "Sorry, Vannah, we run a mystery lovers book club. This just feels natural."

"And good sleuths don't sit around on their computers all day. They gotta gumshoe," Alice chimes in.

"Are you suggesting we … what?" I ask.

"We've gotta take it to the streets. Patricia Cornwell always says crime isn't solved by technology, it's solved by people." Alice stands. "Let's go to his house and see what we can find out. Maybe his neighbors know if he was seeing someone."

Savannah's chair screeches as she stands too. "No. This isn't some book. This is real life. Leave it alone."

Alice puts a hand on her shoulder. "Oh honey, we're just going to poke around a bit. I don't have much living left, and I've always wanted to be an investigator. This is my chance."

Savannah looks like a guppy out of water.

"Why don't you get some rest," Alice suggests.

Savannah pouts but follows us out, shoulders slumped. "This is an awful idea," she whispers to me as she leaves.

I shiver against a gust of wind and get in Alice's car.

"Can you find his address?" she asks. "I don't want to drive around, aimlessly looking for crime scene tape."

"Gimme one sec." I cross-reference the blocks mentioned in the news article with the property tax records. "9951 Sylvester Avenue."

The driving instructions populate the screen.

"Okay, so, I've never been to an actual crime scene before. What do we do first?" I ask.

"We talk to the neighbors. People are naturally observant creatures."

We drive past big trees and a little shopping center, and I try to quell the flutter of excitement tingling in my stomach. This is a crime scene. Someone died here. It should be treated respectfully. But also, I'm doing brain back flips. I take a deep breath as we pull over. Alice does the same.

"Ready?" she asks.

I nod because I don't fully trust my words right now.

Alice parks the car half a block down like a true professional would, and I wish I'd thought of it.

We exit the car, and my first impression is that the neighborhood is nice, clean and well-kept. The houses are modest and mostly ranch-style, with similar exterior designs and color coordinated paint throughout the whole street. All the lawns are gorgeous, with spring green grass and potted plants and landscaping with rock designs and—well, *that* one isn't gorgeous. I eye Alice, and see we're on the same page.

We shuffle closer until we are standing right in front of 9951. David Weiber may have been killed by a garden spade, but it wouldn't appear he was much of a gardener. The lawn is dead with weeds battling the concrete all the way up the drive. The house doesn't look much better. The paint is peeling, a porch swing hangs by only one chain, and the shutters look like a strong wind will blow them off entirely. Crime scene tape circles the front porch.

Alice raises a brow. "This is it, but it looks abandoned."

"You think he actually lived here?"

"He lived here," a gravelly voice says behind us.

We jump and turn to face the man. Alice rolls her shoulders forward and embraces a little old lady stance. She catches my eye and winks.

We both know no one in mystery novels wants to upset sweet old ladies.

The guy facing us wears a potentially permanent frown, and sunspots decorate his forehead and cheeks. Dirt covers his sizable forearms and he looks mad.

"Sorry?" I ask and I'm proud of how innocent my voice sounds.

He steps closer. "Weiber lived in that dump for years. The guy was a loner and a menace. See what he's done to his place? Drives down the property values for the whole block."

"Oh dear. That would be terribly frustrating," Alice says.

"I'll tell you what's frustrating. I'm getting ready to sell, and my realtor suggested we wait till his place is covered in snow. Ridiculous! Who buys a house in Colorado in the dead of winter?"

I take a step back and try to keep on track. "Did he ever have any visitors?"

"The only person I've seen around here is the woman who was screaming at him on Tuesday. I had to close my windows. The only thing worse than a slob next door is a loud slob. So. Much. Shouting." Spittle flies at the space between us to punctuate his last words.

I try not to let my disgust show. "A woman he fought with? Have you seen her before?"

"Did you tell the police?" Alice asks.

"Hmph. I'm not telling the police nothin'."

"Oh?" Any other noise would come out scared.

"They think I killed him with my own spade. They can talk to my lawyer." He gives a definitive nod and spins on his heel, only to squat three feet away and yank at some small offending weed from his grass.

I fidget with a thread in my pocket before calling after him. "Did you see what the woman looked like?"

He turns and stares into my soul as he rips the weed into many, many pieces.

Alice turns my way and says under her breath, "So ... suspect number one is that guy."

I nod. "Definitely. Should we go?"

"Let's knock on the neighbor's door on the other side. Maybe they got a better look at her if she made such a ruckus."

I hesitate, feeling like we might get in trouble, but Alice walks ahead and I have no choice but to follow or be left behind. We walk around the crime scene tape stretched across the driveway to the neighbor on the other side. Their lawn is trimmed but not edged and there are roller skates thrown into the evergreen bush near the walkway. A hole nearly a foot across is dug near the steps.

Alice stands with her chin up as she raps on the door.

Barks erupt from inside the house. Deep guttural barks from dogs that might weigh as much as Alice. I step back.

We wait, but the barking only intensifies. No one comes to the door.

Alice sidesteps some chalk art of stick figures with triangle swords and gushing wounds. "Disappointing, but I think the grumpy lawn neighbor gave us more than he intended." She muses, "Maybe Weiber offended someone. Or maybe he wrote about a real person."

An idea strikes me. "Let's head to the coffee shop on the corner."

"Emma, you don't drink coffee." Alice eyes me suspiciously.

I love her for remembering that. "I'm thinking that if the neighbor kids got to be too loud, maybe he worked at the nearest coffee place. We can talk to the barista."

"And caffeinate." She hurries toward the car.

We are about three feet away when I see the sagging rubber of the flat tire on the front left of Alice's car. I spin and check behind us. No pedestrians. No joggers. The street is empty. Alice is studying the mean neighbor's house up the street. I stare too, hoping to see a shift in his curtains or some other revelation that this might be his doing.

Nothing.

"Maybe we've done enough sleuthing," I say, though disappointment weighs each word.

"Emma, we are either very unlucky or on the right track." Alice is almost giddy with this latest inconvenience. "Do you happen to know how to change a tire?"

"I do. Pop the trunk, and I'll grab the spare."

Thirty minutes later I'm sweaty, and Alice is impressed.

Shivers creep down my spine as we leave the street, but Alice seems totally unperturbed.

When we walk into the nearest coffee shop, a friendly atmosphere and the scent of fresh coffee and warm cinnamon greets us.

I check the faces of both patrons already seated. No threat here. "I'll grab a seat and start reading reviews from my phone."

As she walks to the line, I pull up *Glass Lake Goodbye* by David Weiber on Goodreads and skim through several reviews.

Alice takes a seat across from me. "Find anything?"

"That was fast." I nod toward her cup.

"It's just black coffee. I'm not fussy, just perpetually tired." She points at my phone and raises her eyebrows.

"It's mostly positive reviews." I keep scrolling. "Wow, except this one. It's vile. Says the author is a poor excuse for a human, and they don't deserve their recent success. And here's another that really doesn't like the book and I quote, worst book I have ever read and now I need to wash the filth from my eyeballs, end quote."

"Could be gnomes, right?" Alice asks.

"Gnomes? Oh, trolls. Yeah, it could. Let's look at the profiles." I click on the profile of each reviewer and see lots of reviews, some sound vaguely familiar. "I don't think it's trolls."

"Maybe it's the ex-wife."

"Maybe. Look, this first one read a ton of the same books as our—"

"Have you checked the Amazon reviews too?" Alice asks.

"Good idea." I open the Amazon app and search. "There are a bunch more one-star reviews here. The latest is from GardeninCO22. It doesn't say much. Just that the book sucks."

Alice takes a sip of coffee. "That's not very helpful."

"No. But maybe it's too much of a stretch to think it was the neighbor?"

"Could be."

"There's no line now, should we talk to the barista?"

"Can't hurt. Plus, I can grab a freebie." Alice winks at me.

We approach the counter, and the boy with rectangular glasses smiles. "Refill?"

"Sure," Alice says.

I wait until she gets her coffee then pull up the author photo of David Weiber on my phone. "Quick question: did this guy ever come in here?"

He squints at the picture and nods. "Sometimes. Americano drinker."

"Did he ever have someone with him? Maybe a woman?" I ask.

The coffee guy cocks his head, clearly suspicious. "Who are you?"

"We aren't anybody," I say. I don't want trouble.

Alice tips her cup toward the book. "He's dead."

I cringe at her crass delivery.

The color drains from the barista's face. "Sorry, what?"

"He's dead." Alice says a bit louder.

He shakes his head. "No, I heard you. I just don't believe it. Are you reporters?"

"No, just trying to find some answers about his final days," I say.

He thinks a moment. "He's been grumpier than usual lately. I don't know. He was with a couple of guys and a lady yesterday. They were all very upset."

"Happen to hear why?" I ask.

"Nah, sorry. The group knew each other pretty well, though. I've seen the four of them in here before. They don't usually argue."

Another customer gets in line behind us.

Alice looks ready to attack with more questions, but I pull her away with what I hope is a sympathetic half-smile. "We're sorry to have been the bearers of such tragic news."

I can't help but feel like we should know more now. In books, they'd have a lead by now. "Well, this is frustrating."

Alice raises her voice so I can hear her over the wind as we walk through the parking lot. "Agreed. But we have more than we started with. The neighbor, the shouty lady who may or may not be a crazy reviewer—though that feels very Stephen King—and something to do with a group being mad at him even though the neighbor said he was a loner and menace." She reaches for my arm as we step off the curb. "We have too many bits and not enough bits all at the same time. Like real investigators."

Alice stops just short of the car. "What the—?"

Bright red marker slashes the words "YOU'RE NEXT" on the entire side of the white SUV.

"Oh, Alice!" My chest tightens while my pulse pounds in my ears.

I scour the lot. We weren't in there that long. I see nothing and maybe that's scarier, because someone is following us. It's clear the tire was no accident.

"I'm calling the police," I say.

"Not yet. Emma, don't you see? We're so close! Imagine the headlines when we catch the person behind all this. We'll be heroes, and maybe the police will consult with us on more cases. I could be like Jessica Fletcher without the whole writer thing."

"I don't know. I really don't want to be next."

"Please, Emma. It's my car and I don't mind." Alice holds her coffee so tight the lid pops off. I bend down to retrieve it.

Someone is watching us. I can feel it.

"Let's go back to my house. We can talk there." We need to look like we're giving up the investigation, but I don't say that.

I keep my eyes on the mirrors the entire way back. We're alone when Alice pulls onto my street.

She parks, and we don't talk until we're inside with the curtains drawn and front door locked. I feel much safer in my own home.

I grab *Glass Lake Goodbye* from the kitchen table and flip to the back to read the summary. I only find reviews. Not helpful. I open the front cover and read the blurb. It sounds familiar.

"Hey Alice, did we ever read a book for book club where a murder was covered up by the creation of a lake?" I toss her the book from my spot on the sofa.

She's perched in the armchair. "I couldn't say … wait … actually, I think we read something like that years ago."

"Ding ding. Ten points for Alice." Heels clack from my dining room and Savannah is suddenly standing in my kitchen.

"Vannah? How did you get in my house?"

She gives a wan smile. "Back door. I was hungry and thought I'd check in." She gestures to the sandwich on the counter, but my gaze snags on the knife in her hand. "It was too much to hope for that you two would give up."

I look to Alice, and the color has leached from her face.

"You were just about to say where you've heard of that book, weren't you?" Savannah continues.

Alice nods, eyes darting back and forth to the knife. "It's exactly like your manuscript. The one we read for book club so we could offer our thoughts. You canceled the meeting, though. We never told you how much we loved it."

Her knuckles turned white as her grip tightened around the knife. "My manuscript. Yes. The one David Weiber offered to critique and then handed back with so many notes about how horrible it was. I shoved it in a drawer for forever. I was so embarrassed. He was a professional, and I trusted him."

My heart is racing. I hazard a guess about what happened next. "But he didn't hate it, did he?"

"No, he gave it to his agent and passed it off as his own. He changed just enough so if I took him to court, he could say he might have had the same idea. But ideas can't be copyrighted."

All the pieces are starting to come together. I can't take a deep breath.

"Did you ... did you slash Alice's tire?" She's done it to ex-boyfriends, but to us? We're friends.

"I wanted you to quit snooping. It can be dangerous out there." Savannah cocks her head like a creepy doll.

My palms start to sweat.

"It was you at David's house arguing?" Alice asks.

"I was so proud of him, my writing buddy with his first deal in fifteen years. On a secret book project, no less." A dangerous glint shimmers in her eye. "That deal should have been mine."

I try not to look at the knife she's holding as more answers suddenly make sense. "Your critique group confronted him at the coffee shop? They knew."

Savannah sighs. "They're good people."

She steps right in front of me. The knife is so close I see myself swallow.

"Killing David was so much easier than I thought it would be." She moves fast.

The knife slashes my way, but I shove my foot into her knee and knock her backwards. She screams and lashes out with the knife, catching me in the thigh as she goes down.

The sting hardly registers. I roll to my right and grapple around the floor for anything I can use to protect myself.

Something slides across the carpet and into my fingers. A book. I grab it with both hands and swing hard at the shape trying to stand up in front of me. It connects. Savannah sways, tipping onto her side.

I gasp for air while I stand. The cut on my leg protests but I've got too much adrenaline to care.

"You okay?" Alice asks.

Savannah groans.

I wince. "Yeah. I think you can call the police now and maybe an ambulance."

Alice fumbles with her phone then points to *Glass Lake Goodbye*. "I'll tell them she's been booked for murder … and assault."

PRETTY DEADLY

MELISSA ROBBINS

The tires kicked up dirt and gravel that pelted Ivy Lark's legs as the car fled through the trees. She picked up her duffle and slung the strap onto her shoulder.

Except for the phone in her hand, Ivy's sister Hurri looked like she walked out of a vintage Roaring Twenties magazine with her dark curly bob, black pant suit and white drapey blouse. She adjusted her tortoiseshell sunglasses. "I forget how much sunnier it is here than in Seattle."

Despite leaving Colorado after college, Ivy still embraced the plaid flannel and denim overalls. She had braided her red curly hair into one long plait. Now back, Ivy might use her hiking boots for actual hiking.

The sisters stared at Grammy's timber and stone cottage nestled in the woods. Hurri lowered her sunglasses along her pale nose. "I'm not used to seeing the rosebushes bare. It feels wrong."

When the sisters visited their grammy every summer, the roses burst with colors. This April, patches of snow lingered in the shade.

"We should have come back sooner, Hurri."

"Grammy hid her illness from all of us, including Moonie."

Selini, aka Moonie, their baby sister, had moved in with Grammy five years ago, more for her than for Grammy.

Dread had filled Ivy's heart when Selini had called and said, "Grammy's gone."

Voices rose from behind the cottage. A buxom woman in a hot pink jacket and matching pencil skirt passed through the gap in the wattle fence. Her blonde hair was coifed so stiffly her ginormous pink floppy hat didn't dent it. A man in a white linen suit and straw boater hat walked beside her.

"Who took a wrong turn at the Kentucky Derby?" Hurri whispered to Ivy.

The lady waved her manicured hands at Grammy's house, not noticing the girls. She said to the man, with a southern accent, "And just think of the potential when you buy all this land. You can raze this dilapidated house and build a grand *cabin*." With a tittering laugh, she made air quotes with her fingers. Her nails were painted pink, matching her outfit.

Ivy dropped her duffle with a loud thud. "Excuse me."

The lady jumped. Her startled frown turned into a pink slash. Her eyes darted between the sisters. "Are you here to look at the property, too? I don't think you can afford it."

Hurri straightened out her impressive height. "It's our house. We are Harriet and Ivy Lark, Meadow Lark's granddaughters and heirs. Who are you trespassing on our grandmother's land?"

"Realtor Paisley Vandervender. You probably don't remember me." Paisley whipped a business card from her suit pocket and pointed it at the sisters. "I remember you two now. You spent your summers here with Meadow." She handed the card to Hurri. "Weren't you called Tornado or something?"

A smirk formed on Hurri's face. "Actually, it's Hurricane Harriet, but that still doesn't explain why you're here. We have no intention of selling."

"Here's the deal, peaches. Meadow didn't have a will. District Court Judge Rhett Ballard appointed me the representative to oversee her estate during probate. Once the property sells, you'll get the proceeds. I'm doing you a favor. You'll be rid of this rundown house," Paisley pressed her hand to her face as if to share a secret, "and can use the money to put your crazy sister in a home."

"Our grandmother isn't even in the ground yet." Hurri's fist crushed the business card. Storm clouds formed above them, blocking out the sun.

Knowing exactly how Hurri felt, but not wanting to draw the attention of this vile woman, Ivy covered Hurri's fist. "Selling the property without our consent doesn't sound legal. We'll talk to Judge Ballard tomorrow."

Paisley and the gentleman shared a laugh as they headed to the back of the cottage. "I wouldn't bother," she said over her shoulder. "Rhett will side with me."

A vine snaked its way toward Paisley and wound around her pink pump. She tugged her foot away. "August, you must have the plants ripped out before you move in."

Hurri and Ivy followed Paisley. The din of voices grew louder. The sisters stopped at the fence. The backyard's lawn was still brown from the winter, but people, ten or so, milled around the untamed flower beds.

Selini stepped out from the kitchen's doorway. Her almost white hair floated around her head. She set a cookie tray on a foldable table. Her blue skirt fluttered around her legs as she dashed to her sisters.

Hurri swept Selini's hair away from her eyes. "Good to see you, Moonie."

"How are you?" Ivy hugged Selini.

"It's a new moon. Time of rebirth." Selini offered up a round, iced blue cookie. "Grammy is a star now."

"New moon, eh." Sharing a knowing look with Ivy, Hurri nibbled the cookie.

Selini's attitudes mimicked the moon's phases. Childlike because of the new moon. Once the moon was full, Selini would act more like an adult and downright elderly when the moon waned. She wasn't mental like Paisley thought. Just a little different. They would never put their sister in an institution.

"I'm so glad you are both here."

With her cookie, Hurri gestured to the party. "You didn't mention a wake or we would've come sooner."

"It wasn't meant to be. The librarian brought a casserole. Then, the doctor's wife came with a veggie platter. Even Deputy Flint paid his respects." Selini let out a dejected sigh.

Ivy looped her arm through Selini's and lowered her voice. "What's this about Grammy's will missing?"

"Grammy said Rosemary has it." Selini stuck out her bottom lip. "She didn't know a Rosemary."

"We'll figure it out, but first, I need a drink." Hurri made a beeline for a drink cart someone set up under the kitchen window.

Hurri took a mint leaf from a bowlful on the cart and garnished her mojito. As she sipped it with a glass straw, enjoying the smooth rum, Doctor Owen Abernathy approached the cart and started making a mojito, too. The only doctor in town, he had to be Grammy's. Despite the cool, dry weather, Doc Abernathy looked like he was melting. Paisley joined them. *Can't I even drink in peace?* Hurri thought.

With a fake smile, she asked, "Can I make you a mojito?" *And spike it with something.* Ivy would know the perfect garnish.

Paisley wrinkled her nose and added mint and sugar to her highball glass. "I only drink mint juleps and no one in Colorado knows how to make a good one."

After Paisley finished making her drink with a generous splash of bourbon, she drank a gulp. "By the way, Doc, you haven't written your check to me this month." Her voice seemed genteel, but Hurri detected a threat in those words.

The doctor's face flushed and his drink trembled in his hand. "Yes, of course. You'll get it by the end of the week." He scampered off without taking a sip.

With a smile hidden behind her glass, Hurri conjured a breeze that blew off Paisley's giant hat. Paisley chased after it. Hurri's eyes meet the steely blue ones of a man in a brown uniform. Deputy Flint? More like Deputy Hotness.

To avoid the unwanted guests, Ivy tugged a weed, one of many, from the flower bed next to Grammy's greenhouse. She dreaded the mess awaiting her inside. A tomorrow problem. She stopped when she heard Paisley's trill. Not too many people with that accent around here.

Ivy hoped Paisley wasn't showing someone the greenhouse. She peeked around the building's corner.

Paisley and a man, not the earlier buyer, strolled along the brick path to the greenhouse. Yellow pollen dusted his black trousers. His hair was grayer and he was more portly around the middle, but Ivy remembered Judge Ballard now. Been part of the town for decades. They both held drinks, looking like the mojitos Hurri preferred.

Paisley sipped hers, but wrinkled her nose. "Ugh, Rhett, this mint julep is bitter. Of course, the Lark women only buy the cheap whiskey."

Ivy shook her head. The bourbon didn't come from their stash. Someone else must have brought it.

"Mine tastes all right," replied the judge, but he didn't drink his.

After taking another pull from her drink, Paisley said, "Speaking of the Larks, the sisters are going to cause trouble. I've been trying to get Meadow to sell for years. I shouldn't have to remind you what will happen if the sale of the property doesn't go through. You'll regret it."

"Hand them a check and they'll be on their way. They won't want the old house. The land alone is worth millions. Then, they'll be able to afford the expensive alcohol." Judge Ballard clinked his glass with Paisley's.

Ivy seethed. The judge and Paisley were wrong. Ivy and her sisters did want the cottage. Her family has owned the cottage and land since the 1800s. That meant more to the sisters than the money.

A tree root emerged from the ground, tripping Paisley. She stomped her heel against it. "I can't wait until the buyer digs up this land and puts in a tennis court."

***

As HURRI WAS ENJOYING her conversation with the dashing Deputy Flint, Mayor Grayson tapped his glass with a spoon. "Gather around, all. I wish to toast Meadow Lark." Hurri didn't remember the mayor, but he said nice words about Grammy.

While still holding her glass, Paisley rubbed her temple and seemed to ignore the mayor's words. When the mayor finished his toast, everyone sipped their drinks. Paisley removed her hat and fanned herself.

"Are you all right, dear?" a woman next to Paisley asked.

"I'm fine, Muffy. This cheap alcohol is giving me a headache."

Muffy. She had more wrinkles and whiter hair, but Hurri remembered her now as a foul woman who always tried to get the sisters in trouble with the police or Grammy.

Paisley dropped her hat and pressed her hand to her chest. "I ... I don't feel well." She collapsed on the lawn. Her glass rolled away from her hand.

Gasps flittered among the guests and concerned faces watched as Deputy Flint rushed to her side.

Dr. Abernathy knelt by Paisley's body and took her pulse on her wrist. "No pulse." The doctor administered CPR while Deputy Flint called 911.

After an eternity to Hurri, Doctor Abernathy shook his head. "She's dead. Her bad heart finally wore out."

Unsure what to do, Hurri picked up Paisley's glass. She stared at the mint leaves in the glass. Oh no.

"What is it, Hurri?" Deputy Flint's eyes, the color of a storm, darted between her and the glass she held in her hand.

She replied, her voice barely a whisper, "These leaves aren't mint. They're foxglove." Hurri knew Paisley made her own mint julep, so how did foxglove leaves get in her glass?

With her sister's sixth sense, Ivy was at Hurri's side in a second. "They are similar in shape and texture." Ivy blocked Deputy Flint's hand. "Don't touch them, the leaves are very poisonous."

"I wasn't going to." Deputy Flint removed a handkerchief from his back pocket and took the glass from Hurri. "Poisonous enough to kill?"

"Some of the prettiest flowers can be the deadliest," said Hurri.

Doctor Abernathy joined their little circle. "Foxglove is a digitalis drug. Ingesting the leaves isn't immediate poisoning. If known, steps could have been taken to regulate her heart rate."

"Takes twenty to thirty minutes," Ivy added.

"A bad heart could quicken it though," the doctor concluded.

"Accidental death, hopefully," Deputy Flint muttered under his breath. "I left Denver to get away from murders."

"Murder!" Muffy pointed a finger at the Lark sisters. "They poisoned Paisley. Meadow Lark was a witch and her granddaughters are witches too."

"And naturally the women accused of witchcraft are the prime suspects," Hurri grumbled.

Deputy Flint pressed his hand to his hip. "Mrs. Topper, I'm not going to arrest anyone because somebody accuses them of witchcraft. This isn't Salem."

Hurri liked this man more and more.

"Paisley told me they didn't want to sell the property. That's motive, means, and opportunity." She ticked each off with her fingers and added with glee in her voice, "Plenty of foxglove in the Lark greenhouse."

"Dane, take possession of this glass as evidence." Deputy Flint handed Paisley's glass to another man in a brown uniform who had arrived.

"Coroner is en route," said Dane.

"Collect the remaining mint leaves at the drink cart. They look fresh. Grab all the drinking glasses you can find. Let's hope this is a one-off." He gestured toward the greenhouse. "Larks, show me your greenhouse."

"Hurri and I got off the plane this afternoon. We haven't been inside yet. I don't know if we even have foxgloves growing now," Ivy opened the greenhouse door, "and as you can see, the greenhouse isn't locked. Anyone could have gotten inside."

Ivy stopped short. Selini stood between two tables filled with rows and rows of foxglove plants. Drat. "These are foxgloves and the potted plants behind Hurri are mint."

Deputy Flint looked over at Selini scrolling on her phone and said quietly, "Do you think Selini accidentally chose the wrong plant for the drink garnishes?"

Hurri said, "Don't you dare pin Paisley's murder on Moonie." Thunder clapped outside.

Deputy Flint held up his palms in surrender. "I'm thinking out loud."

Oblivious of being accused of murder, Selini skipped to them and showed the deputy her phone. "Deputy Flint, Olivia Twist knew Senator Pasco had pot-laced gummy bears. Maybe he killed Doctor Dictionary!"

"Add that clue to your journal." Deputy Flint smiled at the other sisters' confusion. "Selini and I are keeping track of a Denver celebrity's murder. The news about it is everywhere."

Hurri said, "Moonie, find Grammy's ledger. We need to check something."

With a nod, Selini weaved around the plant tables to another door that led directly to the house.

Ivy liked how sweet the deputy was to her sister, but that didn't change what he thought of them. "We would fight Paisley in the courts, not kill her."

"If we wanted to kill Paisley, there are better plants than foxglove. Oleander swizzle stick. Lily of the Valley tea." Hurri plucked a mint leaf from a plant and popped it into her mouth.

"Let's not give the good deputy a reason to arrest us," Ivy said with a roll of her eyes.

Deputy Flint stood too close to the jasmine flowers. The yellow pollen dusted his trousers. He tried to brush it away, but it smeared on the fabric. "Why grow so many foxgloves?"

"Selling flowers was Grammy's source of income." And the occasional spell, Ivy thought, but the deputy didn't need to know everything. Let him think Muffy was bonkers. "Foxgloves are popular for their blooms. Most of these will end up in flowerbeds all over town."

Selini returned with a bound leather journal and handed it to Ivy. She flipped to the last page of entries. "The most recent foxglove order was for Doctor Abernathy." Ivy scanned a few pages back. "Wow. He ordered a lot."

With a smirk, Hurri said, "The good doctor was at the cart when Paisley made her drink."

A FEW MINUTES LATER, Deputy Flint escorted Doctor Abernathy into the greenhouse.

Ivy showed the ledger to the doctor. "We noticed you purchased large amounts of foxgloves from Grammy."

"I don't like what you are implying." The doctor's voice rose an octave as he backed into a potting table.

"While watching the full moon last month, I saw Doc give the town librarian a foxglove tincture. She suffers from heart trouble," Selini said nonchalantly.

Staring at Selini, Doctor Abernathy opened and closed his mouth like a fish. "Nosy witch."

Deputy Flint gripped the doctor's jacket sleeve. "How many of your patients are you poisoning?"

"None!" Abernathy struggled against Deputy Flint's grasp. "What's my motive to kill Paisley?"

Hurri said, "Paisley confronted you about owing her money. I thought she was simply after a rent payment, but now I think she was blackmailing you."

"No use denying it, Doc," said Deputy Flint. "I can trace the payments."

Doctor Abernathy removed his hat and wiped his balding head with a white handkerchief. "I supply foxglove to several of my patients, purely medicinal. Digitalis drugs are expensive and many of my patients can't afford them. Greedy insurance cads. Paisley found out and blackmailed me. I paid her to protect my reputation and medical license. I didn't kill her." His squeaky voice almost shattered the greenhouse glass. "I'm not the only one she was blackmailing."

"Don't leave the party. I need to question the other guests." Deputy Flint ushered the doctor out of the greenhouse.

THE SISTERS STAYED in the greenhouse. The plants comforted Ivy as she brushed her fingers along the leaves and blooms.

Selini said, "Doc didn't kill Paisley. He has kind eyes."

Hurri stopped pacing and tapped her forehead. "Why didn't I think of this before? We could cast a tracking spell to find the killer."

Ivy stopped plucking dead leaves from a sage plant. "That's ridiculous. 'Deputy Flint, we know who the culprit is, because our spell told us.' I'm not a lawyer, but that won't hold up in court."

"It will point Deputy Flint in the right direction." Hurri snapped a sprig from a sage plant and ignited it with a lighter from her trousers pocket. She swirled the smoky sprig around the inside of an empty terracotta pot to cleanse it. "We have to be quick before people start leaving, including the murderer."

With a disapproving shake of her head, Ivy plucked red rose petals and dropped them into the pot. For their time restraint, it was the best flower on hand to use.

Selini uncorked a bottle hanging around her neck and added a few water droplets to the pot. "Full moon water."

"Find Paisley's killer," the sisters chanted three times. "Mote it be," Hurri added last. With a wave of her hand, she created a light breeze that picked up the damp petals. They hovered above the pot. The sisters followed the petals floating out of the greenhouse.

The spell aimed for the doctor, confirming what they already thought, but the petals moved to Judge Ballard, who batted them away.

"Judge Ballard has a red rash covering his fingertips," Hurri said. "Could be from foxglove exposure." She scrunched up her nose. "Not washing his grubby hands."

Ivy's eyes widened. Why didn't she notice that before? "He also has jasmine pollen on his trousers leg, just like you do, Deputy. The only way to get that pollen is from visiting our greenhouse."

The judge demanded, "Why would I kill Paisley? We were friends."

Ivy said, "I overheard you talking to Paisley about Grammy's estate. She threatened you if the sale didn't go through."

"That would explain why you appointed Paisley as the representative of Grammy's estate," Hurri added. "She blackmailed you. You saw an opportunity to kill her and blame us."

"That's preposterous. You can't convict me on pollen and a rash."

"It gives me probable cause to take you in for questioning." Deputy Flint escorted Judge Ballard to his patrol car.

THE NEXT DAY, the Lark sisters were repotting plants in the greenhouse. Hurri stared at her hands covered in dirt. She still preferred the cleanliness of storm magic.

Deputy Flint tapped his knuckles against the opened glass door. "Hello, Larks. I wanted to let you know the sheriff's department found evidence of Paisley's blackmail on Judge Ballard, Doctor Abernathy, and several other prominent people in town. The judge had trace evidence of foxglove on his fingertips and the pollen on his trousers matched mine, jasmine, which put him in the greenhouse. The Assistant DA is building a case against the judge for Paisley's murder." He raked a hand through his blond hair and shook his head in disbelief. "I'm impressed you figured it out just by the plants."

"Flower knowledge," Ivy said with a wink to her sisters.

Deputy Flint slid his fingers along the brim of his hat. "Will you three be staying in town?" Although he phrased his question to all of them, those stormy blue eyes focused on Hurri.

"We don't have the best history with this town," said Hurri, wiping her hands on a towel that wasn't much cleaner than her hands.

Moonie yanked an envelope sealed in a plastic pouch from the bottom of a rosemary pot. "I found Grammy's will! Rosemary the plant had it. Silly Grammy." Moonie giggled.

Hurri examined the will through the plastic. "Nice one, Moonie." She regarded Deputy Hotness with a seductive smile. "Maybe we will stay for a little while."

THE PSYCHIC SHRINK

PEG BRANTLEY

Detective Chase Waters and police psychologist Dr. Morgan Blake exited their vehicle at the base of the Cobalt Mountain Resort's main ski lift. Brilliant Colorado skies and a warm April sun made Chase wish he was heading for the slopes this morning rather than a crime scene. He also wished he hadn't felt the need to get Morgan's assistance. Their relationship had always been contentious. He questioned the usefulness of a psychic in a police investigation. Or anything else for that matter. He took off his jacket and tossed it inside the car.

Morgan followed suit, then lowered her baseball cap to shield her eyes from the sun. "It's a perfect day for skiing," she said.

Chase wondered if she was a mind reader as well.

The year had begun well. January had left the detective with time to catch up on his reading, organize his report files, and become better adept at using new software the Aspen Falls Police Department had purchased. He was even home for dinner every night.

It didn't last long.

In early February, the body of Julia Anderson, a young woman and Pitkin County employee, was discovered in the local cemetery. Since there were no obvious external elements which might suggest a cause of death, drugs were immediately suspected. Anderson had worked primarily with Medicaid recipients and wouldn't have been the first person to access prescription drugs she shouldn't have. However, a message was discovered on her back during the autopsy. THIS IS FOR YOU was printed using food coloring. No cause of death had been determined.

A second victim showed up six weeks later. Thomas Brown, an Emergency Department doc at Aspen Falls Memorial Hospital, was an African American with ebony skin. It had taken a close look during the autopsy, but the same words, with the same type of dye, were found on his back.

Besides a slight overlap in their professions, Chase couldn't find any other connection between the two victims. His detectives, all two of them, were still going through records and matching up any connections between Brown's patients, Medicaid, and Julia Anderson. Each time they found one, they had to do a separate interview. It was painstakingly boring, but it needed to be done.

Skiers on the Cobalt Mountain lift had spotted another body this morning. If his fears were confirmed, this would be the third homicide in as many months. He was desperate. That's why he'd finally called Morgan Blake. God help him, he needed her to come up with something for him to run with. If she didn't, his cynicism would win and he could say he'd tried everything; if she did, well, maybe Lucky-Guess justice would come out on top. From minute to minute he altered his preference between the two outcomes.

A snowcat waited to transport them to the scene, then up to Eyrie, the lodge atop the mountain. There, they would interview the people who had made the report, and anyone else present at the time. As they approached the grooming machine, Chase recognized the driver.

"Hey, Sam. How've you been?" Chase called out.

"Hangin' in there, Detective," Sam replied, exiting the car and moving to open the other door.

"Sam, this is Dr. Morgan Blake. She's the department psychologist."

"Ma'am." The older man nodded toward Morgan as she got inside the cabin. He turned back to Chase. "This here murder business has got me lookin' over my shoulder all day long. Might be I need to talk to someone myself."

"Let's not get ahead of ourselves," Chase said, hoping that he'd soon be able to allay everyone's idea that yet another murder had taken place in their mountain community. "I haven't seen the victim yet."

"It's gonna be another murder, I can feel it. And from what I seen, y'all ain't got too far in findin' the killer."

Chase liked Sam, so he bit back a retort. Everyone was on edge, and he was getting used to skepticism from the locals.

As Sam released the door to Chase, their eyes met. "Sorry, Detective. You do a fine job. I know you'll get the dude."

The electric snowcat glided silently on the snow-covered mountain, following the cleared route directly below the lift. Midway between the second and third towers, Sam slowed the machine to a crawl, stopping before the yellow tape marked off by the uniformed officers who'd arrived earlier.

Chase and Morgan strapped on snowshoes before climbing out of the cat. "Wait for us here, Sam. We'll need you to take us up to the Eyrie."

The crumpled body was face down in the snow directly below the lift. Chase noticed a jacket, but no helmet or goggles. From here, he couldn't be certain, but the shoes didn't resemble ski boots.

"Brandon, isn't it?" Chase asked the closest uniform. "Did you take the contact information from the people who discovered the body?"

"Yes, sir. A family here for a wedding this afternoon. They're waiting for you at the lodge."

Chase looked at Morgan. "Getting anything?"

"It doesn't work that way, Detective. At least not for me," the psychologist said softly. Sensing his disappointment, she added, "Something could come later, but right now I see what you see. Nothing more."

Chase gave a grunt, his attention back on the uniform. "Are Dr. Taylor and CSU on their way?"

The officer looked at his watch. "Coroner will be here in fifteen. The Crime Scene Unit is about thirty minutes out."

"Busy around here all of a sudden, isn't it?" Chase didn't wait for an answer. "I'm heading up to start some interviews. Have Dr. Taylor call me when she gets here."

Upon arriving at the Eyrie Lodge, they noticed people gathered by the tall windows, attempting to observe the situation on the mountain. Others were sitting in the main area, talking quietly. A man with a camera was looking displaced in a corner of the room.

Within seconds of their entrance, all eyes were on the duo.

"I'm Senior Detective Chase Waters from the Aspen Falls Police Department. This is Dr. Morgan Blake. We will interview all of you, beginning with those who saw the victim and made the report. Please refrain from discussing what you've seen or heard about this event with others."

Morgan threw him a sharp look. Chase caught it and added, "At least don't discuss things any more than you already have."

CHASE AND MORGAN talked to the family, a husband and wife from Denver, with their ten-year-old and eight-year-old. They didn't learn anything other than what they already knew.

Par for the course, Chase thought sourly. He was so ready for a break in this case. *These* cases. He regretted bringing Morgan along. She was useless and he felt like a fool. He just needed to tough out the afternoon.

In the large room with other guests and staff, Chase

noticed the photographer standing alone in the corner. He believed professionals in that field were nearly as observant as law enforcement. And who knows? Maybe he'd taken a photo that could be critical to the investigation. He pointed to him. "You, sir, I'd like to talk to you next."

The slight, balding man scurried past the others, clutching his camera to his chest as if he didn't trust the straps to hold. As he rushed, his pale face grew pink, obviously not used to being the one in the spotlight.

In the interview room, the photographer handed out cards from his wallet to each of them. "I'm Ralph Ringwald," he said unnecessarily. "Professional photographer, at your service," he added, equally unnecessarily. "This is my second murder in less than a week. Can you believe it? I was at the Twelve Mooses Ballroom in Denver when Doctor Dictionary died. Ever been there? Remember him from TV back in the day?"

Ringwald was a person who struggled to stop talking once he started.

"Well anyway, it was a mess. I was the official photographer. I'd gotten all the shots I needed except for the one with Senator Pasco holding the big donation check. You know? The money shot for me and for the event." He chuckled at his own joke. "Couldn't find him anywhere. Turns out he was in the bathroom with nervous diarrhea, of all things."

Ringwald looked at them, seemed to remember who they were and where he was, and promptly closed his mouth.

"How long have you been here, taking photos of *this* event?" Chase asked, hoping the answer would make room for the possibility of evidence.

"I got here about ten minutes before you did. Haven't taken one shot of the happy couple or any of the wedding party. Don't think they'd want any the way everyone looks now." He seemed to consider something. "You think I'm still gonna get paid?"

Chase felt whatever hope he'd had disappear like an over-exposed polaroid. He handed the little man his card. "If you remember anything significant about this murder, please call me. Night or day."

The photographer quickly exited, likely to inquire about his fee.

Chase's phone buzzed. Jax Taylor. "Hey, Doc," he answered. He listened briefly, then hung up.

"Victim's ID says he's Jonathan Poundstone from Lakewood," Chase informed Morgan. "Business cards indicate he works for a pharmaceutical firm in Denver. Let's see if he was on the guest list." Another person associated with the medical community. What the heck was going on?

"Was Jax able to determine the likely COD?" Morgan asked. Chase wondered for a minute why the shorthand lingo for cause of death came so easily, then reminded himself that she was not only the department shrink, but she'd also been a cop.

"She didn't see anything. Just like the others. But she estimates the TOD to be recent. Between three and six hours ago based on body temp, even in the snow."

He knew she'd find writing on the body when she got it back to the morgue.

CHASE AND MORGAN navigated through the wedding attendees and resort visitors. Jonathan Poundstone wasn't on the guest list, and no one knew him or his purpose for being there if not for skiing. Morgan began to wonder what *she* was doing here. She hadn't heard, seen, or perceived anything that felt off about any of the people they'd interviewed so far, and she could tell Chase felt the same.

Morgan's stomach rumbled loud enough for Chase to hear.

"You hungry?"

Morgan twitched a smile. "That was embarrassing.

Honestly, I was about to get something at the Coffee Pod when you called."

"And then you had to reschedule your appointments for the day. Sorry about that." Chase didn't look sorry.

"I did." Thankfully, the four patients she had scheduled for today were well into their treatment plans, and something had told her to leave openings in her schedule for the next several days. She was able to slot each of them into another time.

There was a knock on the door. "Excuse me, detectives." A small woman wearing a blazer with the insignia of the resort pushed a cart. Neither bothered to correct her, their eyes drawn to the assortment of finger food and liquid refreshments on display. "I'm Wanda Dewberry, Cobalt Mountain's catering manager. I thought you might be getting hungry. These are some of the items we were going to serve at the wedding. The bride and groom suggested I serve them now to everyone who has arrived."

Chase and Morgan both stood. Chase shook the woman's hand and introduced himself. "Your timing couldn't be more perfect." Then he gestured to Morgan. "And this is Dr. Morgan Blake."

Morgan took the woman's hand and was immediately hit with what felt like a jolt of electricity. Muscle memory kicked in and Morgan found her relaxed smile that she knew had momentarily stiffened. She'd experienced this more than once in her lifetime and was adept at hiding her awareness. Surprisingly, Wanda Dewberry's eyes brightened and fixed on Morgan's.

"Have we met?" Morgan asked the woman.

"No, I don't think so. Perhaps we've crossed paths in town or at a Chamber of Commerce event."

"That could be it." Morgan noticed that Chase was about to dismiss the manager so she quickly added, "We'd like to ask you a few questions. Do you have some time?"

Chase gave her a questioning look but pulled out his phone to record the conversation.

"It doesn't look like I have a choice," Wanda Dewberry said with a tight smile.

"Did you know the victim?" Morgan asked.

"Jonathan Poundstone has been a guest at Cobalt Mountain many times. I'm sure you'll see that when you check our records. But I didn't know him personally, if that's what you're asking."

Chase took over the questioning. "When was the last time you saw Mr. Poundstone?"

The tiny woman squared her shoulders. "I couldn't tell you for sure, Detective. I think he was a guest here sometime after New Year's. Valentine's Day, maybe?"

Morgan pulled out her phone and swiped it on. After appearing to look at a text and key in a reply, she held the phone to Chase. It wasn't a text. Instead, she'd typed two words, "push her."

Chase glanced quickly at her phone, then looked at Morgan. "Tell him we'll get back to him when we're done here."

The psychologist keyed in the fake response, then looked at Wanda Dewberry and tried to discern whether the woman bought the ruse. She couldn't tell.

"Poundstone's business card indicates that he works for a pharmaceutical firm in Denver," Chase continued. "Do you know if he was up here to meet a client? A conference of some kind?"

A shield went up in Dewberry's eyes and she pleated her lips so hard the surrounding skin whitened. "We don't have any medical conferences here until July. I would have no idea who he might have been up here to meet. Maybe he was just getting away for a few days." Her voice was forced, brittle. The cheery countenance of the catering manager had long gone.

Chase leaned closer. "I think you know more than you're

telling us, Ms. Dewberry."

"Look, I'll think about it, but I honestly don't know how I can help you." She looked pointedly at her watch. "I have a client appointment to get to." And with that, Wanda Dewberry made her departure.

Chase looked at Morgan. "You got something. What?"

"I'm not sure. Give me a few minutes." Morgan rose and walked to the door. "I need to go somewhere quiet. I'll be outside getting some fresh air."

Morgan Blake left the lodge and walked around the nearly deserted deck. The sun was glorious and warm, but for some reason most people were sticking to the main room. Probably waiting for news, either about the wedding or the dead body on the mountainside.

She found a quiet corner and settled in, closing her eyes and calming her mind. Images began to form almost immediately. Some slowly, almost ephemerally. Others sharp and lightning swift. Breathing deeply and evenly, she willed the messages to clarify her understanding.

The logo of Cobalt Mountain Ski Resort morphed into the one for Eyrie Lodge. A large knife blade, silver and glinting, sliced the logo, then disappeared. Morgan tried to brush her frustration aside. She didn't have time to try and figure out the meaning behind what she was seeing. She needed clarification now, not later.

The images were suddenly sucked into a black hole, and she saw nothing else.

Morgan joined Chase back inside and together they finished interviewing the rest of the lodge and resort staff who had been on duty that morning. Nothing popped from either direct or indirect information.

They were silent as Sam drove them down the mountain to Chase's car. Snowflakes were falling thickly but gently to the ground.

"Looks like we're gonna have some fine powder for tomorrow," Sam tried. When they didn't answer, he gave a little shrug and didn't speak again.

The pair continued their silence as they drove back to Aspen Falls.

THAT NIGHT MORGAN couldn't sleep. She was used to people doubting her; she often doubted herself. However, time after time she'd been proven right, even amidst devasted personal relationships.

Morgan tried reading her current mystery, but gave up and pulled her Bichon Frisé, Quinn, up onto her lap. Petting him gently, she felt herself relax, and finally closed her eyes.

The same images she'd seen earlier in the day began to float into her mind. The logos, the slashing knife. Repeating, over and over. The anger was palpable, but their meaning escaped her.

Finally, she slept, sitting in the chair, her dog on her lap, and didn't move until daylight began peeking through the shutters. She slowly opened her eyes, then closed them again, seeking just a few more minutes of sleep.

She didn't get it. New images pulsated toward her. A cake. A heart. Followed by the slashing knife.

Morgan sat up, pushing Quinn to the floor. There was one person they hadn't interviewed because he hadn't been on duty.

She called Chase.

"HOW LONG HAS your mother been sick?" the detective asked. Chase, Morgan, and Garland Pride were seated at a table in the main dining area of the lodge.

After Morgan's phone call, Chase had done some research. Garland Pride, the head chef of the Eyrie Lodge, was an only child trying to support his family of five on his salary and his wife's disability checks. It only stretched so far in Colorado's most expensive county.

Garland looked at the detective, then at Morgan. "About three years."

"And when did Medicaid review her application and deny her coverage?"

"Eighteen months ago. They found out she'd transferred some assets into my name a few months before we applied." The chef seemed relieved to be telling someone.

Pride's mother had lived in assisted living where she was diagnosed with Type 1 diabetes, congestive heart failure, and chronic obstructive pulmonary disease, all within a few months. Even Medicare couldn't cover the expenses for the medications and doctor visits, which she couldn't afford. She had no other insurance. Her late husband had left her well off, but not well off enough. When she quit taking some of the medications and ended up in the hospital, Garland started getting phone calls seeking payment. That's when he found out how serious his mother's financial situation was, and that's when he arranged the transfer of assets so she could apply for Medicaid.

"And Julia Anderson was your mother's social worker?"

Pride nodded and looked away.

Georgia Pride had died soon after the New Year. Even though he'd been assured that there wasn't enough money in the world that could've helped his mother, Garland's guilt was enormous. It took him weeks to process his grief and resume work.

"How did Dr. Thomas Brown and Jonathan Poundstone enter the picture?" Morgan asked.

"Who?" Garland Pride looked genuinely confused.

Morgan reached across the table and put her hand on the

chef's arm. After a moment, she shifted her attention to Chase. "Can I talk to you? Outside?"

"WE JUST HAVE a few more questions for you, Ms. Dewberry," Chase opened after calling in the catering manager again.

"I'm here to help, but I don't know how I can," she answered.

"Prior to your job here, you were in healthcare. Do I have that right?"

"Well, if you can call working in a retirement home health care, then sure. I was."

"And you administered insulin to the patients who were unable to give it to themselves?"

Her eyes became slits.

"Ms. Dewberry, did you know Georgia Pride?"

A tear slid down Dewberry's cheek.

"You cared about her, didn't you? And no one would help with the costs of her medications. That made you angry, didn't it? And you used food dye in an attempt to throw suspicion on her son, who you also blamed for her death."

Suddenly Wanda Dewberry looked like a cornered feral cat. "I want a lawyer."

AFTER WANDA DEWBERRY WAS PROCESSED, Chase called Jax Taylor with his suspicion of murders by insulin.

"I was just about to call you, Detective. I checked Jonathan Poundstone's vitreous fluid in his eye on a whim. Insulin overdose."

Chase smiled, disconnected the call, and turned to Morgan.

"Dr. Blake? Can I buy you dinner? I have some apologizing to do."

FROM THE DARKNESS

RHONDA BLACKHURST

A door in the back of the house slammed shut, and Jackie screamed like a wildcat and sprang from the sofa. "Someone's here! I knew he'd get back at me. I knew it! And you didn't believe me."

Her friend, Agatha, who'd dropped by for a morning cuppa, gripped Jackie by the arms.

"Get a grip, mate," Agatha said. "It's not the Psycho. And I've never *not* believed you. I only laid out logical explanations. Like now. The ceiling fan probably caused the door to shut. Or the wind. It's blowing so hard that Wyoming's jealous."

"But I didn't open any windows," Jackie said.

"This is an old house. It's *always* drafty."

Jackie started for the hallway to check the windows anyway.

"Would it really hurt to open them when you're home?" Agatha asked. "It's not like you're pinching pennies. Open them and let the wind blow the bad juju out of this place. You've had bloody weird stuff happen in here."

In the past year, several peculiar things had gone down, all of which Agatha and other friends found reasonable explanations for. A coffee cup appeared in the sink while Jackie was at work; she'd been so preoccupied with sales reports she'd forgotten to put it in the dishwasher. The front door was unlocked; she'd forgotten to lock it after Agatha left the prior evening. A bottle of wine had been left on the counter; Jackie's ex still had a key. He'd denied leaving the wine, but as Agatha had pointed out, that didn't mean he hadn't done it. Jackie reasoned it was one last ditch effort, pathetic as it was, to try and change her mind about the split. But if that was the case, wouldn't he have admitted to it? What good would a denial do?

Jackie opened her mouth to speak, but Agatha interrupted.

"Stop, Jackie. We've already gone over this. Each incident has a logical explanation. And remember, the Psycho is still in prison."

A year ago, a customer at Jackie's furniture store began coming in every day, hanging out for longer and longer periods of time. Whenever she'd notice him, he'd whip his head toward a piece of furniture, pretend to scrutinize the price tag, feel the texture, and even make a show of trying it out. But soon she began seeing him and his aviator-style gold-rimmed glasses and full mustache everywhere she went—following behind her on the road in his creepy turd-brown panel van; strutting on the sidewalk across the street from her; sitting on a bench reading a newspaper, directly outside the store she'd just exited.

As much as she complained to the police, they said there was nothing they could do since these were all public places. They told her she could file for a restraining order, but it was unlikely to yield a positive result since the guy had never made any attempt to make contact with her. Soon, Jackie felt like a total idiot, convinced she'd watched one too many horror movies.

But Jackie let her guard down one time. She had closed the

store, locked the door to count the money, and flipped off the main lights. Until that night, she thought it a peaceful glow of ambient light. But then, across the store, the creep appeared from the shadows. She caught her breath and froze briefly before the realization struck her. The money sprayed into the air, raining down around her as if in slow motion. He strolled toward her, whistling a tune she'd never forget—*Tonight You Belong to Me*.

As he crossed the room toward her, still whistling, the self-defense moves she'd mastered the previous year tumbled to the forefront of her brain. With ninja speed, she dialed 911 before perfectly executing a series of moves that landed him on the floor, face down. She planted her foot firmly on the back of his neck until the police arrived. She escaped physical harm that night, but her hyper-vigilant state ramped up out of control. Agatha had come to refer to him as the Psycho, but when she learned his name was Stan, Stalker Stan stuck with Jackie.

Jackie said, "You have to admit I've come a long way. And you also have to admit that a slamming door in the house would set anyone on edge."

"I do admit it," Agatha said. "But you have a way to go before you're free from the dragons in the closet."

Jackie scoffed. "As long as the door to the closet stays closed, keeping the dragons in. But honestly. Eighteen months with credit for five months served prior to trial? That's an insult."

Jackie's testimony is what pushed the needle, leading the jury to find him guilty on one Class IV felony stalking count. The statute allows for up to two years in prison, but the judge apparently didn't agree.

Jackie glanced at the wall calendar with a big red circle around April 24th. "Only two weeks until he's released."

Agatha tipped her chin toward her chest and stared at Jackie. "I'm sure he had much bigger things to worry about in prison than your testimony. They don't just chinwag in there, ya know. He was probably some bloke's princess."

That only gave him *more* cause for revenge, Jackie thought.

Agatha bit her lower lip. "That's all the more reason to hate you, I suppose."

Jackie scowled. "I know. Even if what you say is true, that he doesn't know where I live—of which I'm not convinced, I'll have you know—it's not like I can just pack up and move my furniture store someplace else."

"Hm. Well, think of it this way. At least the police will take things more seriously than before."

Jackie punched her fists onto her hips. "Excuse me? Have you watched television shows? The bad guys get away all the time. Poof! They just disappear."

"Unfortunately, yeah, they do in *American* shows. If you'd watch more British mysteries, you'd see we always get the bad guys. And the detectives don't even need guns to do it."

"All in an hour's time," Jackie mumbled.

As soon as Agatha left, Jackie checked the extra security locks the police had recommended she get installed on her doors and lower-level windows. She glanced at the clock: twenty-five minutes to nine. That only gave her twenty-five minutes to get to the store to open for the day. She'd have to wait until she got back home from the store tonight before checking VINElink, an online notification system that allowed crime victims to check an inmate's custody status and criminal case information. Even though the court assured her she would be notified of any changes in Stalker Stan's status, checking VINElink at least once a week gave her an extra measure of reassurance.

She turned for the door, then back to her laptop. The store be damned. Peace of mind came first. Getting the confirmation she had hoped for, she breathed a sigh of relief and headed out the door.

That afternoon, as she was helping a customer decide on a

bed for their toddler, Jackie noticed a man strolling through the recliners. Her head spun toward him, but she was relieved to see he was a good twenty years younger than Stalker Stan. His upcoming release had her all kinds of wigged out.

Jackie approached the young man, now testing the recliners. She got a sense of déjà vu as a vision of Stalker Stan appeared.

A woman reached the man at the same time Jackie did.

"Are you the one that took down that creepy guy in here last year?"

Taking a moment to recover from the question, Jackie said, "Unfortunately."

The woman clenched her teeth. "You've gotta be so freaked out that he escaped."

Jackie gasped. She felt the color drain from her face, her mouth went dry, and her legs like jelly. She leaned against a recliner and gripped the back of it until her knuckles were white.

The woman looked horrified. "You didn't know. Oh, boy. I'm so sorry to spring it on you like this. I thought they'd have told you by now."

Jackie blanched. "By *now*?"

"It was on the news yesterday evening."

Jackie took a deep breath. How could this have happened? She'd looked on the information system for victims not even three hours ago. And he escaped yesterday? And why? He only had two weeks left. Why risk it?

After flagging down an employee to take over for her, Jackie excused herself and hurried to the breakroom. She closed and locked the door behind her, slid her cell from her pocket, and punched in Agatha's number.

"Stalker Stan escaped from jail!" Jackie said the minute Agatha picked up. "Apparently, he's flying in the wind. Probably trying to find out where I live. Which isn't hard these days with technology and all. Maybe it *was* him this morning. What if he's hiding in my house right now?"

"Whoa, whoa, whoa," Agatha said. Jackie could almost see her tamping the air with her hand. "Back up a minute. How do you know? Did someone from the prison call you?"

"No. A customer told me."

Agatha exhaled loudly. "Okay, first of all, I assume you did your Tuesday online information check, right?"

"Yes."

"And I also assume it showed he's still incarcerated."

"The information system is obviously wrong, Agatha."

"Still, it sounds like you lost the plot. Someone would have called you to let you know." But her tone wasn't convincing.

"I'm telling you, Agatha, he escaped. The woman said it was on the news."

Agatha exhaled loudly again. "Hell's bells. Now you have a legit reason to worry. Call the victim line to be sure it's actually the Psycho, and this woman didn't get her facts all buggered up. In the meantime, and after raising bloody hell with the powers that be, don't close the store at night anymore, alone or not. Get home before dark. After work I need to swing by my house to feed Christie, and then I'll come see you. For now, I must crack on so I can get out of here."

Christie was Agatha's cat, appropriately named.

After Jackie arranged for someone to close the store that night and for the entire next week, she sat in her office to breathe and pull herself together before she called the police department.

During a lengthy, tense conversation, the officer assured her they had cause to believe Stan was in Montana by now with the woman who'd been writing him in prison. They'd alerted the city police there to be on the lookout. The officer said, "He admitted to following you because, quote, 'you led him to believe the feeling was mutual.' Your testimony dispelled that belief."

His assurance gave her the courage she needed to realize it was highly improbable Stalker Stan was in her house, and her home was the safest place to be. Still, she'd take precautions to be sure no one followed her there.

When she opened the store door to the busy sidewalk, she looked both ways, catching someone slip around the corner between two buildings. The opening was just wide enough for a body to fit through. She scurried toward the narrow alleyway to peer down there, to be sure it wasn't Stalker Stan. All she saw was a kid smoking a joint. From his wide stance, probably to keep his sagging jeans from falling completely down, showing more than just *part* of his yellow boxers, she guessed him to be in his teens. He snuck a glance behind him, caught her watching him, and turned toward her.

He narrowed his eyes, jamming the hand with the joint behind him. "Stalkin' me, lady?"

Jackie shook her head, rolled her eyes, and mumbled, "Hardly." *The irony.*

JACKIE STOPPED at the grocers on her way home and made a few creative detours in case she'd missed someone following her. Besides that, other than looking in her rearview mirror more often than she should, the two-mile drive home was uneventful. When she unlocked the front door, a breeze blew through the house and lifted her skirt nearly over her head. A shrill sound escaped her, startling in the quiet house. The sheer curtains were blowing inward on the opened sliding glass door across the house. Her heart sped north of safe as she fell into fight-or-flight mode. *He's here!*

There was a *thump* from upstairs, and Jackie gasped. In one swift move, she dropped her purse to the floor, pulled her skirt back down with one hand, pushed her hair out of her face with the other, and kicked the door closed behind her with her heel. She darted across the house to slam the slider closed.

She scanned the room, then stood frozen, her mind waging war between fleeing or fighting. Gathering enough bravery to move, Jackie twisted around to grasp the pepper spray from the little table alongside the door, and tiptoed toward the stairs. On high-octane alert, she climbed each step, slow-mo and exactly as all the dummies do in slasher flicks as the audience is shouting *Don't go up there! Get out!*

But she'd managed to extinguish the threat the first time around, giving her the gumption to do it again. She steeled herself to keep moving forward. Living in fear zapped too much energy.

When she reached the top step, she paused for a cursory glance behind her, then down each hallway that branched off the stairs, deciding to turn left. She'd only made it a couple of feet.

"Hey!"

All it took was the sound of a voice and the certain knowledge of someone in the house. Jackie spun around and unleashed the pepper spray before she flipped the person over her shoulder. A cat yowled and sprung on her, claws catching in Jackie's dress, shredding the front.

Jackie screeched, prying Christie's claws from her dress.

Agatha lay on her back, sputtering, desperately wiping her eyes with both hands, tears streaming down her cheeks. "You maced me!" she finally said.

Breathless, Jackie dropped to her knees beside her friend. "What are you doing here?"

Agatha tried unsuccessfully to open her eyes. "You gave me a key, moron." She tugged her sleeves over her hands and continued to swipe at her eyes. "I clocked out early, but now I wish I hadn't."

Jackie crossed the hallway to the bathroom, drenched a

washcloth with cold water, nudged Agatha's hands away and dabbed at her eyes.

"I thought someone was in here."

"There was. *Me*. I was in the bathroom." Agatha snatched the washcloth from Jackie. "I'd ask you to open a window to help clear my sinuses from this stuff you doused me with, but an open window is what caused this whole thing to begin with." She groaned, attempted to sit, and winced. "I'd do it myself, but I think you broke my back."

Jackie stood. "It was the sliding door that was open, not a window. Big difference." She shook her head, crossed to the casement window, reached for the lock, and froze. It was unlocked. After a quick recovery, she cracked it open. Fear would *not* rule her life anymore. Out-of-control fear nearly killed the one friend she had left. She shuddered at how close Agatha had come to tumbling down the stairs. Stalker Stan wouldn't steal another minute, or another friend, from her life. She was a forty-eight-year-old woman, for heaven's sake.

Christie stayed hidden the rest of Agatha's visit, and she had to work overtime to coax him out from under the bed when it was time to leave.

***

AFTER AGATHA LEFT FOR HOME, Christie tucked under one arm, Jackie traipsed through the house, checking the locks on the first-floor doors and windows. She pinched the curtains closed one last time before she snagged her chamomile tea from the counter and buried herself beneath a blanket in a corner of the couch. She snatched the remote from the side table and flipped on the TV for the ten o'clock news.

"And now for breaking news in the murder of Leo Linder, otherwise known as Doctor Dictionary." The news anchor looked directly into the camera. "It's been determined that the cause of death wasn't from marijuana at all, as previously suspected. Rather, Mr. Linder died from asphyxiation caused by a plastic bag over his head. Witnesses give differing accounts of the trophy Doctor Dictionary was to be awarded. Some say it had been in plastic earlier, but when questioned, Charlotte Webb, the CEO of the organization, was emphatic the trophy was sitting on a table without plastic anywhere near it."

The female anchor said, "That's a big development, Dylan. That changes things a whole lot."

"It sure does, Samantha."

Jackie sipped her tea while listening to a series of commercials.

"Welcome back. In an update to a story we reported on previously, Stan Stevenson, the man convicted of stalking Jackie Fox of Fox Furniture and who escaped from prison last night, is believed to be the victim in a fatal single vehicle crash in the early morning hours on Fourth and Bennett. Just last week, he was sentenced to ten more years for the assault of a minor that occurred two years ago."

They further explained that Stan had been unofficially identified by his car, the glasses on the floor of the vehicle, his driver's license, and his clothes—an unmistakable prison uniform.

Jackie hit the power button on the remote. Some of her fear melted, replaced with a confusing combination of relief and guilt. Yet, she knew that Stalker Stan was still a threat until DNA tests proved otherwise. Rather than a constant state of fight-or-flight, though, simple vigilance would make sure no one else became a casualty of her self-protection mode. And maybe the friends she'd chased away with her over-the-top obsession would reappear. Hopeful, she decided this deserved something stronger than chamomile tea.

She shed the blanket and trekked toward the kitchen as her phone rang. She looked at the incoming number and leaned against the wall while she answered.

"Hi, Agatha. You heard the news? Stalker Stan is dead. I'm

so relieved. And yet I feel guilty, too. What kind of human wishes another to be dead?"

"Why would you feel guilty? You didn't kill the bloke. He crashed his car."

"But happy he's dead?" Jackie shook her head slowly. "You know what doesn't make sense, though? Why would he have his driver's license? He escaped, so he wouldn't have any of his possessions, right?" The impact of what that could mean was a sucker punch, and she gasped. Did Stalker Stan have an accomplice? That could explain the sketchy stuff that had happened the past year. Maybe it wasn't Stalker Stan's body in that car at all. "No, that's just crazy."

"What's crazy?" Agatha asked.

Jackie shook her head as she pushed herself away from the wall. "I was just thinking that—" She turned the corner into the kitchen and froze. A bottle of Seven Deadly Zins and two wine glasses sat on the old butcher-block table. The whistled tune of *Tonight You Belong to Me* carried into the kitchen from the unlit mudroom.

From the darkness, Stalker Stan appeared, hands casually tucked in his pockets. And from the darkness, Jackie left any buried fear. She reached for a butcher knife with one hand, said into the phone, "He's here, Agatha. Call 911."

Stalker Stan stopped whistling and grinned. "Calling the police won't do any good, Jackie. I'm dead, remember? They won't believe you."

"I knew it wasn't you in the car accident," she said, her mind scraping together a survival plan.

"Yeah? Smart lady. I knew you were special." He cocked his head in a matter-of-fact manner. "I connected with an old friend in prison. He was released a week after I got in. He owed me."

"His *life*?" she said, bewildered. He was more dangerous than she thought.

He shrugged. "Yeah, well, that part was unfortunate." He

lifted his palms. "But here I am, ready to pick up where we left off."

Where we left off? Jackie thought incredulously. For a brief moment, she felt like she'd been flung into some warped version of *Groundhog Day*, when out of nowhere, near super-human strength welled up from within as she transported into the movie, *Sudden Impact*, and she was Clint Eastwood. Stalker Stan was back, but so was she, more ready than ever. This time she wouldn't hold back.

"Go ahead, Psycho," she whispered. "Make my day."

ANOTHER NOTE TO READER

There you have it, Readers.

All the clues to solve Doctor Dictionary's murder have been revealed. If you'd like to stop here and try to figure it out, go back to the character page at the beginning and look over your notes. (You did take notes, didn't you??) To check your work, read the denouement after you read about all of our fabulous authors.

If you solved the murder of Doctor Dictionary, let us know by visiting the anthology page at SistersInCrimeColorado. org/anthology. (There might even be a surprise for you there!)

If you enjoyed this anthology, please drop a review—no spoilers, though—and tell your friends!

MEET THE AUTHORS

When not actively engaged in defending New Mexico green chile as the best in the world (sorry Coloradoans), **Amy Rivers** splits her time between writing dark psychological suspense and dabbling in a new adventure/cozy/romance series. AmyRivers.com

Ann Dominguez writes suspense and is on the hunt for the perfect cup of tea—will she be able to finish it before it gets cold? AnnDominguezBooks.com

Award-winning author **Becky Clark** is the seventh of eight kids, which explains both her insatiable need for attention and her atrocious table manners. BeckyClarkBooks.com

Brooke Craig writes cozy mysteries and decorates and declutters other people's homes as she attempts to recover from decades of teaching math to teenagers. BrookeCraigBooks.com

Donnell Ann Bell has never performed an autopsy but she does watch Quincy and reads Rizzoli and Isles novels. She also writes bestselling Romantic Suspense and an award-winning Cold Case series. DonnellAnnBell.com

When **Fleur Bradley Visscher** isn't writing, she's watching bears run down the street from her fixer-upper cottage in the Colorado mountainside. FleurBradley.com

Francelia Belton writes crime stories because committing a real one would disappoint her family. Francel.Be/Writing-Stories

G.P. Gottlieb's motto is, "never pass up a piece of pie," but she's open-minded about other desserts. She writes culinary mysteries and has interviewed over 230 authors as a podcast host on the New Books Network. GPGottlieb.com

When not stringing words together, **Holly Harris** can be found out riding one of her horses with Wyatt, her Australian Shepherd, trotting alongside. HollyRHarris.com

Jenna Lincoln loves martinis, smart women saving the day, and labradoodles. instagram.com/LegionOfJen

Kerry Hammond immerses herself in writing mystery stories because she's been told that real murder is wrong. KerryHammond.com

Award-winning author **Leanne Kale Sparks** is a coffee mainlining dog mom who spends most of her days coming up with exciting ways to kill people ... for her books. LeanneKaleSparks.com

Linda Solaya is an intermittent writer who has attached herself to the wonderful women of the Colorado Chapter of Sisters in Crime in a desperate hope that some of their talent will rub off on her.

Marie Sutro writes dark thrillers by the light of a thousand suns to keep from scaring herself silly. MarieSutro.com

Mary Birk, a retired trial lawyer, writes mysteries when she isn't gardening or wrangling German Shorthairs. MaryBirk.com

Meagan Dallner is not a race car driver (much to her dismay) or a sky diver (probably for the best), but instead gets her thrills from books she reads and stories she writes. MeaganDallner.com

Growing up with copious amounts of tea, mysteries, and fantasies, **Melissa Robbins** was destined to write historical mysteries with magical twists. Melissa-Robbins.com

Multi-award-winning thriller/suspense author **Peg Brantley** likes to start conversations because she isn't adept at actually finishing them. PegBrantley.com

Rhonda Blackhurst pens mysteries and romantic suspense stories. She enjoys hiding behind her computer screen, where she can unashamedly enjoy her addictions of dark chocolate and coffee. RhondaBlackhurst.com

DENOUEMENT: MURDER AT THE TWELVE MOOSES BALLROOM

What a stupid way to die, Doctor Dictionary thought. Those brownies must have been laced with pot. He thought the magic ingredient had been cinnamon.

He clutched at his throat and sucked in as much air as possible. The doctor told him his allergy to marijuana wasn't life-threatening, but it would cause constriction and dilation of parts of his body Doctor Dictionary couldn't remember right now. He hadn't paid much attention because once he was diagnosed—along with his allergy to legumes and pumpkins—he simply decided not to imbibe anymore. He figured he could live a full life without pot, lentils, or Thanksgiving pie.

He stumbled to the table that held a pitcher of water and some glasses. He filled one for himself. The first sip was tight, but maybe the ice had relaxed his throat? Perhaps wishful thinking, but he took another sip. Yes, his breathing was indeed becoming easier.

Doctor Dictionary calmed a bit, but was relieved when he heard someone enter the room behind him.

"What's the matter, Doc?" Senator Pasco's face registered concern.

Doctor Dictionary squeaked out, "Allergy to pot."

"Oh no! Why did you indulge if you were allergic?" Senator Pasco stepped toward him, pulling out his own bag of gummy bears. He reached an arm around Doctor Dictionary's neck and crammed the last few remaining gummies into his throat. He pushed them down as far as he could, then clamped Doctor Dictionary's mouth closed so he couldn't gag or spit them out.

Doctor Dictionary thrashed and struggled, finally stomping on Pasco's foot hard enough to shock him into releasing his neck. He had no choice but to swallow the gummies, but chased them with a large drink of water.

"What do you think you're doing?" Doctor Dictionary was finally able to sputter.

"Something I've wanted to do for a long time." Senator Pasco rubbed his foot through his loafer.

"Why?" Doctor Dictionary's voice was a hoarse whisper.

"Are you kidding me? How many times did you share that viral video of me? How many times *just tonight* did you bring it up?" Senator Pasco smirked. "And now I get to watch while you die from an overdose."

Doctor Dictionary took another deep swig of water then a deep breath, finally feeling his chest opening. "I'm not overdosing, you twit."

"Oh. How disappointing. Back to Plan A, then." In a flash, from his jacket pocket, Senator Pasco produced the plastic bag that had encased the trophy. "I was a Boy Scout, you know. Always prepared."

Before Doctor Dictionary could react, Senator Pasco had slipped it over his head and pulled it tight.

Doctor Dictionary's eyes widened, then bulged as his breathing became more rapid. Soon he was practically sucking the bag into his throat in his ever-increasing panic to breathe.

Senator Pasco held tight until he felt Doctor Dictionary go limp. They both sank to the floor. When it was clear Doctor

Dictionary had taken his last breath, Pasco removed the bag and stuffed it back into his pocket.

Senator Pasco glanced around the room, making sure nobody could tell he'd been there, then inched open the door and peeked into the hallway. It was clear, so he hurried away. At the corner, he veered to the left as he saw Charlotte Webb coming from the right. He slipped around the corner, sure she hadn't seen him.

He knew he needed to return to the ballroom before he was missed, but he'd made a vague reference about nervous diarrhea earlier so people would drop the subject immediately. He was on his way when he heard Charlotte Webb scream. Suddenly there were people everywhere, rushing toward the noise. He followed them.

Charlotte was hysterically trying to rouse Doctor Dictionary, and the crowd surged forward to help, or at least to gawk.

Senator Pasco took charge, pushing through the bodies between him and Charlotte. "Call 911. Turn him over. Give them some room. Call an ambulance!" His drill sergeant voice finally got some response and phones were whipped out of pockets. "Tell them we're in the Antler Room."

"No, this is the Ungulate Room!" Charlotte said.

"Pretty sure this is the Proboscis Room," someone from the back said.

Senator Pasco had to hide his smile. *That'll slow down the paramedics.*

When the paramedics finally arrived, he put a comforting arm around Charlotte Webb's shoulders and steered her out of the way. "You have to go make an announcement," he said softly.

"I can't!" she wailed.

"Would you like me to do it for you?"

"Would you? I just can't. Look at me ... I'm shaking."

She was indeed quite shaky and he gently pushed her into a nearby chair. "I'll take care of everything," he whispered.

As he strode to the ballroom, Senator Pasco worked on his opening line, the one that would prompt everyone to pull out their phones and start recording what he was about to say. His new viral sensation.

A WEEK LATER, Charlotte Webb was idly sipping a glass of merlot in front of her television. She hadn't done much since the night Doctor Dictionary died. Tidbits of the investigation flitted in one ear and out the other, but early on it was determined he'd been murdered. Her mind replayed the event over and over, but she still couldn't make sense of it.

Who would murder Doctor Dictionary?

She herself had been a suspect early on; they all were. She'd had some 'splainin' to do to the detectives about her purse Glock and her penchant for threatening to shoot people dead a million times a day. She vowed to work on that. Thank goodness Doctor Dictionary hadn't been shot. And Jack Como's explanation of his surprise proposal did not look good for either of them until he produced the banner, the ring, and his auntie who corroborated everything.

Wendy Bilbersteen was lucky her gummies not only were worm-shaped, but also not edibles. Until the coroner had confirmed the marijuana hadn't caused Doctor Dictionary's death, Wendy seemed a likely candidate due to her decades old hostility toward him. She would have been off the hook anyway, because she was so busy at the event, someone could always pinpoint her whereabouts.

When Charlotte told the detectives that Olivia Twist lied about being Doctor Dictionary's assistant for the event, they scooped her up in a hurry. But when the story of how Olivia sought him out, sure he was her long-lost father based almost solely on the fact they both had an allergy to marijuana, everyone learned that an allergy to marijuana wasn't uncommon, nor did it have to be fatal. Her doctor confessed he just told her that to keep her away from drugs. Olivia probably would never know if Doctor Dictionary was her father or not.

Ryan Rizzuto—The RizzBizz online—had to do the most to clear his name of the murder. As soon as it was revealed he was at the event, all of his prank videos shot into the stratosphere, which was all he'd ever wanted. He had set up an elaborate prank with a partner. At the precise moment when Doctor Dictionary was to receive his award, his partner would brandish a firearm, threatening Doctor Dictionary. Ryan Rizzuto would "rescue" Doctor Dictionary, it would all be filmed and uploaded to the internet, and he'd be a hero, gaining eyeballs and advertisers for his RizzBizz. His partner had gotten cold feet, though, and disappeared, but not before ratting him out in a chatroom. The detectives made Rizzuto sweat, reportedly in an effort to put the kibosh on his online tomfoolery. "Dangerous and stupid," one of the detectives had pronounced his antics. It might have worked. Charlotte hadn't seen any RizzBizz videos lately.

Charlotte had been stumped by the appearance of Lois LaLanne's pot-laced brownies. But as Lois was not a criminal mastermind, her garbled confession spewed forth the minute it was determined she was the one who brought the pot brownies to the event. She kept saying, "Not him! Not him!" When pressed, she revealed she'd wanted Wendy Bilbersteen to eat them so she'd mellow out enough that Lois LaLanne could worm her way into the television news game instead of the print media. Wendy hadn't been giving her the time of day—ignoring every single phone call—but all Lois wanted was a well-placed mentor, someone who would help her. Fat chance of that now.

Charlotte started at the mention and photograph of State Senator Manfred "Freddie" Pasco on the television. It was so kind of him to take charge when she'd found Doctor Dictionary's body that night. She turned up the volume in time to hear the on-air reporter say, "… arrested for the murder of Leo Linder, known around Colorado as the beloved Doctor

Dictionary. Pasco is alleged to have asphyxiated Linder with the very same plastic bag he used to transport Doctor Dictionary's trophy, honoring him for his work with the organization Kindhearted Individuals Dedicated to Dreams and Opportunities, or KIDDOs for short. Pasco's motive is yet to be revealed, but the murder at the Twelve Mooses Ballroom seems to have been solved."

She stared dumbly at the TV through the next segment, trying to wrap her head around Senator Pasco's arrest. His "Pasco Fiasco" suddenly seemed tame compared to this. She could only imagine what the internet would do to Unsteady Freddie.

THANK YOU

- to Sisters in Crime for promoting the ongoing advancement, recognition, and professional development of women crime writers since 1986
- to the members of the Colorado Chapter of Sisters in Crime for offering educational opportunities, unwavering support for their fellow mystery writers, obscene amounts of fun and laughter, and the occasional kick in the butt
- to MB Partlow for her help brainstorming the "Murder at the Twelve Mooses Ballroom" and for lending Becky some desperately needed critical thinking skills
- to Jessica Cornwell for her eagle-eyed copyediting and proofreading
- to our spouses, kids, parents, grandkids, besties, and everyone who offers snacks/coffee/encouragement while we write early in the morning, late at night, or in brief snatches of time whenever we can find it
- to booksellers and librarians for placing books in the hands of readers who will love them
- and to you, Best Beloved Reader, for championing your favorite authors to anyone who will listen, enthusiastically attending author events, and indulging your passion for getting lost in the pages of a book

WE THANK YOU FOR HELPING US DO WHAT WE LOVE TO DO